"A luscious, mesmerizing tale of the dangerous land that lies between the art and the artist, and the deep, profound emotion we find there."
CHRISTINA HENRY, author of *Alice* and *The Place Where They Buried Your Heart*

"Dazzlingly lush prose marks a series of unforgettable character portraits in this literary fantasy masterpiece."
CAITLIN ROZAKIS, *New York Times*-bestselling author of *Dreadful*

"Equal parts enchanting and horrifying, *The Apple and the Pearl* is a stunning meditation on art: the gritty emotions that make us human, and the monstrous appetites an artist must cater to. A shocking sensual story wrapped in glossy ethereal tulle; a tale that is deeply nuanced, yet deceptively effortless."
KRITIKA H. RAO, *Sunday Times*-bestselling author of *The Legend of Meneka*

"A taut, soaring dance of a novel formed from precision, muscle, and grace; it moves through your body and lingers long after. Superb."
TASHAN MEHTA, author of *The Mad Sisters of Esi*

"Shadowing a touring company across a single day, *The Apple and the Pearl* is an intricately woven tapestry of hopes, fears and dreams, as its ensemble cast wrestle with the things they can't escape and those they must leave behind. At once deeply human and gorgeously strange, this is a fierce and tender portrait of life in thrall to art."
E. J. SWIFT author of *When There Are Wolves Again*

"Kechacha's skill is matchless. *The Apple and the Pearl* is an evocative, beautifully weird celebration of performance, desire, and camaraderie."
ALIYA WHITELEY, award-winning author of *The Beauty*

"Poetic, witty, relatable and bewitching ...
Readers are sure to be entranced."
LEXY HUDSON, author of *Wonders Never Cease*

THE APPLE AND THE PEARL

RYM KECHACHA

TITAN BOOKS

The Apple and the Pearl
Print edition ISBN: 9781835414156
E-book edition ISBN: 9781835414163

Published by Titan Books
A division of Titan Publishing Group Ltd
144 Southwark Street, London SE1 0UP
www.titanbooks.com

First edition: February 2026
10 9 8 7 6 5 4 3 2 1

A CIP catalogue record for this title is available from the British Library.

EU RP (for authorities only)
eucomply OÜ, Pärnu mnt. 139b-14, 11317 Tallinn, Estonia
hello@eucompliancepartner.com, +3375690241

Designed and typeset in Agmena Pro by Richard Mason.

Printed and bound by CPI Group (UK) Ltd, Croydon CR0 4YY.

For my daughters

The Crow welcomes you to this evening's performance.

DANCERS OF THE COMPANY, MUSICIANS OF THE ORCHESTRA AND MEMBERS OF THE CREW OF

The Apple and the Pearl

2nd NOVEMBER, 7.30PM

Dancers of the company, Musicians of the Orchestra and members of the crew

King .... Gregory STEVENS
Queen .... Mara PAULSON
Crow .... Joshua MICKELSON
White Princess .... Stephanie OLIVIER
White Suitor .... Stuart BLOW
Red Princess .... Harriet PLOWSON
Red Suitor .... Benjamin ATKINSON
Blue Princess .... Zuleika AHMED
Blue Suitor .... Romero DUPONE
Pages, pearls, hunters and orchard dancers ....
Luke Benson, Matthew Prove,
Theo Watson, Richard Smith,
Daniel Blackman, Solomon Grahams,
Bella Williams, Jessica Turner,
Anita Walsh, Sarah Forde, Lucy Hughes,
Emily Knight, Dora Lewis, Felicity Jackson

Company manager .... Belinda VRYDER
Ballet mistress .... Cecile FOURNIER
Company chef .... Gino DiANGELO

Technical director and stage manager .. Mackenzie MACKENZIE
Deputy stage manager.... Charlie JERRYSON
Assistant stage manager .... Shirley WILDE
Wardrobe manager............ Alina BAKER
Wardrobe assistant........... Milly OWENS
Fly operator.................... Kavi BHATT
Lighting director .... Zachary TAYLOR
Lighting assistant .... *position vacant*
Follow spot .... Derek JONES
Stage right.................. Daniel PETERS

Conductor...................... Aleko JONES
First violins.......... Michael HAYWARDS, Roberta SIMPSON
Second violins .... Max MOORHEAD, Henry MAY, Sarah MILLER
Viola .... Eleonor NORMAN
Cellos....................... Wilfred ROOT, Anna BULSOM
Double bass................ Jack BESTING
Harp .... David JOHNSON
Flute........................ Yolanda ROY
Oboe .... Jean PETERSFIELD
Clarinets.......... Sandra BELLINGHAM, George DAVIES
Bassoon .... Steven ADAMSON
French horn............... Wendy HARRIS
Tuba.................... Eddy ROBINSON
Trumpet .... Lancelot BARNES (orchestra leader)
Trombone................ Jack BLOSSOMS
Percussion .... Jasper ALLEN

ACT ONE

Once there was a Queen who had three daughters. As they come of age, her husband the King persuades her to throw a party, inviting all the suitors in the land. But, unbeknownst to the rulers, a mischievous Crow has cast a spell on the princesses; they are each to marry their own true loves, as long as they can traverse lands of dreams to find their princes.

In a flash, the castle tumbles into ruins as if it has been standing for a thousand years, the three princesses are in rags, and the Queen and King dance mournfully among the wreckage of their lands as their daughters set off on their quest.

ACT TWO

Princess Sapphire arrives on the seashore, searching for her mate. She dances with the waves, dives for pearls and finds her suitor at the bottom of the ocean. Princess Opal searches the skies for her prince and finds him in a maze of clouds.

ACT THREE

Princess Ruby searches in an orchard filled with exotic fruits and finds her prince among the boughs. A group of hunters escorts the princess and her mate back to the castle, which is restored to its former glory. The three princesses wed their suitors and the Queen and King celebrate all being well in the land.

The honoured Lords, Ladies and gentlefolk of our audiences are respectfully reminded that the auditorium opens after the sounding of the Angelus bells, at 18.55 GMT each evening.

Payments are gratefully received. Please leave your tokens on your seat as you leave us at the end of the performance.

We kindly request that our honoured guests refrain from touching, tasting, or otherwise interacting with our performers and musicians.

Just before midnight the cast and crew of *The Apple and the Pearl* are aboard their train, not a one among them left by the boulder-strewn river where last night's performance took place. The shriek of a whistle – the very last warning call to stragglers – and the train starts to heave itself along the track, a groaning moaning sound of carriages awakening, spitting and spluttering as they gather speed. The *chug chug hmisssss* of the curved steel on the track. The sigh of cool air on the nose of the locomotive as it hurries through the darkness, its lurching the loudest thing in the night. A hunting owl's wings brush the air; tiny icicles dangle from the fir trees growing a hair's width every hour as the snow water *drip drip drips*; a fox cub snuffles as he digs at a hedgehog nest.

Now the bell rings, tolling in the new day and bidding farewell to the old. It rings loud outside the train, echoing solemnly in the valley.

A clang for the King, a clang for the Queen,
three clangs for the sisters never to be seen.

In the first carriage, behind the set and costumes and paraphernalia a touring ballet takes on the road, a woman named Belinda sits with a heavy hidebound ledger open on her lap. She scrawls down the columns quickly, dropping coins and earrings and watches and tiny gleaming jewels into the iron-bound chest at her feet. As the fifth bell tolls she puts the ledger in the chest, locks it and puts the key on a chain around her neck.

A clang for the orchard, a clang for the sea,
three clangs for the suitors who lie in a dream.

In the dining carriage in the middle of the train, the cellist, the percussionist and the bassoonist are drinking, sipping from shot glasses and slamming on the tables in syncopated rhythms. They hum Verdi and Puccini as they get drunker and drunker, and when the tenth bell comes they weave its note into their wobbly melodies and toast the coming of the new day.

A clang for the curse, a clang for the quest,

The sleeping cabins in the back half of the train are filling up with those who hear the curfew of the midnight bells with relief rather than as a challenge. Yawning, the assorted dancers and stage managers and woodwind and strings spit out toothpaste, pull pyjamas out from under duvets and slip on eye masks, rolling out their shoulders and necks from another day of leaping and turning and humping and hauling and blowing and plucking to sink into the soft lull of the train gently rocking their tired bones.

And one last for the crow who sings in its nest.

At the very back of the train in the caboose, a woman sits with her legs dangling off the deck, a broom across her lap. She wears a voluminous dress of black serge and hums a little tune as she points her toes and swings her legs. Beside her is a tray bearing a half-finished plate of garlic risotto, a few crumbs of a shortbread biscuit and two empty shot glasses. She watches the dark hills of the day dissolve as the train staggers into a new landscape, and with the toll of the thirteenth bell she opens her beak and caws out into the night.

Nine o'clock in the morning is the first reveille on the Grub. For most, it sounds like a light burble of running water; it's cheerful piano scales for those who do not consider themselves morning people; and for Zach, the lighting director, it's a foghorn that sounds over and over like a ferry in a storm until he gets up out of his bunk, opens his cabin door and presses the button above the door two cabins over. By that time, standing barefoot in the corridor with his hair rumpled, a pillow crease on his cheek and last night's garlic risotto wafting out from between his molars, he is fully, furiously awake and swearing at the cacophony that yanks him this way from the sweet oblivion of his dreams every single morning.

'Fuck you, Grub,' he mutters, as behind him Alina the wardrobe mistress leaves the bathroom and the pungent, lavender-scented steam of her shower seeps out into the corridor.

'Morning Zach!' she calls brightly as she squeezes past him. 'It's a beautiful day to put on a show.'

He pulls up the closest blind to see that it isn't a beautiful day at all. He drags a finger through the condensation on the window to see fine, drizzly mist. He lets his forehead fall onto the cold glass and watches as Belinda marches past, with one gloved hand gripping a tray bearing an empty plate and two shot glasses, and the other clamped around the Pearl. Already he can hear the doors of the cargo carriages creaking open; Danny shouting to Charlie as they unload the first of the crates containing the set; the hiss of the hydraulic lifts and the *thump thump thump* of the broken wheels of the stage left props crate. The musicians are still in bed, the bastards. Maybe he should learn to play an instrument, the drums or something: that can't be too hard. Then he'd get a blasted lie-in for once in his life.

He needs a shower. A coffee. A double helping of whatever Gino's doing for breakfast today, more coffee and an extra jumper because it's bound to be cold in the Grit today with that creeping fog out there.

Belinda is waiting for him in the dining car, gloves tucked away, her clipboard clutched tight.

He holds up one hand. 'I haven't had any coffee yet, Belinda, so if you're coming at me for that expenses form I'm just going to grunt until you give up and go away.'

'Good morning, Zachary,' Belinda says smartly. 'May I introduce you to Lara.'

He squints at the blonde woman beside Belinda, dressed

in a black t-shirt and black jeans with her hair tied in two long plaits over each shoulder. The dress code makes things tricky here, especially as he's not great with faces. Everyone dressed in raven black but the dancers, who all look the same to Zach anyway with their hair slicked off their faces and their sharp, sticky-out bones and their turned-out, froggy feet.

'She'll shadow you today, and if she likes what she sees she'll take her pledge tonight and be your new lighting assistant.'

'Am I being promoted?'

Belinda raises one eyebrow. 'Do keep up, Zachary. Juliet left six weeks ago and you've had your pay rise for at least a month, so I hope you've been doing the job I've been paying you for.'

He pulls the lever on Gino's coffee urn and watches it splash into a mug.

'Joking. Everything's under control.'

Belinda hands Lara a thick black folder. 'Here's your contract and code of conduct. Have a little look at it when you get a chance today and ask Zachary or Mackenzie if you have any questions. I'll keep your things in my office. After the show Zachary will bring you back and we can see what you want to do.'

The blonde girl nods. She looks composed enough but a little twitch in her top lip gives her away. Belinda sweeps out of the dining car, leaving an awkward silence behind her. Zach wonders where to start.

'Have you had breakfast?' Zach asks, finally. He'd like to be a good boss, and as far as he's concerned a good boss concerns themselves with their employees' stomachs first.

'I'm not hungry. Thanks.'

'Right. Well. Hold on while I get something.'

Gino, who never seems to have the problems with mornings Zach suffers from, greets him cheerily.

'I've made your favourite, Zachary, and I'll keep some aside until lunch if you fancy a snack.'

He passes a plate of pancakes and blueberries drenched with shiny rivulets of golden syrup across the serving hatch and Zach's mouth waters.

'You're a god among men, Gino, I really mean it.' Gino has given Zach extra helpings since his very first day. Gino had raised his eyebrows, looked the almost seven feet of length of him up and down and made an Italian sound of admiration. *You'll need quite a bit extra to keep that frame going,* he'd said. *Do not go hungry, you hear me? If I am starving you, ask for more.*

Zach takes his plate and coffee to a booth on the other side of the dining carriage. Lara follows him, the ring binder tucked under her arm, hovering awkwardly by the booth.

'Sit.' Zach gestures to the bench opposite him and she perches on the corner. 'Have some pancakes.' He pushes his plate towards her and she tentatively tears off a corner of the dough and holds it lightly between her fingers.

'Where did she pick you up from?'

She stifles a yawn. 'Southampton.'

'Have to get up early?'

Lara nods, a wry smile beginning on her lips. 'Left my mum's at four thirty. It's not always this bad, is it?'

Zach wants to tell her no. He wants to say that today will be the hardest day she'll ever do on *The Apple and the Pearl*, even if she stays another ten years. And in some ways that will be true. But he can't lie. So he makes the kind of non-committal grunt that used to have Juliet throwing her hands up in frustration – *Are you an animal? Fucking communicate, please!* – and tears off another corner of pancake to pass to her.

'So how much did Belinda tell you in your interview?'

Lara shrugs. 'She mainly asked me things about my life and my experience. She said it was a ballet and we travel from venue to venue on a train.'

Zach spears a pancake with his fork and eats it in one bite. 'Anything else?'

'She asked me if I'd had any contact with the supernatural.'

Zach cocks his head. 'And have you?'

'My auntie Doreen was a medium. She ran seances in Nana's front room. After a few years she'd earned enough to buy the house off the council and Nana was thrilled. But then my granddad turned up and started throwing things about because he was a union man and he didn't agree with privatisation. So we moved, but he followed us.'

Zach wrinkles his nose. Sensible, really, how this

show attracts people who are already acquainted with the workings of other worlds. He thinks of his own mother, picking mugwort and elderberries on the common behind their house, muttering under her breath as she stirred that sludge in the saucepans.

'Is that what this show is?'

Zach takes another bite of a pancake. 'Sort of. A bit weirder sometimes, but that's the general gist.'

He watches Lara's face for a moment to see if she's afraid. A flicker of curiosity, but otherwise she seems admirably composed.

'Right. Well, I think the easiest thing to do is for you to stick by me.' He has a gulp of coffee that almost scalds his throat but feels good – he needs that warmth in his bones to get them going. 'Ask me any questions you like but I might not know the answers.'

Zach finishes his pancakes and goes back to the serving hatch, where he swaps his empty plate for two more plates stacked with pancakes and a fresh mug of coffee.

Gino nudges the jug of milk towards him. 'Lighten it up a bit to stop the jitters?'

Zach grimaces. 'No thanks. Milk's always dodgy these days, Gino. No offence.'

He brings his plates back to the booth and pushes one towards Lara.

'Eat. You'll need it.'

She pokes her plate with a fork but she doesn't put it to her mouth. Zach wonders where he should start. On the day of his first pledge – almost eleven years ago now – they had stopped in a deserted seaside fairground with water slides and sandpits and a lagoon filled with pedaloes and dinghies. Juliet had pointed to the Grit, wearing the gaudy colours of a Neapolitan ice cream, and told him that nothing else mattered but the show. *All the rest,* she said, *is noise.*

Zach wonders if Juliet ever thinks of him now, knowing it's unlikely. 'First I'll tell you about the show. Have you ever worked in ballet before?'

'This is my first job. I saw an advert in *The Stage*, I rang the number and now I'm here.'

'Right.' Zach feels a little pang of disappointment, although he knows everyone's got to start somewhere. 'Well, ballet's tricky because the buggers move around, but it's fun. This show is a dream to light, really. LX department is you, me and Derek the follow spot, but in the mornings and before the show he does stage set up, and he spends most of act three in the stage left wing.' *Which is a blessing, really,* Zach thinks. He won't scare her off yet. Plenty of time for her to learn about Derek.

Zach spears another pancake, eats it in two bites. He tries to finish the whole mouthful before he starts talking again. *Your table manners are atrocious,* Juliet used to laugh.

'Mackie's our direct boss, he's a good egg. Knows the show inside out, has our back when Belinda goes on the warpath. We set up in the flies, wing booms and footlights, but sometimes the Grit fucks around and we lose a few wing flats if it decides to be smaller that day.'

Lara stares at him, a fork poised in her hand, the honey on her pancakes glistening undisturbed on her plate.

'You look like you've got a question.'

He can see her thinking back over everything he's just said, trying to find something to latch on to that she can make sense of. 'What's the Grit?'

'Ah.' Zach finishes his mouthful and drains his coffee. 'Bring that plate and follow me.'

He fills a mug again from the urn and bounds down the aisle between the booths. He's starting to feel like himself, more than himself really, with someone to watch him. He's putting his best foot forwards, as his mum would have said, showing himself to his best advantage. He feels self-consciousness settle on him. He better not fuck it up, as his mum would also have said.

'Ta, Gino,' he calls as he slides his plate across the serving hatch. 'We'll bring hers back at lunchtime.'

Gino gives a mock salute as Zach pulls open the door to the carriage and holds it open for Lara behind him. He jumps down from the train and turns to see her gazing out at the mist. He wonders if he should offer his hand to help her down or if she would consider that patronising. If he'd offered to help Juliet she'd have taken his hand and crushed it. He settles for taking Lara's plate and folder from her and standing aside in what he hopes is a gallant manner. She jumps down, landing clumsily on the carpet of evergreen needles.

'Okay, I know you asked something else but we'll start

here. This is the Grub, our train. Home.' He gestures towards the carriage behind him, sleek and shiny and speckled with condensation. Today it appears as an old-fashioned steam train, painted forest-green with little black bolts holding each iron sheet in place. He can just about see the bell frame through the mist, a large bronze bell hanging in a grid from a gigantic iron scaffold above the engine car at the front.

She looks sharply at him, fear starting to shadow her face.

'Did it look different to you earlier?'

Lara nods.

He sighs. How did Juliet describe this to him? He can barely remember now. Something about the way that although everyone's dreams are different they all share symbols.

'Don't worry, it does that. It plays all kinds of tricks and it pisses us all off but you get used to it. We call it the Grub because it's the ugly side of things, the maggot in the fruit.'

He gives her back the plate of congealing pancakes and beckons for her to follow him. He walks confidently into the mist as he sips at his coffee, his warmth dissipating the water vapour. After a few paces Zach trips and smacks his knee on a boulder sticking out of the ground.

'Fuck!' He holds on to the offending stone to rub his knee and groan a little.

'Is this a graveyard?' Lara asks, her knuckles white around her plate.

Zach looks around and sees she's right. He has tripped over the grave of a Desmond C Jones, which is covered in patches of yellow and white lichen and half buried in brambles. He picks his way around the thorns to find a path through the rows of graves, which stretch as far as he can see into the mist. He shrugs. 'We stop in funny places. You get used to it.'

She follows him, her footsteps light and wary, until Zach finds himself in a patch of clearing mist on a wide, cobbled avenue between the graves. He can no longer see the iron carapace of the Grub but he can sense its bulk somewhere behind him. Directly ahead at the end of the avenue there is a shadow looming. It's the tallest thing around, spiky and threatening like a haunted house from a horror film. And although he can't think how he's going to explain to this girl that their theatre doesn't always look like that, he's got to hand it to whatever imagination it is that powers this thing – today the Grit is seductively spooky. Zach has the feeling it's revelling in its uncanny new clothes.

'Okay,' he says. 'That's the Grit. It's our theatre, and we call it that because it's another ugly part of the show, the speck of dirt that gets trapped in the oyster shell. We store all the set and gear in the first few carriages behind the locomotive: there's a whole system but Mackie will tell you where to put everything.'

Lara looks puzzled. 'So does the theatre kind of – travel with you – or is it a completely new theatre each show?'

Zach sighs. This is why Belinda's paying him the big

bucks now. Juliet would have known what to say. She would either have described all the specific ways the Grit disobeys the ordinary laws of the universe, or she would have told her not to worry about it with such a tone that Lara could find herself all the way at her next pledge without ever having wondered what the fuck the Grit really was.

'Both. Neither. We take down the things inside, like the lighting rig and the stage – that definitely travels with us – but we leave the actual building behind. It turns up at the next venue a bit different but essentially the same.'

He can see by the twitching of Lara's fingers on her plate that he's doing a terrible job.

'It's like that boat.'

Lara frowns.

'You know, the boat that has all the planks and sails and whatnot replaced. But it's still the same boat.'

She's still looking nonplussed and Zach feels a little bubble of hope pop inside him.

'Look, don't worry about it for the moment. If you think too hard about it, it'll trip you over.' He turns away and walks up the avenue.

'The best way to understand is just to come inside and see. There's a point where you have to accept it or go home. All shows have quirks, this one just has a few more than most.'

The graves lining the avenue start to become marble mausoleums, complete with rococo carving and gold inlaid writing, and Zach finds himself reading the messages etched for eternity, things about sleeping with angels and perpetual peace. Not for the first time, he wonders if this is a real landscape. *What do you mean, real?* Juliet had scoffed when he'd asked her years ago. *Real as in, it's still here when we're not, has a life outside what we see here on the day the Grub arrived.* Juliet had shrugged. *Does it matter?*

Now Zach has reconsidered how he defines the word 'real'. He thinks about the creatures revealed as the house lights come up for the curtain call each night, the improbable shapes that flicker at the edges of your vision at dusk, all that stuff inside the box in Belinda's office that looks like diamonds and is really only dust. He thinks of all the mischief and malevolence he's seen from the Crow as it cavorts around the theatre and the train, and he wonders if he left everything that was 'real' that night when he waited at Manchester Piccadilly, or if that world had whirls of weird hiding in plain sight too.

The quick, light footsteps of someone running towards them sends Lara scuttling towards the safety of Zach's bulk until the silhouette of the black-clad figure sharpens in the mist.

'Phone signal!' the man pants as he passes them on the avenue. He's wearing a headset with the microphone poised at his lips. 'And internet too! I'm just off to tell Gino!'

'That's Charlie, deputy stage manager,' Zach explains as the man jogs away. 'Good bloke. Everyone likes him.'

Juliet would have followed that up with telling her about the members of the cast and crew who are not so popular. *Mackie's grumpy in the morning but he's a good boss, the best you'll ever have I reckon, Alina gets antsy if you nick her pens or soap and for the love of all that's holy keep away from Derek.* But thinking about the tangled webs of love and hate and indifference that stretch between the Grub and the Grit makes him feel tired again, so instead he focuses on the crunch of his boots on the leaf skeletons. Lara follows him, quietly chewing on her pancakes and Zach feels the knot of nerves in his stomach loosen a little. Eating is a good sign.

The foot of the stone staircase up to the doors of the auditorium is crowded with battered black flight cases. Zach sees Lara lean over to read a few of the labels written in black marker on white gaffer tape. *KING AND QUEEN COSTUMES, X 4 WING BOOMS, CROW HEADDRESSES LARGE AND SMALL, PEARL.* He remembers Juliet smirking at him in that annoyingly knowing way of hers. *Are you the kind of idiot I need to spell things out for, or have you got a brain between your ears?*

He's just started the long climb up the steps – the Grit doesn't always position itself so high up but today it's leaning into the drama – when Zach hears Lara clear her throat gently.

'Excuse me, Zach?' He turns to face her, one foot on the bottom step. 'Do you have a watch? I need to take some pills at about ten.'

He slaps one hand to his forehead. 'Shit! I forgot! I'm so sorry.'

'It's okay, I—'

'Listen, I have to tell you something really important.

Juliet would never forgive me and Belinda would have my guts for garters. There are two curfews here and they're timed to the second. You absolutely must be inside the Grit by the half – that's five to seven every night – and you absolutely must be inside the Grub by midnight. There's a bell, it's really loud, you can't miss it. Eighteen chimes before the house opens and twelve at midnight. You don't have to count them, but you got to get inside.'

'Do you mean I'll get in trouble if I'm not there?'

'Big trouble. Bigger than you can imagine. So get yourself a watch and sync it to Belinda's.'

Zach remembers Juliet strapping a cheap watch with a canvas strap onto his wrist the first time she took him into the Grit. *Don't take it off, don't mess with it, if it starts to slow get a new battery from Belinda immediately. You don't want to know what'll happen if you're caught out after curfew.* He misses Juliet, gone off to her retirement flat in Brighton only six weeks ago. Twenty years on the show and she made it out not just alive, but thriving. *I thought demons had me in their grip when I came here, young buck. Now I know the real demons don't want anything to do with me and I'm free.*

'Sorry, Zach? I do actually need to know the time.'

Zach glances at his wrist. 'Ten seventeen,' he says. 'Honestly. Wear a watch. If Mackie sees you without one tomorrow he'll tell you one of his horror stories.'

He takes the rest of the steps two at a time and veers sharply to the right towards a rickety wooden door marked *ARTISTES* in faded yellow paint.

'Stage door,' he calls over his shoulder. 'Moves around and looks different but always to the right of the auditorium entrance.'

He pushes the door and holds it open for Lara. 'After you.'

With a caw, the Crow settles on a lichen-spattered headstone engraved with the name *Desmond C Jones* and looks around the graves with satisfaction. An avenue of ivy-cloaked mausoleums, yews draped in cobwebs, holly studded with ruby-bright berries. *All Souls',* the Crow thinks happily, *and yes, this is the place to bring the humans to mourn their dead. A gift from Crow to her beloved cast and crew, the day of the year for the ancestors. Dead mothers, dead fathers, dead lovers, dead dreams.*

She turns on the pocked stone to face the Grit and rearranges her wings. *Every night the show is the same, curtain up seven thirty sharp on these old dances to older tunes, but every morning the Grit sinks itself into different earths on the thresholds of different worlds and it is Crow who guides them. Today on the day of dead things there's a new crew member to pledge a year and a day in service of the Crow, and what does she see when she looks around her? A king and a queen – or she will tonight, when the dancers take their cloaks about them and parade afore the proscenium. Three sisters, naturally: what is a ballet without a princess poised in her pointe shoe? An orchard – no, this is the land's winter now and there is nothing growing but poison seeds nestled in the holly and the yew. The sea – no, Crow has brought the Grub far inland to celebrate the dead on this day. Three suitors, then? Yes, and more. A curse – oh,* The Apple and the Pearl *is full of them – and a quest, of course. That's what you get when you deal with humans.*

And last of all Crow, singing in her nest, bringing all these people here, luring them out of the world to present The Apple and the Pearl. *Crow has been doing this for a long time now. Crow the impresario, Crow the mistress of the ring. With any luck that's what they're telling the new girl, how to do the show properly as it's been done for hundreds of years now, how to do this show so you don't piss Crow off because you don't want a Crow for an enemy, girl.*

The Crow looks up at the Grit, caws appreciatively and takes off into the mist with three great tugs of her wings.

When she hears the little sighing click, Belinda opens her arms and the Pearl falls into them. She clutches it securely to her chest and flicks on her torch to inspect every single rope, lever and pulley criss-crossing the old hornbeam joists, checking for any tears, frays or fissures. Every morning she wakes with a bubble of dread that something has gone wrong and today is one of those days she'll have to spend in here with Mackie and the Crow while they re-knot some rope or weld some part of the chassis, but mercifully that is not to be her fate today. She steps down from the carriage and elbows the door shut. No need to lock it. It will only open for her.

She shifts the Pearl under one arm – it's always light and cold in the mornings, its energy spent by the night's exertions – and angles her torch to inspect the bell, mounted on the great iron frame above the engine carriage. It's covered in dancing particles of mist and the bronze is dull in the weak winter sun, but still it glows. Belinda spots a little patch of rust on the headstock. Hmm. She will need to get in touch with the bell smith.

The crew are in the middle of unloading the flight cases from the storage carriages behind the engine, and she can see Derek wandering towards her with a toolbox balanced under each arm. She has no desire to be harassed about some irrelevant detail of what Mackie said yesterday so she quickly settles the Pearl inside its case, shuts the latches and hurries down the train just past the dining car to her cold, damp office.

Belinda locks her office door and pulls out the portable heater from under the desk. She plugs it in and sits in her chair, basking in its red glow as the smell of dust charring in the heat fills the space. She checks her watch – eleven twenty-two. Plenty of time. She likes mornings; the most troublesome members of her flock are still in bed and she stands a chance of getting something done without the constant interruptions of *sorry-Belinda-can-I-just*.

She leans back and shuts her eyes, running through her to-do list in her head: chase down the last expenses forms; put in Alina's order for pointe shoes; email that pawnbroker in Edinburgh to apologise for that amethyst necklace that turned out to be a bit of rope; email the bell smith. All of it can wait for her to warm this mist out of her bones. The day – and night – is long yet.

All Souls', and the year is turning to winter, everything shrinking back into its roots. Stopped in a graveyard roiling with mist around the yews of course, but the Grub likes its little jokes.

All Souls', and still they're safe for the year. She's thought about writing it up in the dining car, like they do in hospitals, *no deaths on this ward for ~~8~~ – ~~3~~ – 5 days!,* just to focus people's minds. She suggested it to Mackie once, in a half-joking way. He became very still, took a sip of his lager and frowned. *But what of joy, Belinda? Don't you think people deserve to just live, here and now, without fear?*

She thinks back to the last incident, only forty-six days ago. A dancer, one of the young men in the corps de ballet. Alex, on his third pledge, disappeared after class. Cecile had looked a little sad for once. *Excellent allegro,* she'd murmured as she filled out the accident form. *I'd planned for him to learn the Blue Suitor.* Before that it was Bobby, that French horn taken on a rainy day in September. Stupid man. Shuffling about with his shoes undone. AJ had given her the accident form two days later. *I don't see why I have to fill one of these out every time we lose a soul, Belinda. Sometimes their luck just runs out and that's that.* They all rail against the paperwork. Cecile flounces as she takes the forms and makes her provocative sounds of disgust, Mackie gives one of his heavy sighs, and AJ fills them out in unreadable handwriting – deliberately, she's sure – but they take the smooth, safe passage of their lives here for granted. Either they don't know or don't care that she pores over each form for days after a snatching, trying to tease out any lessons she might find, wondering how to stop it happening again. But sometimes, even she has to admit there's nothing she could have done. The dancer went back to the Grub alone – which is against the rules – and the French horn was being chased, tripped and fell into the Otherworld. Wilf saw it and spent a long hour detailing here in her office detailing every movement. *He was just unlucky, Belinda,* he'd said, staring out the window. *Simple as that.*

Replacing the French horn had been relatively simple, but hiring dancers never is. There was no time to hold an open audition; instead she wrote to an old friend who worked at a ballet school and asked her to send someone. *I've got just the young man for you: solid, dependable, won't set the world alight with his intellect but sweet enough. No family left, brought up by his grandmother who has recently died.* Belinda winced when she read that. It makes this show seem like some kind of dumping ground for orphans and runaways, given to *The Apple and the Pearl* because they've got no one in the outside world who'll miss them when they're gone.

Luke turned up at London Bridge the next day with a backpack and a too-big coat, smelling of mildew. The Crow had taken one look at him and rolled its eyes, though it let him pledge. Cecile had been horrified not to be consulted on his hiring, and has been making his life a misery ever since.

Belinda shrugs her coat off and switches her laptop on. As it whirrs and grumbles into life and she untangles the lead, she thinks about that silly little rhyme the dancers mumble to each other to say good luck before a show, that doggerel about the king, the queen and the suitors in a dream. *Where did it come from?* she asked the old company manager, Percy Montgomery, during her first week. *No idea,* old Montgomery had shrugged. *I leave them to their superstitions. Their lives are ruled by luck, can you blame them?*

Yes, there's luck here, and you want your fair share of it, but there are also rules. Keep a perfectly timed watch, don't move between the Grub and the Grit alone – never bloody obeyed, that one – don't touch the Pearl, don't look at the creatures in the auditorium. There are curfews and salt everywhere, and vast sheets of iron in the Grub and the Grit. There's Gino to feed every single one of them exactly what their hearts desire, there's Belinda herself, who – while she would not like to overstate her abilities – has a few tricks up her sleeve. There's the Crow, though the vast majority of the cast and crew will never understand it. There's a bronze bell cast by the latest scion of an ancient metalworking family—

—Ah, the bell smith. She needs to get back to him. The laptop screen blinks on and Belinda types in her password. She clicks on her email, finds the message from the bell smith and begins to write: *Are you able to get to Didcot Parkway on the 12th? I'll pick you up from the ticket office and walk you through the guest cabin, as usual. I'd like you to look at the hinges of the bell frame which are a little rusty and you know how we feel about rust here!*

Midday and it's musicians' reveille in the cabins. For Michael it sounds like a tumbling, tinkling harp but he barely hears it because his ears are plugged with foam earplugs he buys in pharmacies on days off. He doesn't need an alarm anyway. He's awake: he has been since the vibrations of the technical crew's stomping boots woke him.

Like yesterday, and the day before and the day before that, he is lying in his cabin re-reading his notebooks. He flicks through the pages quickly, the words hurtling back to his mind from the forgotten place he had stashed them.

The Grub has stopped in an orchard of mulberries and quince and as they were setting up the Grit for the show we walked together among the trees, pulling fruit off the boughs and biting into it, black and yellow juice making bumblebee stripes on our chins.

He turns the page to read a detailed and appreciative description of Evelyn's unique tuning, written while he sat with her in the pit after rehearsals as she moved her levers and plucked her harp strings. Once he had thought of his notebooks as a record for their children and so he did not write about the shape of her bare white thighs around his waist or the long moan of her juddering climax as she clung to him. But now it is an exquisite torture to him that these things are missing. He is living on the lingering scent of her and these chaste cliches in his diaries, with nothing of substance to his fantasies, nothing to fill or nourish him.

The reveille ends, but in Michael's cabin there is still an echo of the harp burbling away in a stream of arpeggios. This is why he uses the earplugs. There is always a harp playing in his ears while he's inside the train, all day and all night. He is never free from it. That's what the Crow does when he's in here, it reaches inside him and pulls out threads of melody to hum his obsessions back at him, singing songs he barely remembers, snatches of nursery rhymes he's not heard since he was at his mother's breast, and weaving it all into whatever reality he's currently swimming in with a kind of childish glee, careless of whether that music might be sweet to him or if the last thing he wants to hear is a fucking harp.

Evelyn's introduction to the Pearl waltz tonight was so beautiful I almost missed my cue. My bow was poised, I was looking at the exact bar in the score, but her vibrato just went on and on, right through my bones.

The new harpist is fine. He's competent, his instrument gilded finely enough to sit at the front of the pit and look plush, his manner affable enough, but there is no more sparkle of a black sequinned dress as the orchestra stands during the curtain calls, no more vibrato before the second act waltz and no more stray red hairs in his bed.

Dinner with Lance after the show and we were talking about the music we loved as children and right at the same time Evelyn and I started talking about Sandy Denny and we looked at Lance and held hands under the table and sang 'Who knows where the time goes…' and he laughed and she leaned in to rest her head on my shoulder and I have never been so happy, so right, so light in all my life.

Enough. He wedges the notebook back on the shelves in a place he tells himself he will forget by tomorrow morning and pulls on his trousers and an old jumper of Lance's. At the door he takes a battered satchel off the hook on the back of door and slings the strap over his shoulder. There is a brief, agonising whisper of the siren arpeggios as the earplugs slip a little but he does not let it pull him into madness. He hums 'The Wheels on the Bus' to distract himself and shoves it back in. His cabin door clicks shut behind him.

The dining car is right in the middle of the Grub, the centre of everyone's world. At this time of day it's filled with technical crew just finished setting up the Grit, pouring themselves cups of thick black coffee from the urns beside Gino's serving hatch. Michael joins the end of the line and shuffles along. He is hungry, but it is almost indistinguishable from all the other emptinesses he feels. He stands between Danny and Kavi the stagehands, skinny among their burl, and each of them nods good morning without speaking. Everyone knows about the earplugs.

'Afternoon morning,' says Gino as he passes Michael a knife and fork through the hatch. 'I never know which one. I'm still serving some breakfast so you can have roasted millet pancakes with a variety of toppings or celeriac soup, which is the lunch option.' Michael can barely hear Gino through the plugs and the thrum of voices in the dining car, but his beard makes the movements of his lips very obvious and he's got very good at reading lips.

'The soup please.'

'Good choice.' Gino slides a plate across the hatch. 'And there's phone signal, by the way. In case you want to contact anyone.'

A slick of ice along his spine. 'Why are you telling me that?'

Gino sighs. 'I'm telling everyone, Michael. I'm supposed to spread the word like I always do.'

Michael takes his plate and moves away without a *thank you* or a *sorry*. He's a landmine these days, that trips only explosions of grief inside him. He sees Henry the second violin in a booth, both hands clutched around a mug of herbal tea. Perhaps Michael should like him more, as one of the only people here who didn't know him as Evelyn's other half, but there's something both cold and over-eager about him that is exhausting. He clearly wants to be Michael's friend – or something more – but Michael can't imagine getting through a conversation about the weather, let alone explaining that he's flattered, but not interested.

Henry smiles but Michael pretends he hasn't seen him and sits in a booth at the far end of the carriage with his back to everyone. He alternates sips of coffee and spoonfuls of soup because everything tastes like sawdust. He's only eating because hunger is one pain too much to deal with and because Gino would know if he didn't and tell AJ. The black tuxedo he wears for shows hangs on him as if on a wire hanger, his skin is sallow and flakey and his hair is lank. He stares at the fogged windows, all that water condensed on the glass from cooking and breathing and the spray of taps and the steam of tea. He reaches into his satchel to take out his notebook and pen and writes:

I wonder if any of this water passed through her body to become a little bead on this window, or if there's no longer anything here in the Grub which she once touched.

He returns his plate and mug to Gino, smiles contritely and pulls the door to the gangway open. The air outside is chilly and damp, mist curling between the cars. He jumps the three steps down from the Grub and lands with a squelch in wet, loamy soil covered in a carpet of rotting evergreen needles. Instantly, the distant hum of harps is gone, and Michael pulls the plugs out of his ears and stuffs them into his pocket.

Before him is a graveyard straight out of a storybook, the most misty, overgrown, haunted-looking graveyard he could ever have imagined. *It likes a sense of theatre,* Michael remembers writing in the diary of his first pledge, *it sucks at the essence of what you think a place is like and spits it out at you in technicolour.*

Michael wanders among the graves, picking his way between the drooping yews and the ivy creeping over the stones tumbling this way and that like the earth beneath them is buckling, trying to release the bodies buried within.

Wandering alone like this is against the rules but he's beyond that now, even Belinda would agree. Damp spreads inside his shoes and his skin pimples with cold and something else, an eerie sense that come seven thirty tonight the dead could heave themselves out of their coffins and come shuffling into the auditorium just as they are, flesh falling off bones, formaldehyde leaking from their skulls.

He turns onto a wide avenue flanked by marble mausoleums, and the Grit looms out of the mist at him. He sees a familiar black-clad figure standing in the middle of the avenue, fog curling like ghostly hands around his ankles.

AJ's brilliantined silver hair is speckled with dew and he wears a black suit with a mandarin collar and black patent shoes with gleaming white spats. Michael has never seen him in anything else, except for the time when there was a fire scare before reveille and they all stood in a dark field waiting for Belinda in her hi-vis jacket to inspect the Grub, where he waited next to Cecile in a wine-red velvet dressing gown and matching monogrammed slippers.

Michael comes to stand next to him.

'A little melodramatic today, don't you think?'

AJ gives his enigmatic little smile.

'It's All Souls', Michael.'

'Oh yes,' he murmurs, a little ashamed. He wants people to think he's recovering and coming back to himself, and he especially wants AJ to think that, but losing track of the date is a clear sign he's still floundering. For Michael, there is no difference these days between the dead and the plain gone. He should light a candle for Evelyn, the way his mother will be lighting one tonight for his grandparents. Let the wick make a deep well within the wax and splutter into darkness.

'Too on the nose.' AJ sighs. 'The Grub's always been obvious in its metaphors and mockeries.'

Michael thinks of the harp music and the vibrato that plays over and over and over until everything in him is jangling with the note.

Not everyone can feel it, you know. AJ said when he'd tentatively broached the subject with him in the first month of his pledge. *For some the Grub is just a train and the Grit just a theatre and the only thing unusual about this job is the audience.* Evelyn was the only person – other than AJ – who'd felt it as he did.

He'd been sitting in the dining car after the show, the crew pulling the Grit apart and hauling it back to the cargo carriages with the Grub nestled peacefully in a dark valley blanketed with snow. Everyone was drinking aniseedy liqueurs from the bottle. He felt a light tap on his shoulder.

He looked up from his notebook to see the new harpist standing by his booth, clutching a glass of red wine. His fingertips started to fizz at the nearness of her. He'd been with the company for two years and in that time he'd lived in shy, bewildered celibacy, watching Lance work his way through the dancers, orchestra and most of the crew, standing alone on the edges of a raucous, never-ending game of musical beds.

Hi. I'm Evelyn. AJ sent me to you.

He'd known her name. Her first show had lit him all over with electric pleasure. Her playing was exquisite. She drew tones from the score he'd never heard before and he'd fallen halfway in love with her before he'd even seen her face. A few days later, Lance had hurried into the dressing room at the five-minute call, grabbed his laundered shirt from the rack and kicked his trainers off in a huff.

New girl's not for playing, although I don't know why I'm telling you that.

Maybe she just doesn't want to play with you?

No. Lance had looked genuinely horrified. *Not possible.*

With Evelyn in front of him, smiling, her fringe falling deliciously across her face, the Grub had started to play wheeling, spitting fireworks in his ears, so loud he could hardly hear her. A swelling in his trousers and a twisting in his belly, the agony of the humiliation – he felt fourteen again.

Can I ask you a question? she'd said.

Of course. His heart soared and plummeted at the same time. The fireworks kept sparking, mockingly. He thought she'd probably ask him if her tuning was right in the third act, which it was, or something about per diem payments. She slid into the seat opposite him and put her glass on the table.

What do you hear when you're in the Grub?

A thrill slid through his blood that she heard it too, this beautiful woman with hands that pulled such grace from her instrument, so near to him, asking him something so intimate.

He smiled broadly to mask his nerves and clasped his hands tight in his lap, hoping to hide his ridiculous hopes. *Right now I can hear a mash-up of the John Lee Hooker my dad used to play and the hello song from a music class my mum used to take me to when I was three. But I've got used to it. I just ignore it most of the time.* That was a lie. He never managed to ignore it and there was no way he was going to tell her truth; that the fireworks were blasting, and that as she flicked her hair over her shoulder and he got a waft of some kind of fruity shampoo he heard a long, low blast of a saxophone, like a joke sexy noise, that went straight into Marvin Gaye.

He wished he could have painted her face, the delight, the relief. That was when he fell the rest of the way in love with her.

But that's so nice! She took a swig of her wine and it left a purple stain on her lips that made his groin twitch. *I hear nothing but these hokey old Irish folk songs I used to have to play for weddings when I was a teenager.*

I used to do weddings too, he said. *I don't ever want to hear that Mendelssohn march again.*

Something bitter passed across her face and she took another gulp of wine. *Yeah. My mum pretended she was my agent. She booked me almost every weekend for years and years and when I asked for the money to go to Guildhall she told me to leave and not come back until I was grateful for her sacrifices.*

There had been a moment of awkwardness. She had

cracked open a little door of honesty and he wanted to stick his foot in it to wedge it open. He could feel the smirks of Steve the bassoonist and Wilf the cellist burning into his back, and the fireworks spitting and shrieking in his head were starting to make his temples throb.

Do you want to get some air? he'd asked. *It's really noisy in here.*

A couple of weeks later they discovered that if their bare skin was touching they could hear each other's private music, and the more of themselves they pressed together the louder it was. They'd lie entwined in his cabin after curfew, the movement of the Grub rocking them like babies, and they would listen to the music it played them and giggle together at the cacophony. At those times it was like the Crow was playing along, the jester to their king and queen, telling jokes only for them. He had never been so bare, so raw. The Crow teased out every loving, obsessive, jealous, doting thought of her, gave it melody and played it to her.

But Evelyn would say, *I don't know how long I'll be able to stand this, Michael. It's only in here with you that I can get any peace.*

Sometimes the Crow repeats these words in the middle of the night and he wakes up, his cheeks wet with tears, reaching for her in his bed, fingers clawed with regret at what he didn't do and didn't say to keep her. *Just wait, will you, I'll leave. Just let me finish out this pledge and I'll come with you.*

But she hadn't waited. She'd left, walked off the Grub

at Liverpool Lime Street dragging a suitcase and the harp inside its scuffed, taped-up case. *I think it's best if you stay, Michael. I'm not sure what we'll mean to each other out in the world.*

Michael looks at AJ, his hands clasped behind his back, staring up at the Grit.

'Can I ask you a question?' AJ inclines his head. 'What does the Grub play for you?'

It's an intimate question, like asking to peer into his dreams, but there is no one left who understands what it's like. AJ thinks for a moment. 'Rachmaninov, mainly. My mother was a very fine pianist, and he was her favourite.'

Michael envies that clarity. How restful to only hear what you could hum along to, something that could comfort you instead of drive you mad.

'I missed it, though. During the years I've spent away. There's nothing out there in the world but silence. It can be lonely. Perhaps that's why I keep coming back.'

Michael nods. He knows about loneliness.

'Do you still hear the harp?' AJ asks delicately.

Michael says, miserably, 'Yes.'

'You won't forever, you know. It will get better.'

This is the first time they have ever spoken about Evelyn, or the lack of her, and Michael is winded by it. Everyone else has done him the favour of pretending she never existed, letting her name lie silent as if she'd been snatched, at least in his morose presence, and although he knows AJ is trying to be kind, he rears away from it.

'I have to go,' Michael says. 'I'm playing for class.'

'Of course.' AJ gives the funny little bow he does when you leave him and Michael walks quickly away, his footsteps echoing on the mausoleums, up the wide avenue leading to the steps to the Grit, leaving AJ among the graves staring up at the theatre.

It had been AJ who had suggested Michael might play for ballet class. He'd missed three shows, which everyone knew about, even Derek the follow spot operator, and he'd missed nine meals, which only Gino knew about. He knew there'd be a knock on his cabin door any moment, he just hadn't known how to say what he was going to say when it came.

When the knock came it wasn't Belinda but AJ, standing elegantly in the corridor, his slick silver hair glinting.

I understand you have not been well, Michael.

He could not answer. He knew he looked wretched, dismantled like a broken puppet. He had not slept, he had not eaten, he was standing in the wreckage of his room as he'd torn it apart packing everything he owned into two bulging suitcases. He coughed. There was something trying to escape from his throat, something scratching and clawing at the tender, aching skin of his gullet. He coughed again to dislodge it.

I have been sent by Cecile to ask if you are available to play for ballet class today.

He coughed again. He was trying to say, *No, I am not available and by the way I cannot see out my pledge, I have to leave, I will pay any forfeit the Crow asks, thank you for everything you have meant to me,* but the thing was stopping him from talking, like a plug holding back the river of tears, and he was choking on it. AJ stood watching him, inscrutable as always. Michael coughed and coughed until the thing came loose inside his chest and he hacked it up. It slid up past his tonsils and burst out of his lips to splat on the floor, right by the toe of AJ's gleaming black patent shoe.

What is that? Michael had whispered, hoarse, dizzy.

AJ looked at the pulsing crimson thing, leaking some kind of black fluid. He sighed.

That is your heart, Michael, he'd said. *A cruel forfeit but the Crow never pretended to be kind. At least you can take comfort in being safe now. Better protection than salt or iron.*

And he pulled a white handkerchief out of his breast pocket and swept up the throbbing, meaty mass of it and tucked it into his pocket. *Cecile will be expecting you at one thirty on stage,* he said as he walked away.

Michael unpacked his notebooks. He has not seen his heart since.

He looks at his watch as he pulls open the stage door. Five past one. There are so many hours in the day now he doesn't sleep and he barely talks, so much time to sit out and watch pass. The minutes ache, the hours stab.

He goes to the musicians' dressing room first, where he checks his tuxedo is hanging on the hook that bears his name – it is, it always is – then brushes a bit of bow rosin from the lapel. The melancholy of the place begins to bruise him, so he shuts the door again. He climbs three flights of stairs to the stage, pausing to look at the noticeboard in the corridor, which is more or less the same as yesterday, give or take tonight's casting for the dancers and a handwritten note from Mackie the technical director inviting everyone to celebrate his pledge day after the show tonight – *dressing up optional* – and Michael sighs. Lance will escort him there and give him a beer to hold while he stands in a corner of the bar, ears plugged, ignored by everyone except possibly Gino who will offer him a slice of halva or cherry cake. Henry might try to talk to him, which will be excruciating in its own way – *look, just tell him he's not your type, or let me do it for you,* Lance has said a few times, *but you've got to let the poor man know where he stands. It's starting to tip into stalker behaviour.* Then, while Lance occupies himself with whoever he's currently sleeping with – Yolanda the flute, if his information is still up-to-date – Michael will put the untouched beer back on the bar and slip out of the dining car and back to his cabin to lie in the dark alone, waiting for the bell to toll midnight and the soft swaying movement of the Grub to draw him into his restless dreams.

He pushes open the heavy door that separates the corridor and the stage, and lets it swing behind him. The blackness of the as yet empty theatre is comforting to his eyes. In here there is no night or day, only illusion.

The wings are crowded with the dancers' things: canvas bags spilling over with pink ribbons; water bottles; a careful heap of jewellery on the props table; ankle supports; and back braces. The stage is criss-crossed with portable ballet barres, the dancers draped over them. He crosses to the downstage right corner where the piano is always set up and waves to Romero, who lies on his back with his legs twisted around each other, wearing that grimace all the dancers wear at this time of the day before the bending and swooping of the ballet class smooths their pains away.

He watches Anita, sitting on the floor at the back of the stage, tying her pointe shoe ribbons around her ankle. A couple of weeks ago he'd had three beers on an empty stomach after the show and when he'd passed her waiting for a shower as he went back to his cabin he'd recklessly tapped her on the shoulder.

Do you miss him?

Anita's face had creased in panic. She looked quickly around her and shrank back towards the window, holding her towel in front of her like a shield.

Michael, please don't—

Because you seem to be fine, yet you'll never see Alex again and I could walk off this train any time I like to see Evelyn if the bastard Crow would let me. Don't you long for him? Don't you want to shout his name? Don't you want to jump off the stage in the middle of the Pearl waltz and beg one of those creatures to take you to him?

She had covered her face with her hands but tears leaked through her fingers. *Please don't do this, Michael. I understand you're hurting but please please please don't do this to me.*

Michael had woken up more than usually ashamed

of himself. He'd written a note and put it in the cubby in wardrobe where she kept her shoes. *Very sorry for my behaviour, please forgive me. I'm glad you have found some peace, I admire that very much.*

'Morning, Michael, how are you?' Romero says brightly. He always begins ballet class right by the piano. All the dancers have their places on stage for class the way all the orchestra have their places in the pit, although it is more obvious where a new flute would put themselves than where a new dancer would. When there's a new pledge, they hover in the wings until the very last moment to pounce on the free space, which will be theirs until someone leaves and vacates a spot. Like hermit crabs, Michael thinks.

He smiles at Romero, murmurs something non-committal. They'd first met at Waterloo station one summer evening; Michael with his violin and two suitcases at his feet and the Kinks' song tripping through his mind, Romero sitting on a bulging backpack with his long legs stretched in front of him, toes dropped away from each other in a perfect quarter-to-three position. Michael had played plenty of ballet music at the conservatoire but Romero was the first dancer he'd really met. He couldn't stop staring at him, the lithe lines of his body, the way he fully inhabited every inch of his skin, the catlike grace of him.

Belinda was there, handbag in front of her like a weapon. *Gentlemen of* The Apple and the Pearl*?* Romero had sprung to his feet and Michael had slung his instrument over his shoulder. *Follow me please.*

Now he suspects Romero has been deputised among the dancers to try to be nice to him, seeing as they're pledge-mates. He is waiting for Romero to ask him some small-talky question with a tactful, sympathetic smile. Lance told him all the backstage tannoys leak salt water during his solo in the second act Blue *pas de deux* and it's annoying everyone, but Michael had told him to take it up with the Crow. *Do you think this is how I'm choosing to live?*

He adjusts the piano stool, sits on its padded leather and pulls out his latest notebook and a pen. He writes, *We are stopped in a graveyard filled with ancient graves with moss grown in the carved names to obscure them and–* He stops. It is harder and harder to know what to put in his notebooks these days. He keeps starting sentences and abandoning them, the ink trailing across the paper, his thoughts drifting to a halt. This whole notebook, the one he started after Evelyn left, is made up of sad little fragments like this, random disconnected thoughts that never connect into a text. He keeps thinking of who will or won't read all the hundreds of pages he's filled and what they'll find about him. He's settled recently on it becoming more of a record of whatever it is that powers the Grub and the Grit and so he tries to write less around the raw, jagged edges of his emptiness and more about what he sees and hears and feels. But it always ends up circling round to her, his thoughts like a hungry buzzard over a meadow.

All Souls', he writes, *and I had forgotten, but it makes little difference to us. The show is the same.*

That was something Evelyn had hated, the way the day started again and again with the same shape to it – set up the Grit, ballet class, rehearsals, show, pack up the Grit, get moving, do it all again.

We play the same thing over and over and over and the tunes are boring, Michael, don't you think? Don't you yearn for some complexity, something other than waltzes and marches, something just to sink your teeth into?

He had tried to understand, he really had. Taken her on fun, unexpected dates on days off, tried to be spontaneous, tried to make things exciting. But then they came back to the Grub, to the Grit, to the show. To their lives. *It's a ballet score, Evie,* he'd said with impatience one night off after they'd been to see a kora-harp fusion band in Liverpool. *You can hardly expect it to be avant-garde.*

She'd made a face and turned away. He was worried. Two weeks off her next pledge and she was saying she didn't want to renew, making noises about them leaving the show together and going back into the world, teaching maybe. She wanted to record, she wanted to compose, she said performing was becoming like a chain to her, tying her down.

I don't want to teach, Evie, I want to stay here.

But what do we make here, Michael? What do we create, what do we leave behind us?

You could compose here. He had been baffled by her restlessness, but he hadn't known what to do about it. Now that's what wakes him early in the morning and stops him getting back to sleep, all the things he should have said to her. He writes them down instead.

Let's ask Belinda for a couples cabin and those stupid songs won't bother you so much.

What can I do to help you? I couldn't bear it if you left.

Why don't you write down the things that lurk and hurt you and we can exorcise them and get them out of your head so the Crow can't reach them?

Maybe she was right to leave. Writing down his heart-breaks isn't making him feel any better and it isn't starving the Crow of ammunition. He doesn't know why he thought it might have helped her.

Twenty-five past one and Cecile sweeps onto the stage from the prompt corner surrounded by her usual haze of lily-of-the-valley and hairspray. She reminds Michael of a bat. Skinny limbs swathed in black – black legwarmers and a long black skirt, and a black silk blouse held at the throat with a string of pearls. Michael shuts his notebook and slips it into his satchel. The dancers clamber to their feet, pull their hair into ponytails, peel stripy woollen leggings from their thighs and push their insteps into their pointe shoes.

Cecile sits on a stool and raises one hand, fingers poised to click the rhythm she wants for the first exercise. Michael pulls up the piano lid and places his hands on the keys. He closes his eyes. A tune comes to him for the warm-up stretches and he feels a tiny rush of warmth in his fingers. The closest thing to joy he feels these days is the flicker of gratitude that, no matter what else has gone, he is still able to conjure melodies from the strings hidden in this box and the strings under his hands on his violin.

Cecile has a voice like a frog but still she sings to count Michael in and her words are a spell, drawing a soothing balm from the bare, black box of the Grit to tend to the dancers' aching muscles and swollen joints.

'Five,' she croaks. A slow, echoing click of her fingers.

'Six.' Click.

'Seven.' Click.

'Eight. Maestro.'

Four bars of introduction while Mara lets the sound of the piano seep through her skin and into her bones. The music is the spark that lights the engine: she can go nowhere without it. The first soft notes soothe the roughness in her muscles and then, like a marionette, she finds herself moving, pulled by the invisible strings of melody that stream across the stage. She stands facing the barre, toes squashed into still-too-hard pointe shoes, pedalling through her feet, releasing each raw muscle.

She stretches one calf and then the other. They ache from the Achilles tendon to the back of her knees. She danced the Red Princess last night and all those balances on the right leg are now etched into the meat of her. It will take until the end of the class to wipe them away, to erase all yesterday's aches and set herself straight again.

She sweeps her arm over her head and bends, first to one

side, then the other. The feeling of release in her middle is never enough, she yearns to stay curved until whatever tightness lingers in the muscles holding her ribs to her spine has eased away. She rolls her neck and shoulders, and reaches her hands up to the flies to greet the familiar grid of the backdrops and the lighting rig. She stretches, hears little cracks and pops in her spine, and dives to press one hand against the cool vinyl of the stage floor and knead her aching calf. *Here we go again*, she thinks. Another morning, another day.

'Now we go into *pliés*,' calls Cecile over the music and there's a shuffling as everyone moves to place their left hands on the painted steel of the barre. Mara brings her heels together to stand in first position. Jessica stands in front of her in exactly the same position, the delicate blonde hairs on the back of her neck a little lifted against the chill of the Grit.

Every day the same start to class, every dancer everywhere reciting their alphabet anew each morning, the basic bend-and-stretch that sits underneath all the complex grammar of classical ballet.

Bend the knees, straighten – in first, second, fourth and fifth. Swoop and stretch the arms, extend the right leg *a la seconde* and pull up the muscles on the standing thigh. A gentle curve in the arm, keep the neck long, relax that supporting hand on the barre, track the knees over the toes. She turns to the other side to place her right hand on the barre and stare at the back of Ritchie's head. Everyone stands in the same places every day, one of those bullshit tradition things she's tried to persuade everyone out of, though she might as well have been trying to make sheep somersault for all the luck she's had. *The dancer is a creature of superstitious habit,* she imagines the narrator of a nature documentary whispering, *and instinctively hierarchical. There is a feeling – unsubstantiated but present nonetheless – that a comfortable spot for daily ballet class can make or break a show.*

That means Mara has spent quite a while contemplating first the fine golden necklace Jessica wears, and then the fluctuations of Ritchie's hairstyles. She stood here on her first day because it seemed like there was a space and she's been stuck here singing the ABCs of ballet ever since.

Michael finishes the *plié* music with a flourish; Cecile stands from her stool and places one delicate hand on the barre at the front of the stage to mark through a *tendu* exercise.

Mara barely watches. It's an easy day for her, only the Queen tonight. Not that the Queen is an easy role. You're on stage a lot and Mara always has the feeling that she's holding the show together, like she's its seams. But physically she can relax. There are no pointe shoes, no jumping, no holding it all in for endless lifts and turns in the *pas de deux* that leave her ribs and hip bones raw. She'll take class easy, maybe skip the jumps, keep her pointe shoes off for the centre. Chill.

As she puts her left hand back on the barre and Michael plays the first chord, she shuffles into fifth position with an automatic squeeze of the glute muscles to protect her knees. She stretches her right leg in front of her, to the side and behind, always half a beat behind Jessica because she's copying her. *Tendu* and fifth, *tendu* and fifth. The music is always a little too fast at this point in the class. She's not ready to move quickly yet, she needs more time to luxuriate in the movements. Ideally, she'd like to do the exercise half time but Cecile would not be amused. *You think you know better than me?* she'd drawl, with one long, painted fingernail shot in her direction.

You'd think after nine years and having danced every role in the repertoire she'd be allowed a little bit of autonomy, a little bit of trust to know what's best for her own body, but no. Ballet is obedience, often blind, to an authority often taken by force and Cecile is as bad as any other ballet mistress for her insistence that things happen as they have always happened, because they always have. Mara's lucky. She's never been on Cecile's really bad side, never been reduced to tears in rehearsals – except that one fucking awful rehearsal of the Crow, but rehearsing any part of the Crow's sections of the show always puts Cecile in a foul mood – never been beckoned to the front of the stage, flicked on the stomach or thighs and told to stop eating dinner. Although, to be fair, that's hearsay, from Cecile's first pledge as ballet mistress. Apparently she hasn't tried that one in a good few years. Gino put a stop to that. That's why they don't talk.

There are privileges she has earned. Like her baggy woollen trousers and jumper. Jessica hasn't, not yet, and she stands in leotard and tights so that Cecile can see and comment upon every twitch of every muscle. A strange kind of privilege, to have the privacy and warmth of your clothes, but there you go. Batshit. Ballet.

Mara can't say when exactly she started wearing her baggy things during class. Sometime after she was regularly dancing each of the three Princesses and the Crow but before she did her first Queen. She thinks about the icy way Cecile would glare if one of the new pledges in the corps de ballet were to get to the end of class still swathed in a tracksuit. None of them ever do. They're too well trained from ballet school. Your bodily autonomy is something you've got to prove you deserve, and it's toxic. In this world you're nothing but your body and everyone knows it.

There have been days in the winter when the mercury in the Grit was stuck at ten degrees and Cecile made Mackie drag out the heaters and blast them from the wings rather than let the corps de ballet stay in their tracksuits. *Lazy clothes, lazy muscles* she'd trilled and wandered among them draped in her cashmere shawl as they shivered.

'*Glissés*!' Cecile calls, demonstrating with neat, tight movements as her feet leave the floor just a couple of inches. She must have been a beautiful dancer, Mara's always thought. A bitch, but wonderful to watch. Michael starts to play something a bit too plinky-plonky for Mara to really get into and she yawns a little, watching Jessica's sharp feet fly in and out of fifth position. *All too fast*, Mara grumbles as she turns to the other side to watch Ritchie, also entirely too perky, do the exercise half a beat ahead of her. *Please just let me wake up.*

Cecile marks through a *rond de jambe* exercise and Mara watches upside down as she stretches her hamstrings. This is the point in the class when Mara starts to feel her body come alive, the point where her muscles start to glide over each other and her joints become silky again. She never used to take such care with her body, oiling it and tending to it like a precious car. She could just throw her shoes on and bounce into class. But she's thirty now and that's what? *About a hundred and ten in ballerina years*, Josh said the other day with a smirk.

She won't pledge again. She's decided. She celebrated her birthday a couple of months ago with the Grub stopped in a field of freshly cut hay bundled in golden stacks. After ballet class everyone gathered outside the Grit, waiting for Gino to bring out one of the cakes he only makes if you're having a birthday with a zero in the number. That day the Grit sported hanging baskets of pink and white petunias and she stood between Cecile and AJ on the steps while Gino carried the cake towards them. The whole scene was a perfect version of itself. The haystacks absorbed the slanted September sunlight until they glowed, the shards of grass stubble shone, blackbirds pecked softly at the earth.

It is as if Monet is in our minds, painting all that we can see, AJ had murmured and he was exactly right. It was a gift from the Grub, this kind of place, the kind of gift the train gives them sometimes just to fuck with them.

Saying – cackling – *look what beauties it's in my power to gift you, and you'll never know why I choose not to do this every single day.*

Gino lit the thirty candles on the cake and the dancers, tech crew and musicians all mumble-sang 'Happy Birthday' in various keys while lights flickered at the edges of their vision as they always did at times like these. *Harmless enough at the minute*, Mackie had said when the flute and the trombone started to get twitchy. *They just know we're here having a good time.*

She sliced her cake and she smiled until her mouth twitched but something was flailing inside her. Thirty. She knew she wouldn't have long left. She had the sensation that with every movement of the knife she was severing everything she had built around this show for the past nine years.

That night she danced the Crow, and when she took the tray to the caboose after the show she waited until she heard a loud caw. She turned to see a huge black bird on the railing.

Mara carefully pulled a slice of birthday cake wrapped in a paper napkin out of her pocket and put it on the tray.

It's my birthday. One with a zero. Gino made a cake for me.

But the bird had not even glanced at it. Instead, it hopped over to her and dropped something at her feet that made a small clinking sound.

Oh. She picked it up and turned the coin over in her fingers, let her hands warm the metal. It was an ordinary fifty pence piece. She had known exactly what it meant. *I get it. Redundancy pay.* The Crow often had a sense of humour.

The bird said nothing. She turned to face it to find it staring at her, the black eye gleaming even in the dull light of the lantern swinging from the ceiling. *Do you know what?* she said, trying to hold back the tears. *I'm actually grateful. I've always wanted to retire at my peak, you know? Not hang on when I'm long past it. I had this ballet teacher at school once and she said that dancers are the only artists who destroy their instrument. I mean, mine's not entirely destroyed but it's not doing that great either.*

But the bird was no longer listening, so Mara pocketed the coin and went back to her cabin. How life changes in an instant, she thinks, lying awake all night, willing those swelling tears to come at last. Everything over, so quickly and yes, just as she has become the best dancer she has ever been. A daylily blooming for just one day before withering, that's her. That's all of them. That's ballet.

And is it worth it? she wonders, as she watches Cecile demonstrate the *fondu* exercise. Have these nine years of class, rehearsal, show, class, rehearsal, show been worth it? The question has niggled at her for years, since well before her birthday. *Worth it? What is anything worth, Mara?* Stuart said, after too much wine one night. *What price are you asking for?*

Michael starts playing the seemingly obligatory tango rhythm that always accompanies a *fondu* exercise and Mara stands in fifth position. She sinks into the *coupé*, then extends her leg in front of her.

She kept that little silver coin. It lives in her make-up

bag now. Every evening, as she gets ready for the show, she sees it and it reminds her that she's almost done.

Done, she thinks as she extends her leg to the side. *It's almost over.* And she's found herself feeling more and more all right with that with every show that passed. *I did it, I danced. I was here, and I danced and I did it well.*

And wasn't that the dream, those days when she was sixteen and turning up to ballet school each day, desperate to be one of the lucky ones who got a career?

It didn't always seem like it was going to happen for her. After graduating, she spent a horrendous six months in Florence doing *Swan Lake*, then a desperate round of auditions as she did class each day on her own in her childhood bedroom with the rug pushed back. Eighteen and what did she know about the world? She'd got to the point where her mother was making noises about getting a job in a cafe, *not too late to go to university you know,* when she saw it, scanning the noticeboard before an open class. *Open audition for* The Apple and the Pearl, *4.30.* She had nowhere else to be, so she went into the room. A woman she now knows as Belinda gave her two safety pins and a paper number *46* and told her to take a spot at the barre. The ballet mistress – Cecile – sat silently at the front of the room, swathed in black, a notepad on her lap.

Half the dancers were told to leave after the barre, another five after the first two exercises in the centre. It was gladiatorial, like any of these cattle call auditions, but there was something else in the room, watching along with Cecile and Belinda's shrewd eyes, a pressure that sat on Mara's shoulder blades.

By the end of the class there were four dancers left in the room. Cecile thanked the pianist, crossed the room to open a window and in swooped a huge black crow, which perched on a chair next to Belinda and cawed twice. There was a long silence. That place between Mara's shoulder blades started to itch.

Number 46 and number 15, please see me. The other dancers gathered their bags and left.

Cecile smiled at them. *Congratulations. I would like to offer you both positions in the corps de ballet of* The Apple and the Pearl. *If you accept, please be at London Marylebone at sunrise on Saturday 24th of this month.*

A suitcase at her feet, her mother's worries echoing in her ears. *If you don't like it just come home, don't suffer like you did before, do you promise me?* She saw the other girl from the audition and smiled tightly at her. Annie, who became a good friend. She stayed three pledges before she injured her knee and left to become a dentist.

A tall man with a head full of golden ringlets stood near them, an instrument of some kind by his feet. He looked at them and grinned.

Are you for The Apple and the Pearl? She and Annie had nodded. *Me too. I'm Lance.* And he'd shaken their hands one by one and looked deep into their eyes, and Mara had thought *Oh fuck.*

A year and a day, that's how long she managed to resist

Lance. Longer than Annie, who she found creeping out of his cabin at musician's reveille a month after their pledge. She'd found it funny, and slightly romantic too. Lance was handsome and talented, and Annie was beautiful and sweet. That's all you needed, surely? But then it got messy. Lance left the dining car one night very publicly with Juliet, the old lighting director and everyone saw Annie crying. Charlotte, who was then the most senior dancer at *The Apple and the Pearl*, made it known that she was sleeping with him and she would destroy the careers of anyone who dared look at him. But a few weeks after that, Jennifer, who was junior in the corps de ballet like Mara and Annie at the time, was seen leaving his cabin after curfew, and then Belinda had to step in.

The day of their first pledge renewal came and she, Annie and Lance gathered in Belinda's office after the show. Annie was over it by then, and Mara pretended Lance didn't even exist, never forgetting that sensation of tumbling into his eyes when they'd first met at Marylebone.

You joining the party? Lance had asked afterwards. *I've persuaded Gino to do happy hour for us.*

Glasses of wine, a sambuca shot with the second violins, some kind of tequila cocktail Zach brought out of his cabin, then another and another and everything blurred and the bell was tolling curfew and somehow – she has never worked out how – she was in Lance's cabin and he had his hands on her and her clothes were on the floor and his hands were on her skin and her memories flicker like a tuning radio.

Morning. She woke up naked in Lance's cabin with the musicians' reveille which sounded like a long, low blast of a saxophone, horrified by the sight of him. *Did you drug me?* she hissed, gathering up her clothes in a panic. He caught her wrists, actually upset for once. *What? Of course I didn't! You wanted it.* And she ran out into the corridor, mercifully emptied by the thick hangovers, and straight into the shower. She never spoke of it again.

But there hasn't really been anyone since. Jason, the old assistant stage manager, which progressed in a lukewarm kind of way until he left to go on a world tour of *Cats* and it was silently agreed that whatever they'd shared had been mainly for convenience and wasn't worth eking out across the distances and worlds between them. A brief fling with a clarinetist who drank too much and would pass out on her bed before they'd even got their clothes off and keep her awake all night with his snoring. Everybody else fucking like rabbits, emotionally incontinent and calling it love, and her alone, trying to pretend she didn't care.

'Sixteen bars for your own stretches!' Cecile calls and Mara sinks to the floor to bend over her legs, massaging that fragile place on her left instep with all the scar tissue from the multiple sprains.

Perhaps she'll meet someone when she leaves here. A kind man, the owner of a bookshop maybe, someone with his own flat with a balcony where he grows sweet peas in the summer and they'll sit together on sunny Sunday mornings with a cup of coffee and he'll lean to her and say something like, *Tell me about your dancing life* and she will think back to moments like this, hamstrings finally warm and supple from the *fondu* exercise, Michael banging away at the tango rhythm, fingers resting on the scuffed vinyl floor and she will not know how to answer. *Every day we did ballet class,* she'll say hesitantly. *And it was neither good nor bad, it just was.*

She watches Cecile demonstrate a *frappé* exercise and stands in fifth again. Flex the foot at the ankle and brush the ball of the foot against the floor as the leg extends, to the front, to the side, to the back, like striking a match on the squeaky floor. Her first ballet teacher was called Mrs Jeffers and she taught after-school classes in the church hall down the road where her mother went to WI meetings and one of her sisters did judo. Mara can still hear her voice calling over the music, *You are preparing your body to jump, you are telling your legs to get ready to propel you into the air.* And although she does the *frappé* with everyone else, because you can't pick and choose the ones you like, she has never seen the logic of this match-striking movement helping her to jump. She closes her right foot into a neat fifth position and turns to the other side to make sparks with her left leg.

It gets to the point – and truthfully she is long past it – where you forget what the point of these individual exercises are and you do them faithfully every day like you lay down in your bed, because to not do them would be a rupture with everything you know to be good for you. Every day she does ballet class and that's what she's been doing for what?

Fifteen years now? And maybe there's something released by the combination of these movements, some hormone that lingers in the fibres of your muscles that acts like a drug, keeps you coming back for more. Is she addicted to ballet class? She feels like she needs it to function, her body will not obey her until she's finished at least the barre and her mind is scattered and distracted until the end of *allegro. Part of the brainwashing,* she said to the lads once, but Stuart had laughed and Josh had rolled his eyes. *I know you're on a crusade to make this place into a hippy commune, but I don't think you'll manage to get rid of class.*

What will happen to her without daily ballet class? Withdrawal, perhaps. An uncontrollable shaking that won't stop until she gets out of bed, pushes the rug back and starts doing *pliés.* Grief, likely, like someone has died, and to be honest they might as well have because she will never come here again and she will probably never see these people again.

And yes, people have left before and she got over it. She and Annie were inseparable for a couple of years and now Mara doesn't know a thing about her life. They've passed out of the realms of long-distance friends, through the land of old mates, and now they're merely two women who used to share everything but sex. She looks across the stage to the place where Greg and Stuart stand opposite each other at the barre, concentrating on each flex and stretch of their legs. Never to giggle with Stuart again, never to feel the judder of his shoulders next to hers as they sit in a booth in the dining car, laughing at something Cecile said. Never to hear Greg's soft taps on her cabin door in the morning, never to sit with them after shows nursing a beer and talking about nothing in particular. She might even miss Josh, grumpy old git that he is.

A niggling ache of cramp starts in her left arch.

The music finishes and Mara holds the balance in a low *arabesque* for longer than she really wants to, just to show herself she can, and she stays there while Cecile bustles to the front of the stage and starts to demonstrate a difficult *adage*, full of long holds of the legs in positions that will make the thighs ache and calves burn.

'Today we will fight the damp outside and put fire in our muscles!' Cecile trills and there is a groan from the place where Greg, Romero and Stuart stand draped over the barre. She gives them a mock-flirtatious smile filled with steel. 'And the principal gentlemen shall show us all how it's done.'

Mara smirks; after all these years she has learned to appreciate Cecile's sense of humour. But everyone else looks somewhere between reluctantly stoic and mutinous, and as Cecile strides to the front of the stage and looks at Michael to count him in, there is a barely suppressed groan.

'Give me your juiciest melodies, maestro,' she calls to the front of the stage. 'I need something to get them going.'

'Never a break, never a chance to just chill,' Jessica mutters as she wearily crosses her thighs into fifth position. 'Always there with the whip.'

'Hold!' Cecile calls. 'Three and four. Use the stomach, keep the shoulders still. *Bien*, Harriet.'

Mara has always accepted this – the burn in the thigh, the pouring sweat, the feeling of I-can't-go-on-I-must-go-on. The incessant practice of one tiny movement; the scrutinising of the line and form of the body in the mirror; the desperate horror of the gap between you and what you want to be.

It's all the other bullshit she can't accept. The artificiality of it, the arbitrariness of the rules. The insistence on being as bony as a corpse. Some French king long ago liked to boogie and he had the power to make his friends do it too, and one thing led to another and now ballet is this strange, diamantine thing, made of equal parts cruelty and beauty. The bullying passed on like a chain, each generation forging its own link, misery hooked onto misery, supposedly in the service of this thing.

The fetish of the blood pouring out of the pointe shoe; the insistence that you abdicate your selfhood to a teacher you don't even like; the demand to punish the body for existing as it does, unforgivably imperfect. It attracts the sadists and the masochists and now, after nine years, she's worked out that's why the audience of *The Apple and the Pearl* keep coming back. They want to see pain and they want to see beauty and they want to sip at that space between pain and beauty.

Perhaps there's a point to all the suffering. She's never found it herself, but it's clearly there for others, some deeper meaning to the tortures they all endure. It has been her undoing sometimes, to think *but why*? When ballet teachers have acted like no one ever gets a career unless some great sacrifice is given, like you need to throw your true love down a well to be able to dance one *Swan Lake*, she's just been baffled. People lap it up: she knows, she's seen it. Anorexia, psychiatric units, double knee replacements at thirty-nine, and all for what? To stand on stage and be applauded? Not that you even get that, here at *The Apple and the Pearl*. For the thrill of it, to be admired, to be loved if only for the hour or two a night you spend on stage? It's no life at all, for her.

Tell me about your parents, Annie had said one night in the Grub when they were talking about something like this.

Mara had shrugged. *Nothing to say. Both nice. My dad died a few years ago. We were sad but we live with it.*

There you go, Annie said. *Most people are trying to fill a void in themselves, Mara. Drugs, booze, ballet. It's all the same.*

For Mara there is only one reason to dance, and it's being beautifully demonstrated right at this moment by Michael. He's taken Cecile at her word and is playing the act two *pas de deux* from *Spartacus* as if his life depends on it, as if Kachaturian himself is standing next to him. All swelling arpeggios and thundering chords, she lets her body soak it up and pour through her skin as she squeezes her back muscles to hold her *arabesque* a little higher, lets her arm extend from the shoulder a fraction, everything pulled and stretched like she's on an exquisite rack strung entirely of the notes of this *adagio*.

She remembers a car journey as a little girl, sitting in the front seat beside her father as her mother tended to the twins in their bulky car seats in the back, wiggling her shoulders and swinging her legs in the cavernous footwell to a song with a bouncy, cheesy beat that came on the radio. And her father asked her with a twinkling smile if she liked the music and she said, *Not really, but my feet do.* And she'd thought it a reasonable thing to say, an accurate way of describing how the music moved through her body without passing by her brain or her heart, but then she had caught her father look at her mother in the rearview mirror and seen the amusement in their shared glance and felt shrunken. She stopped swinging her legs, held herself still. It truly wasn't a very good song.

Twenty-five years later, she thinks it would not be possible to say it any better than she did that day in the car. The music makes my body dance and I like it. That's it.

Because they are not saving lives. They are not making history. They are not one of those people who put their shoulders to the creaky wheel of society to shift it somewhere better. *You are the artists,* her mother once said, when things were bad at ballet school and she was considering – not for the first or last time – stopping completely. *The feeling people get when they watch you is what they're all living for.*

She would like to believe that. It would make it easier. Easier to stay, easier to leave, easier to think back fondly on this time in her life when she's out in the world doing something else, something boring, something more necessary.

She closes her feet into a neat fifth position, rises onto the balls of her feet and turns to the other side.

The piano roars as she draws her left foot up her shin, and the stage starts to smell damp like the graveyard outside, like the lichen in the stone, like the mist dripping off the yews. There's a commotion in the right downstage corner, near the piano. Growing in ripples from the vinyl dance floor are tiny mushrooms, slick and shiny, the colour of bleached bone. All the dancers have stopped now, gazing at their feet, trying to avoid stepping on them as they sprout under the soles of their shoes. Mara glances at Stephanie, who shakes her head with tears welling, murmuring, 'That poor man.' Stephanie has always approved of Michael but now he's tragic and lost she nurses an enormous crush on him.

'Maestro!' Cecile shouts over the music, the only sign that she's at all perturbed the wrinkling of her nose. But Michael can't hear her. On he plays, letting the piano swell and roar and Cecile walks quickly to the front of the stage where he sways on his stool, eyes shut, humming along with his music. She lays a hand on his shoulder.

'Michael.' He stops mid-phrase and looks up at her. With a small flick of her hand she gestures behind her, and as he sees the tiny pale globes all over the stage his face reddens. But before he can say anything Cecile claps her hands.

'Okay, we start this side again!' Cecile calls. At her voice the mushrooms instantly shrink and the dank smell is gone. There are quiet mutters and groans. 'You may thank him later for giving you a few seconds' rest.'

Mara keeps her legs low, conserving her energy on the other side of the *adage* exercise, and yes, it's a privilege of seniority but she didn't make the rules. She remembers Michael's ex-girlfriend vaguely – red hair, harp, seemed all right – but it would be fair to say the woman is having more of an impact on the daily life of *The Apple and the Pearl* in her absence than she did in her presence. Mara imagines there are already meetings between Belinda, AJ, Cecile and Mackie. She can almost hear their aggravated conversations.

Cecile: *I cannot put up with it any longer, he is making a misery of act two for everyone.*

AJ: *Yes, I can see it is upsetting but I think he deserves a little understanding.*

Belinda: *I've offered her a pay rise, but she's determined not to come back.*

Mackie: *I just feel sorry for the man.*

'*Grands battements*!' Cecile calls from her chair at the front of the stage. 'You know it!' All around her are Lycra-clad legs flying past shoulder height, but Mara keeps her legs low again. It's only the Queen tonight. She remembers her first rehearsals for the Queen a couple of years ago. *Do not raise your legs above knee height, you are not doing the can-can!* Cecile spat. *You are a sovereign!*

She had laughed about that with Greg and Stuart in the Grub that night because what the fuck did Cecile know about historical queens, but really it was typical of what she definitely wouldn't miss about this place and the show.

The fake medieval shit, the artifice of it. The storyline that doesn't make a bit of sense, the pretence that you can even tell anything approaching a story with ballet. *Why the fuck does the Crow care about the Princesses?* She and Annie used to laugh at the ridiculousness of the show. *Where do the Suitors come from? What if they don't fancy the Princesses when they wake up?*

Greg used to shrug, a small smile playing on his lips. *Just another one of those old stories. They never make sense. Doesn't matter to me.*

And then Stephanie would lean in and start talking very earnestly about Jung and matriarchal societies and Stuart would roll his eyes, pat her arm and say *I'm going to get you another drink.*

'*Alors*!' calls Cecile, clapping her hands. 'We come to the centre.'

The men take away the ballet barres, lining them up neatly at the back of the stage where Mackie and Charlie will dismantle them later. Mara, along with the other women, disappears into the wings where she left her bag filled with pointe shoes in varying stages of newness and comfort. She changes from flat shoes into pointe shoes, quickly wrapping the rubber pad around her toes, stuffing her feet in and lacing up the ribbons. Soon there'll be no more pointe shoes and it won't be a moment too soon. No more blisters and ingrown toenails and corns. No more squashed and sweaty feet.

A tap on her shoulder.

'Do you have a pair of scissors?' Zuleika asks. Mara roots in her bag and hands her sewing kit to Zuleika who is sitting on the floor with one pointe shoe on and the other in her hand. A long thread dangles from the ribbon.

'Thanks,' Zuleika says. 'I'll put them in your bag when I'm done.'

Zuleika will be someone who will benefit from her leaving. Like she's an old mother beech falling in the forest, making light for the saplings beneath her to thrive. Zuleika's a good dancer, but anxious. With Mara gone she'll learn the Red Princess, and probably the Queen too, and that will give her some confidence.

Cecile marks through the first exercise in the centre and Mara steps onto pointe, pushing her arches into her shoes which are a little too soft to perform any of the Princesses but comfortable for class. She watches Bella manipulating the toes of her pointe shoes with her hands. She's another who will thrive without Mara's shade. White or Blue Princess for her, probably starting rehearsals in the next couple of weeks. She's reliable, strong and has a lovely quality in the upper body.

The men go first and Mara stands in the wings, half watching the exercise to know it well enough to do it in a minute or two. *Find your balance now, girls,* Mrs Jeffers used to say when they'd leave the safety of the old, splintered pews at the side of the room and stand facing the mirrors streaked with rust. *Allow your pelvis to settle in gravity and support the spine with the tummy muscles.* All this nonsense ballet teachers tell you, lodged in your brain like toffee in a tooth.

'Four bars for the women to come in,' Cecile calls over the music and the men leave the stage.

Mara starts the exercise herself, moving through the *tendus en croix* and in *effacé*, thinking of Mrs Jeffers. She should find that lady, if she's still alive. *You'll never guess where I spent the last decade of my life,* she'll say, though how on earth will she be able to describe the reality – the unreality – of *The Apple and the Pearl* to anyone? *And you know what, I heard your voice almost every single day.*

'We repeat the *adage* from yesterday,' Cecile says, quickly marking it through. 'Because I did not see a single one of you perform it correctly.'

Cecile looks at Michael with an uncharacteristically nervous eye, and she indicates to him to start. He plays the adage from *The Two Pigeons*, another ballet class pianist staple, but this time he keeps his eyes open, fixed on the keys, alert with no possibility of allowing the Grit to take him over.

The men finish and the women replace them on the stage. Mara stands on her left leg as she draws her right toe up her shin and extends it to the side. She intends to keep her legs low, but the music gives her muscles a little push. Where else will she get this feeling? In nightclubs? In a group exercise class at the local leisure centre? Perhaps she should look for another dancing job. One last heist before she hangs up her shoes forever.

And now it's *pirouettes* from the corner, the part of class that starts to feel like really dancing rather than just training and sculpting the body. She watches Benji moving across the space, eating it up with joy. He's good at that. Even in class he covers the floor like a panther, his heart beaming out into the empty auditorium. A nice lad. A considerate partner. Making his debut tonight as the Red Suitor. She's written him a card with a few words of encouragement he'll never get from Cecile and the traditional lines from the rhyme – *three clangs for the Suitors who lie in a dream*. She'll give it to him at the half.

She steps out of the wings just as Romero shuffles his feet into fifth position to start the exercise. He gestures to her to step in front of him, and she hops forward in the final bar of the last phrase before the exercise starts.

Chassé pas de bourreé, double *pirouette,* finish cleanly in fourth. Nothing revolutionary about the combination, it's as staid and stolid as a roast dinner with overcooked cabbage. But every day it is subtly different on her body, every day she needs to greet the steps again, try them on, adjust the fit.

Michael is playing the waltz of the flowers from the *Nutcracker*, unusually mechanically. Mara sighs. Someone really should do something about him. She asked the Crow a few months ago, when the tannoys started crying during his solo during the Blue *pas de deux,* but it just smirked and rolled its eyes as if it were tired of people interceding on Michael's behalf and went back to its tray. Tchaikovsky shouldn't be played like this, like it's the hokey-cokey. It should have some soul. Annie used to make fun of her when she said that. *What, the workhorse of ballet music? Good old Pete, beloved of Christmas adverts and stupid jingles the world over?*

But that was the point, they shouldn't use the *Nutcracker* to sell plastic tat or *Swan Lake* to inject some drama into a scripted reality TV show. Some things should be sacred.

She lands the double *pirouette* cleanly in fifth position. Will she still be able to do these basic movements after a year with no ballet class, two years, ten? How long does it take the muscles to forget that they were long and lithe and supple? She catches sight of Cecile, sitting on her stool with her long neck and back as straight as a poker, as she turns. How long has it been since Cecile took a ballet class? The body remembers.

It might be time to get sentimental about this ordinary combination of steps. How many more times will she do it? *Chassé pas de bourreé,* double *pirouette*, finish in fourth. Pledge day is just before Christmas. There are between forty and fifty ballet classes and shows still to go, depending on when Belinda decides their days off will be. Forty to fifty days marked with that strange light of the blessed or the damned, she's never figured it out, when the creatures in the audience will be able to tell that soon she'll be out of their grasp.

It's happened before. It happened to Charlotte a few years ago. She was forty-two and limping but still commanding on stage, and a week after Cecile called her into her office and told her she absolutely had to leave she was snatched while walking to the Grit before class. Mara had seen the whole thing from the doorway of the Grub while she waited for Stuart. A tall figure dressed in a deep purple dress, strolling along a cobbled lane between two hay meadows, opening their arms as they came towards Charlotte. Mara had opened her mouth to call to them, smirking at the thought of what Alina would do when she discovered someone had taken one of the page costumes for a walkabout but then Charlotte had begun to shimmer and the cobbles beneath her feet glowed and she gave a fleeting glance back to the Grub, nodded, and vanished.

Mara relayed the story to Belinda an hour later, sitting in her office with the Crow perched on the desk. She'd been shaking so hard Belinda had poured her a shot of brandy. *Was it because Cecile sacked her?* she'd whimpered. Belinda had taken off her glasses and rubbed at the bridge of her nose. *Maybe. But it could have been you, or Stuart, or anyone else.* To the best of Mara's knowledge, Cecile hasn't sacked anyone for being old and broken since. She would rather die than admit guilt to anyone but she's not a complete monster.

That must be what's keeping Greg here. Really, it should have been Greg who received severance pay from the Crow – though who's to say he hasn't, the Crow certainly doesn't keep Mara updated with its plans for their destinies. Greg is thirty-seven and *fit only for the knacker's yard*, he says glumly when he's had a bit too much to drink. Recently, Mara has caught Cecile watching him in class with something like pity. She imagines Cecile opening the window to her office at the interval to let the Crow perch on the sill. *For the love of God, creature, tell him to go before something seizes him from the stage.*

She still hasn't told Cecile about the joke coin from the Crow. It won't be real until she tells Cecile.

Mara finishes the exercise and moves into the wings, watching Cecile as the last group finish the exercise from the left. She gives no corrections, just nods and glances at her watch.

'You know it.' She calls from her stool. 'Eight in first, eight in second, eight *changements*, four *echappés sautés*. Maestro.'

In another life, if Cecile were ten years older and Mara hadn't been told to leave, and if she cared a fraction more about the minutiae of ballet technique and the staging of the show, Mara could imagine herself becoming the ballet mistress here. Sitting in Cecile's office doing the casting, meetings with AJ, Mackie and Belinda, watching class with narrowed eyes, looking to see who is getting strong and competent and needs to be doing soloist roles. Maybe that's what Charlotte was holding on for.

The men go first again and Cecile clasps her hands in her lap, eyes low and narrowed, watching the way her dancers' feet leave the floor. Mara retreats to the back of the stage and sits on the floor under the ballet barres. From this angle she can join Cecile in one of her obsessions – *I see ninety-nine per cent of injuries in the second you leave the floor* – she shouts at least once a week, and she watches the feet of the three newest pledges as they spring up and down.

She winces as she sees Luke land poorly. He's not a bad dancer, if a little shy and boring in style, but he's a bit odd. Any conversation she's tried to have with him in this past month since he turned up to replace Alex has petered into awkward silence. Cecile is trying to bash him into shape in the only way she knows how – by shouting at him – but Mara worries for him. He doesn't seem to be weaving himself into the social fabric of the place. Like the straggling antelope at the back of the herd, loners get picked off on *The Apple and the Pearl*. If she were Cecile she'd set Luke up with a buddy, maybe one to help him learn the choreography and another to be a mate outside of rehearsals and class. Michael, perhaps. Kill two birds with one stone.

Yes, she can imagine herself in charge here, the changes she'd make. She'd let everyone keep their baggy things on for class for a start. She would never, ever make a comment about anyone's weight. Let everyone get as fat as they like, what do their audience care for skeletons?

But Cecile is going nowhere, and she is going home. Well, back to her mother's house, a place which is no longer her home but will have to do until she figures something out.

But what will that thing be? What will she do with the rest of her life, where will she go? The whole wide world is hers. There are two obvious things that retired dancers do when they stop dancing and she dreads both. She could train to teach something like pilates or yoga or zumba to middle-aged men and their paunches and menopausal women and their hormones, living out the fiction that the body she's spent more than a decade sculpting can be attained through an hour a week in a sweaty leisure centre. Or she could do a certificate to teach ballet to kids, filling draughty church halls and youth centres with toddlers in pink skirts, ten-year-olds with pushy mothers and the occasional truly talented kid who'll she'll have to bully and abuse into a career, completing the cycle to become everything she's ever hated about this world.

You're being unfair, her mother would say. *To yourself and others.*

She sees why everyone does one of these two things. Mara has no qualifications outside of the dance world, she knows almost nothing of how the world works. She's never worked in a bar or a shop or a cafe, has no office skills. She has no degree, only two A levels, and her references would be who? Cecile, who would write something about how she's worked very hard on her *allegro* over the years. Belinda could, at least, be relied upon to come up with something suitably corporate and dull. *Mara is a reliable team player who works well within existing structures while making projects her own.*

She has savings, that's about all that can be said for her situation, a bank account fat with years of salary and little spending. And she has a mother still rattling around her childhood home, which is a stroke of luck. At least the twins will be pleased. She thinks of the messages her phone picked up this morning, long streams of frustration from her sisters. *She only wants to eat toast and peanut butter and when I told her she needs some vegetables she said she'll do whatever the fuck she wants. The doctor said gentle exertion only but of course she was up on the ladder messing about with the wisteria.*

So she'll leave the Grub at some random station of Belinda's choosing and get an ordinary train home to Three Bridges, where she'll ring and ask her mother to pick her up. That home smell, the mix of furniture polish and butter, will hit her as soon as her mother opens the front door.

And then she'll never do ballet class again.

I will never do ballet class again, she makes herself think as she watches Zuleika practice an *assemblé*, neatly joining her ankles in the air to land in a dainty fifth position.

One more time: *I will never do ballet class again*.

Yes, it's all right. She can bear the thought so she can bear the reality. She might miss performing, she definitely won't miss rehearsals, but yes, she will miss this daily ritual, this medicinal torture that sets her straight, this communion between her, the piano and the dance that itches inside her.

As the music starts for the next *allegro* exercise, Mara goes into the wings to put her jumper back on. A tendril of guilt in her belly. With her ballet classes numbered, should she be stopping early? Shouldn't she be squeezing every last movement out of every last moment, wringing each exercise for all its worth?

When she tells Cecile she's leaving and it becomes common knowledge, maybe she will. Maybe she'll let her inner child take over and she'll be that little girl letting her feet dance to the music every single day, and she will no longer have to worry about the old sprains on her left ankle, those aching places in her back, the sharp tugs on her knees.

She'll tell Belinda first – no, it should be Cecile – no, telling Belinda is the smart thing to do in case there's some admin that needs doing, in case she says something like *a fifty pence piece? No, I think that means I need to give you a pay rise.* And then she'll tell Cecile, probably after class one day when she's feeling fortified, and they'll plan her farewell show.

She'll ask to dance the Crow so she has one last chance to go to the caboose and say goodbye – even though it probably won't even show up, it often doesn't – and she'll ask Gino to make enchiladas for afterwards. She'll spend the day packing up her cabin and hauling her stuff along to the guest cabin that Belinda will turf her out of the next morning. She'll go to Belinda's office in the Grub after lunch to sign the forms and see her vial of blood destroyed and she'll ask her, just for shits and giggles, all the questions the Crow has ignored. *Doesn't it bother you, handling the Pearl like that? What if it breaks and whatever's inside it bursts out and spills all over you? What happens if you're taken, Belinda, who looks out for us then? Do you feel scared of the creatures of the audience? What hocus-pocus is it that connects the guest cabins to the real world? Why did you choose me all those years ago at that audition? What the fuck will I do with the rest of my life?*

The mood in the dressing room that night before the show will be charged, tearful and joyous. She'll have all her farewell cards arranged around her dressing table, all the heartfelt messages, all the gifts. Someone, probably Stephanie, will have written out that random little poem about the show and she'll have to hold back the tears when she reads the line about the Crow who sings in her nest.

Alina will give her that choker to tie around her neck, that one with salt in the lining and fortified with iron studs to keep her safe, because the audience can always tell who is saying farewell to the stage that very night. That is when you are most in danger, they can smell it on you like the electrical charge of thunder in the air. And she will finish the third act Crow's solo on one knee, the rest of the company waiting in the wings for the curtain call, everything she has been for the past decade dissolving around her.

And as the first group of men leap across the stage in the *grand allegro*, Mara wipes away the first tear she has shed since the night the Crow gave her that coin.

Dance only exists in the single instant of the dancer moving. Before it is only potential, an itch in the muscles, a yearning between two bodies. Afterwards it's at best a sheen of sweat on the skin, panting breath and the music lingering in your fingers. There is nothing else. If you are not dancing right now, perhaps you are not and never were a dancer. Until you dance again.

And if you never do? she wonders as she watches Romero soar into the air in the *jeté*. One day you dance and so you're a dancer, and the next day you don't and so you're a… what? She'll find out soon. In forty to fifty days, depending on when Belinda arranges their days off.

'Thank you, everyone,' Cecile calls. 'Good work. Take fifteen and I will see tonight's cast of the court scene back here.'

Blast. That's her.

Two thirty, and downstairs in the musicians' green room Henry sits on the edge of a chair with his score spread on the table in front of him and his violin on his lap. He follows a few bars with his fingers, shakes his head and tuts, goes back to the beginning of the page.

The door opens and Henry looks up expectantly, although he knows exactly who it'll be. He has been waiting for him to finish playing for ballet class and come here for the break before rehearsals.

'You don't mind, do you?' he asks, rubbing rosin on his bow. 'There's a bit in act three I find a bit tricky.'

Michael sits down in a chair by the door and pulls out his notebook. 'It's fine. I have these.' He rummages in his pockets, pulls out his earplugs and presses them into his ears.

The thing about this score – and he's only been playing it a few months, not like some of the other musicians who are decades in, could hum it in their sleep – is that it sounds like everything else Henry's ever played. There are a few nods to Tchaikovsky – the marches and the harp, the way the Suitors and Princesses solos all match their *pas de deux*, and you can hear the pomposity of Elgar in the court sequences. The hunting dance could be Mendelssohn, all quivering and lush, and parts of act two could be Prokofiev, teetering on the edge of discordant. It's confusing, and if you don't pay attention you'll slip into some other score you used to know from years ago.

Then, to complicate things, there are all the parts of the score lifted directly from the Fae. The Blue Princess's solo reminds him of the song that used to open one of the lavish winter balls. The melody of the White Suitor's solo is very like the one that he used to play while the Fae supped on dessert at their banquets, and the Pearl waltz is based on an old Fae lullaby. It makes his heart ache. He spent his childhood humming those tunes and his youth practising them note by note on his violin. For the past twenty years this music has lived only in his mind. Until he came here.

He's put it together piece by piece in the years since he returned, taking out each memory, shining it, putting it carefully in its place. The earliest thing he remembers is a hawthorn grove in full bloom, the wizened trunks of the trees alive with insects and warm to the touch. He'd been lying in a willow basket – as his nursemaid told it – wrapped in a flax blanket and giggling at the clouds as they passed by on their white-as-cream mares bedecked in ribbons and tinkling bells. *You not three years old and your golden curls shining in the sun there, oh! You were gurgling and singing away – the sweetest sound it was, and the Queen couldn't resist you!*

He never asked about his mother, a woman long dead by now, her bones mouldering somewhere in the earth. Never wondered aloud what possessed the woman to leave him on a bright summer's afternoon at the foot of a tree in froth with may blossom, without so much as a nail to protect him. Never considered her shriek when she came back and found her basket empty.

The door to the musicians' green room swings open with a long creak and Sandra the clarinet shuffles in.

'Hi Henry, you okay?' she asks in her quiet, mousy voice.

He smiles tightly. 'Yes thanks.'

She glances at Michael slumped in the chair and her face darkens with disapproval. Sandra is a joiner-inner, a helper, a let-me-know-if-I-can-help-honestly-it's-no-trouble kind of woman. She's a Miss Bates who wants to be a Jane Eyre and secretly worries that she's a Mrs Bennet.

'Act one Crow's solo, is it?'

'The Red *pas de deux*, actually.'

'Oh yes, that one is tricksy for strings. I'll leave you to it. Just let me know if I can help you at all, it's no trouble.'

He pulls his lips back in another approximation of a smile and she adjusts her lank hair in its chipped barrette and settles in an armchair just opposite him. He tries not to growl. He's learned that kind of behaviour doesn't help you fit in among humans. She opens a bag and takes out a package wrapped in white paper and blotched with grease.

'I can't tell you what a happy day it was here when Gino finally agreed to do takeaway!' she giggles, unwrapping a sandwich and releasing a waft of hot brie into the room. Annoyingly, Henry's mouth waters a little. The chef here is surprisingly good. Not as good as what he was raised on, of course. It's a myth that you'll never leave if you eat fairy food. Every time he's read it in a stupid mortal-written book he's wanted to scream and strike it out. He ate nothing but buttermilk, honeycakes, pears and mallow fruit every day of his childhood and still he's here, exiled in the cold, stinking hell of the human world.

He goes back to the score and tucks his violin under his chin. He can feel Sandra's eyes lingering on his instrument which makes him soften to her a little. Carved from a single piece of juniper wood, its grain ripples along the f holes, and in certain lights the wood appears to move with the vibration of the strings. The bow used to be strung with human hair, but over the years it's proven too much effort to source it and now he uses horsehair like all the others. It was given to him by the Queen herself, at the beginning of a May Day banquet when he was about ten years old. He remembers how the wood warmed to his touch as soon as he took it, how the strings sang as he plucked them, how the living pulse that flowed from the scroll poured into his palm.

He adjusts his chin rest, raises his bow and begins the Red *pas de deux* at half tempo. This part of the score is odd, a Fae jig turned melancholy in stateliness. Not for the first time, Henry wonders about the traffic between the two worlds. The other musicians have only a few topics of conversation and most of them make him feel like pulling out his eyeballs from boredom. The only discussions he can bear to listen to are where the score for *The Apple and the Pearl* comes from. They debate it endlessly without resolution, the Jarndyce and Jarndyce of the green room. *The Fae gave it us, note perfect. It evolved from a single song like us from the amoebas that float in the sea. Every hundred and one years there is a new composer, a new choreographer and a completely new set design and that's how the Crow keeps immortals coming back for more.*

He stops playing and starts flicking through the score. He comes to the last few pages, to the Crow's solo in act three, and looks through the mess of notes. Sandra's right, the Crow's solos are difficult. Human and Fae music – which seem to amount to the same thing – are based on fours and threes. Either the *da-dum da-dum* of a heartbeat and the *da-da da-da* of footsteps, or the swaying *ONE-two-three ONE-two-three* of a baby rocking to sleep in warm arms. It's fed to you from birth, dripped into a place beneath memory, beneath language, etching itself on the spiralling ribbons of your DNA.

But the Crow's music comes from an entirely different kingdom. There are no melodies and you can't sing it. The time signatures are all over the place; it's muddy, atonal and as soon as you catch onto something familiar it flies away. The closest thing to a tune happens in the act three solo where there are a few bars of sevens lent a bit of pulse by the timpani, before it dissolves into a random mixture of fives and nines with no phrasing, no breath, no roll and bounce in the notes.

His violin hates it. It quivers with distaste under his

fingers and all the way down his arm. The instrument is Fae-crafted and it just about tolerates the human world, but it rears away from whatever the Crow is. Everyone thinks it's the salt and the iron that keeps them all from being snatched into paradise but they're wrong. It's whatever black, flapping, cawing thing lurks in these parts of the score that leaves the Fae bamboozled.

It was only after he joined this show that he discovered there was anything in any world that could bamboozle the Fae. In his childhood he'd regarded himself as a worm among gods, living in an ever-deepening state of panic and disgust. The sweat from the creases under his arms, the stickiness of the saliva in his mouth, the flaking of his skin, the moulting of his hair. And always the stench of him and all his effluvia, lingering in the air, leaving must on his clothes. *Leaking again,* his nursemaid would sigh. *Clean yourself up, boy. Before the lords and ladies catch a whiff of you.* He learned to hide the foul parts of his human nature in Fae. He learned to pretend that he didn't piss and shit like the other changelings, he was – if not perfect – trying his best in an endearing kind of a way.

He was perhaps fourteen years old, it was hard to tell, and he was miserable because his body was betraying him, a different blow every single day. Tiny eruptions of pus on his face, coarse hair the colour of straw sprouting under his arms, at his groin, on his chest, on his sweaty upper lip. A voice that careened between a growl and a squeal, dreams of burning and drowning that awoke him with a raging erection that shamed him. Human desire was taboo in Fae. Every day he would stare at himself in the looking glass, despairing. His nursemaid, who still retained her old affection for him would wince when she saw him. *Try to hide yourself away until you're presentable again, won't you dearie.*

A Fae of low rank, and full of spite with it, arrived one day in his chamber and wordlessly beckoned to him. He was practising for a banquet and so he kept hold of his violin and his bow as he followed the creature through the court. In the years that followed, he has frequently been moved almost to tears to think of what might have become of him had he not had his violin clutched in his hands that day. A coincidence like the one that saw him taken as a child, a circumstance that has coloured everything since.

The Fae led him out of the filigreed gates and across the buttercup meadows to the border of the woods. He'd tried to ask where they were going but the courtier had ignored him. She led him through the beeches until they came to a ramshackle cottage. He remembers that he was nervous. He remembers that he thought he might be sick if it was the Queen in there. He remembers that he was holding his violin so tightly the strings were cutting into his palm.

She shoved the door open. *You're going in there,* she'd hissed, baring her pointed teeth, whiter and sharper than mistletoe in the oak. *Do you know why you have to go? Because the Queen's had it with humans and she's most specially had it with you. Ugly, stinking oaf you've become, she loves you no longer.*

She pushed him through the door and he arrived back

in the human world, dressed in ugly, drab human clothes. It was precisely the same spot they'd taken him from – though it took him years to work that out – except the trees had long gone and in their place was a car park and four huge buildings like luminescent temples arranged at its northern end. *HOMEBASE*, read one. *HOBBYCRAFT* said another. *KWIKSAVE* and *DFS*. He blinked in the unnatural glare and coughed from the fumes. By the time he thought to look, the portal was gone and all he had were the human clothes he stood up in, his violin and his bow.

Even now, all these years later, the memory squeezes at his chest. He rubs his thumb over the wood of his violin to calm himself, closes his aching eyes. He starts to hum the Pearl waltz, one of his favourite parts of the score. Like wrapping a warm, heavy blanket around himself and sinking into darkness.

That's what he'd done that first day, hummed and sang to stop himself from screaming. He'd wandered the edges of that car park until dusk, watching the steel carriages come and go, bewildered by their speed and noises and lights. He slept on its edges that night, bedding down among the thorny branches of the box trees with his violin tucked between his knees, broken glass stuck in the tread of his trainers and the stink of foxes acrid in his nose. It was May 2, 1998. He saw it on a newspaper.

By the time the winter set in, he'd got himself in hand. He'd made his way to the city where he spent his days busking outside train stations for pennies, and his nights collecting banknotes in hotel rooms and saunas. He had enough changes of clothes to fit into any social situation, a bed to sleep in each night, a case for his violin and a rough understanding of how the new world worked. It turned out there wasn't much difference between the mortal world and the Fae court: that first delighted, then depressed him. You needed to be beautiful, and you needed to be able to wander about the world without a care, unattached, tethered by nothing more troublesome than gravity. Those with power expected to be able to look and touch as they pleased, and if you were smart you'd let them, and pocket their favours while you could.

There's a loud knock at the green room door and without waiting for a response, Derek the follow spot strides in, power drill in one hand.

'Mackie sent me to have a look at a loose shelf,' he announces and gives the drill a little blast. Sandra hurriedly opens her book and pretends to read. Michael ignores him. Henry shrugs. You have to pretend he doesn't get to you, Henry's found, this Uriah Heep with the manners of Mr Collins. You have to hold your face blank and your nerves steady until he goes away and torments someone else.

'Go ahead.'

Derek puts his drill to the shelf bracket above the mirror and aggressively drills a screw into the wall. 'Sorry!' he shouts. 'I'll only be a minute!' Henry stares at his score, thoroughly jangled and trying not to show it.

'All done.' Derek giggles, an unpleasantly high-pitched

noise that doesn't match the paunch, the wisps of straw-like hair over his bald scalp or the steel toe-cap boots. He gives a silly little shudder. 'Sorry, I had to have my coffee black this morning. Milk was off.'

And with an aggravating smirk, Derek saunters out, letting the door shut softly behind him.

Henry's stomach swoops. How long before everyone starts to put two and two together about soured milk and a changeling aboard the Grub? How long will Belinda – who must know – shelter him? Will the Crow sling him out on a day off, or will Derek move first? What exactly would be the consequences of everyone finding out? A stoning, the silent treatment, a public repudiation back into the human world? But that would be breaking his pledge, so what would the Crow do about that?

As usual, he feels like mad Bertha in the attic after an encounter with Derek, so he flips back through the score until he comes to the wedding scene, a lilting 6/8 that is almost the exact tune as the song he used to play each year on Queenday and plays the first few bars to comfort himself. A new problem to worry about. As if his life hasn't been hard enough. How the fuck did Derek guess? Who or what is he?

Five months here and still Henry understands so little and yes, it makes him respect the Crow, if only grudgingly. The magic tricks are perfect, the illusions seamless. Why, for example, doesn't anyone notice the Grub when they stop in ordinary train stations? Does anyone ever tell the people they know on the outside the truth of this show?

Why did he take so long to find out about it? More than twenty years he's spent poring over human-written books of what they call folklore, long pages of mostly nonsense about the fairy world and not a word about this show. Ever since the internet became widespread he's been searching, scouring squillions of terabytes of bollocks, wading through endless message boards of people emoting at strangers about their problems, trying to find one, just one, like him.

All these years alone with himself and his violin. All these years wandering through the greyness of the human world, never even catching a glimpse of magic from the corner of his eye. The only person who'd ever come close to knowing the truth of his life was Nora.

He met her on a carnival when he was maybe seventeen. He was still stumbling around the human world, confused by light switches and bewildered in a supermarket; she was a teenage runaway with a shaved head and burn marks all along her thighs. Six months they spent together, getting stoned behind the haunted house, telling each other their dreams, carefully talking around the holes in their childhoods. She was the closest human to a Fae he had encountered out in the world; capricious, carefree and cursed – perhaps – with a clairvoyance that saw her stuffing her bra with twenties on a Saturday night after a few hours in a tent dressed up as Esmerelda. He modelled his speech on hers, copied her inflection until all traces of a bygone time were gone from his tongue. *Jesus Christ, Henry, you know life has moved on from those chonky books about dead people you love so much?* He did know that, but he didn't much care. He'd learned everything about humans from long afternoons in a library, the only place he'd been able to get warm. He swapped Fae masters for human ones as he worked through the shelves: Austen, Brontë, Carroll, Dickens, Eliot, Hardy, Thackery, Tolstoy, Zola.

Nora disappeared with a tattooed dodgem operator and Henry had taken it as a sign to wise up, forget about having friends and get on in the world he'd found himself in. Then, last year, on a warm Monday evening in July, he had a night off from *Turandot* at the Coliseum. Restless in city smog that only trapped him in his gasping, sweating body, he did what he used to do when he was a kid and had nowhere else to go – he got on the Tube and rode until the end of the line in any direction, until the city petered into scrub. He would wander into scrawny, forgotten copses littered with fridges and mattresses and he'd stand with his eyes shut, breathing in the green, trying to hear the pulse of Fae beneath suburban drone.

Down the escalator at Notting Hill, into the clay-bound bowels of the city on the Central line, thundering east. He got off at Loughton and wandered until the lights of a fairground lured him off the road and onto the common.

He went to the fortune teller for the memory of his old friend. And there, in the corner of the booth, was Nora herself, conjured like a spirit. Her tears drew black streaks of eyeliner down her face as she watched him walk towards her and sit down at the velvet-covered table.

He was not a man given to sadness or pity, but when he saw the track marks up her arm as she reached lazily for his hand he felt something squeeze in his stomach. She traced one blackened fingertip from his thumb joint to his little finger and she folded his fingers into his palm.

They don't love you back, you know.

His breath hitched.

But there're ways in again, if you can find them.

Do you know how?

She leaned back, her eyes fluttering closed. He could see her pulse flickering at her throat as her breath slowed and her body sank into the chair. *You've spent your life on the fringes of this world because you think that's where you'll find them. Carnie folk, deadbeats and junkies like me. But they don't think as much of us as you do. You need to try going somewhere else that's neither here nor there.*

How?

The Apple and the Pearl.

What's that?

She'd shrugged. *I can't see any more than that.*

She dropped his hand and folded her hands in her lap. He understood – go chase your ghosts and leave me alone with mine. He rode the Tube home, each stop a rush of warm, fetid air as the doors opened and shut on the almost empty carriage, diving underground as the city began to flicker with light and thrum with noise. As soon as he got home he sat at his laptop and set up an alert for the phrase 'The Apple and The Pearl'.

Eleven months later, deputising on a touring musical in Nottingham, a hit. *Seeking violin, harp and French horn for a touring ballet* The Apple and the Pearl. *Ask for Belinda.* He had joined the Grub at Leicester at sunrise in June and the next day he watched the dancers warming up from a chair placed just behind the deputy stage manager as he called beginners. The oboe sounded, the orchestra tuned, and the curtain rose and immediately he knew – if there was a door to Fae that might open to him, if he was ever going to get back home, this was it.

The score stitched together from all those tunes from the Otherworld. The story an almost-lucid version of an old Fae folktale. The shrieking noise they made instead of applause, their wings glittering in the reflections of the stage lights, the bell that chimes at precisely the same note as the one that used to call the court to hunt that gives him a shiver of pleasure every time it tolls.

He pledged that evening without a single hesitation, Belinda the tricoteuse squinting at him over the half-moon of her glasses, his instrument thrumming happily in its case. He'd seen immediately that she was a woman who bore more than a drop of Fae blood herself, but he kept that knowledge tightly guarded, ready to deploy like a cyanide pill in case of emergency.

That night he slept deeply and dreamlessly for the first time in years. Swaying with the movement of the Grub, lulled by the hiss and chug of the wheels. By the time he opened the score and started to learn it the next morning, all his doubts and suspicions that he had never really been taken to Fae as a child at all, and that the architecture of his mind was instead cracked and broken in some way so as to make him believe so, were gone. If he is mad then here, at last, are people as mad as him.

Not that he intends to stay here for very long. From the moment Belinda pricked his finger on that first day, he was making plans. Because they all think it's random, like the wheel spins and if your number comes up then you're unlucky, but Henry knows that's not true. Henry knows the type of humans the Fae wish to pass their eternity with and by the end of his first week he'd seen several of them sitting in front of AJ in the pit.

There's the oboe, a mousy middle-aged woman who nonetheless draws the sounds of heaven from her instrument, a woman born aboard the Grub – how could a creature from the Otherworld resist *that* – struck by some kind of melancholy she thinks she hides, but Henry can hear it keening from her music as soon as she purses her lips. Lance the trumpet has that swaggering, aggressive heterosexuality the Fae Queens adore, leaving a trail of broken hearts and misplaced virginities behind him like a cross between Sergeant Troy and George Wickham. Jasper the percussionist is blind in one eye – how's that for a mythological symbol – and then there's AJ himself. Something Fae in his bones, for sure. The longest serving member of the company, although apparently not continuously. When he found that out, Henry put the knowledge in a little box to consider later, because what exactly was AJ doing out in the world when he left and why did he come back again?

True, the last person to be taken was a dancer, a month or so ago and Henry was savagely disappointed that he hadn't seen it coming. He'd joined the vigil in the dining car while the Crow shrieked around the Grub that afternoon and tried to keep himself from throwing a salt pot at the wall.

But if Henry were a betting man – and he's not, but he knows Fae and he knows the fair folk and he knows that they love musicians above anything else – he'd put money on it being a musician. Not just any musician, but Michael, the first violin, a man so drenched in misery you could almost smell it coming in hot waves of grief from his skin. A potent mix of Jean Valjean, Miss Havisham and Heathcliff.

What happened to him? he asked another of the second violins, hoping it was a dead parent, a depressive episode, a diagnosis of terminal cancer.

Max had shaken his head. *Heartbroken. His girlfriend was the harp, she left a few months ago. He's not been the same since.*

Shit, Henry thought. If there was one thing the Fae couldn't resist it was a mortal – a mortal musician – suffering from unrequited love. Henry started to shadow Michael everywhere. But Michael's misery is not enough. When Belinda had held out her watch for him to sync to her own, Henry had looked obediently at the digital numbers, wound his own watch slightly late and strapped it back on his wrist. When Lance had told him about the salt in his pocket he'd nodded earnestly, but before every show he conscientiously dips his hand into the huge vat in the dressing room then empties his suit jacket down the toilet near the stage. He takes care to leave the Grit after each show at the back of a crowd and only drifts away from them when he's sure they've forgotten about him. From the very first night he's stayed outside the Grub in wind and rain until a few minutes before midnight, sitting on rocks and sand and itchy grass, waiting for twinkling lights, for the scent of peaches, for the sound of hoof-beats, anything. And always, nothing. Every night he's climbed aboard the Grub as the engines start to heave and made his way in despair to his cabin full of pranks and lain down for the night fit to weep. *When will I go home? Tell me, when?*

Although – and go on then, he'll admit it – being here has done him the power of good. This is the closest he's come to the Fae in years. The stench of magic here, the sour tang of it everywhere, the nearness of the creatures that fill the auditorium each night, the wild roar of them, the full blast of their glamour. Never his court, never his Queen, sometimes beings more like goblins and gnomes, but still, it feeds him.

So let the bastards complain about the soured milk. Let them work it out, if they can, let them realise he's the changeling, he's the reason they've got to drink their coffee black, let them go to the Crow itself and complain. He's going to stay. Being here – despite all the shit – is healing the crack forged in him as he was pushed through that door. No, not healing. Filling it with molten gold, like those Japanese vases. If all else fails he'll go to Belinda and beg, *is there really nothing you can do for me, use me as a sacrifice, swap me for someone, use whatever influence you have?* He is almost – not quite, but almost – prepared to concede that even if he can never return to Fae, he will stay here for the rest of his natural life, playing this score, pretending to fill his pockets with salt, lingering outside the Grub until the warning whistle, waiting for death or Fae, whichever comes first.

Voices outside, then a humming rumbling baritone as someone begins to sing. The door to the green room gives its long creak again, and in come Steve the bassoon, Jasper the percussionist and Wilf the cellist. Oh fuck.

This is the very last combination of souls he wants to see. The three musketeers, as they call themselves, with Lance their occasional, mocking D'Artagnan. They spend their days talking absolute bollocks in the Grit, and their nights getting drunk and talking even more bollocks in the Grub. Jasper is in the middle of a torturously circuitous story, Steve is singing over him and Wilf stops, hands on his belly, and belches. They settle in a corner and Steve takes out a pack of cards and begins to deal a game of rummy.

Sandra has finished her sandwich now and she's slowly wiping her hands with a napkin. Henry carefully avoids eye contact. Sartre – not that he's the kind of pretentious idiot to quote Sartre, at least not out loud – must have done a pledge aboard the Grub. There are people everywhere; it is almost impossible to have a moment to yourself. You either shut yourself up in your cabin or you take a long, long walk between the Grub and the Grit and hope you don't bump into someone else who's had the same idea. You can't even eat on your own. People like Sandra come and sit next to you, to 'keep you company' and 'make sure you're settling in all right'.

It was for lack of space to himself that everything went wrong two days ago. He'd thought it was a sure thing. Halloween, the day he'd been longing for, his best shot since leaving that car park. He'd woken with the midday reveille – which naturally sounds like hoof-beats for him because the Crow is a bastard – and his chest had been fit to bursting with the thrill of it. Halloween. The night the Fae came. The night he'd go home.

He'd spent the afternoon seeing to his suit, brushing off each speck of dust. He'd showered and dabbed himself with the rose oil he's been oiling his skin with for years, ever-hopeful something would take him based on the scent of flowers alone. He examined himself in the mirror. He's more than forty – well, his *body* is – but he hardly looks a day older than twenty-six. Long ago he decided he would rather die than moulder in the human world, ageing and sagging and rotting from the inside out. Creams, skin treatments and a strict gym regimen have kept him looking like the airbrushed images on the front of magazines. Women do double takes and men lick their lips at the sight of him, and although it gives his ego a boost, he ignores it all. He hasn't taken a lover in fifteen years. The thought of all that slick wetness, the smells and the *leaking* makes him want to heave. When he goes back to Fae – and he *will* go back to Fae – he will go as a princeling, not the troll he'd left as.

Two nights ago, he'd stayed outside the Grub after the show. The train was stopped by a river and he'd seen lights flickering on the bank, a warm smell of peaches drifting in the air despite the autumn chill and he'd walked towards the glow, violin slung over his back, his heart singing, the kind of broad, boyish smile on his lips that he hasn't had in years.

But they were uncatchable. Every time he thought he was near, the world would go topsy-turvy and they would move off to the side, behind him, somewhere just out of his vision that he couldn't quite see. He wandered, following the lights, until he came to the caboose. In the glow of the orange light he saw a huge black bird pecking at one of Gino's bread rolls. An old-fashioned lantern with a thick pillar of a candle sat beside it.

The Crow looked up at him and cocked its head.

But it's Halloween! he'd said in desperation.

The Crow gave a soft caw and went back to its soup.

He'll try again tonight. Fae time doesn't run parallel to human time – and hasn't he found that out the hard way? – but the veil is still weak. Whoever turns up tonight could be powerful, maybe even wanting to keep the merriment of the Hallow's Eve feasts going with a little mortal sport.

All Souls', the day of dead things. Henry could almost hear them, hooves thundering, horn blaring out into the mist to call the hunt, bells tinkling with the frost. He shut his eyes to the graves and took a long breath of the damp air.

From the corner of his eye he sees Michael stuffing his notebook into his bag and starting to stand. Henry takes that as his cue. He puts his violin back in its case, flicks the latches and follows Michael out of the green room, along the corridor and through the door to the stage because he does not want to take any chances, not on All Souls', not surrounded by graves, not here in this in-between place where up is down and in is out and there is nowhere in the world better for him to get home or die trying.

'*Alors*!' Cecile claps her hands and the stage falls silent. Michael slips into the chair at the piano and folds his hands into his lap. 'We begin with the court procession. The spacing was atrocious last night so I'll give you five minutes – ten, I am feeling generous – to work it out and then we'll run it.'

Belinda lets the heavy door from the corridor shut behind her and sees the dancers already moving about on the stage. She checks her watch. Two forty-six. Bugger. Cecile always starts rehearsals bang on time, she'll have to wait until later – maybe even tomorrow – to get her to sign off on these expenses.

'Belinda? Can I have a word?'

Hot breath on her neck and a waft of something frying in old, rancid grease and Belinda turns to see Derek standing too close, hands deep in his pockets, staring at her intently. She suppresses a shudder and takes a discreet step away from him.

'Of course. Everything all right?'

'Depends on how you look at things. I saw hoof-prints, on the earth, by one of the graves out there. Name of Desmond C Jones, if you care to see for yourself.'

'Right.' The man makes her skin crawl, she can't help it. When she pricks his finger to take his blood on his pledge day what she squeezes into the vial is a bright, mossy green. The Crow has brought him here for reasons it has declined to share with her but now she has to put up with the sour stink of him, the litany of complaints he produces and the vaguely menacing air of threat that he knows something she doesn't.

'I just thought, All Souls' and all that. You–'

'Yes, thank you Derek. I'll look into it.' He shrugs in a maddeningly casual way and walks off, a little, taunting whistle under his breath.

Belinda sighs, pulls out her clipboard and shuffles the papers there. She'll go find AJ and remind him, once again, that Madagascan vanilla macarons and pots of loose leaf lapsang souchong from Fortnum & Mason are not reasonable company expenses.

In the musician's green room, Wilf the cello, Jasper the timpani and Steve the bassoon are introducing David the new harp to one of their favourite discussions – the timbre and pitch of the Grub's bell, its esoteric meanings and its role in the music of the spheres.

'Well.' Wilf leans back, takes a swig from the plastic water bottle in his hand which mostly contains vodka. 'We're pretty sure it rings on D when it does the single peal before we leave the Grit at the end of the show. That's the note we hear, mind, not necessarily how the bell smith cast it, because of the… What does Lance call it? Time and space warp of the Grub when it gets going at midnight—'

'—we should ask that fella, next time he comes—'

'—not likely, Belinda keeps him on a tight leash—'

David is interested in this conversation, and in general finds these three men good company in many ways, but he is feeling quite bleary after last night's whisky and struggling to hold back a yawn. Wilf talks about the bell smith often, and always in tones of hushed admiration. David has the idea of some kind of consultant wizard who graces them all with a visit every couple of years to do arcane magic around the bell and leave Belinda with a signed year's warranty that guarantees absolutely nothing but the sheer existence of the peal.

'—but we disagree about what we hear at the half when the bell rings the Angelus – just another of the Crow's jokes – because Jasper swears it's D again, how could it be otherwise? But Steve has always said he hears E in winter and C minor in summer. And the weather does matter you know, the sounds bleed, you can't quite make it out–'

Up in the lighting box, Zach shows Lara each of the buttons and dials on the lighting board and talks through each lighting cue of each act.

'I feel a bit awkward asking this, Zach, but who am I replacing?'

Zach knows what she's trying to say but his stomach swoops at the thought. Harder than he thought, to explain all the little pieces of etiquette here, all the stupid dos and don'ts.

'Me.' He smooths his fingers across the folder of cues, buying himself time. 'The old lighting director just retired, she was called Juliet, taught me everything I know. Mackie promoted me and hired you.'

She exhales. 'So I'm not replacing someone who got snatched.'

'No.'

'When was the last time that happened?'

Zach winces. 'To be honest, it's not something you're supposed to talk about. People get twitchy about it. Superstitious. About a month ago, maybe two, a dancer went missing after class. No one saw what happened.'

She frowns. Zach can see she's not satisfied but he can't bring himself to give her more details. What would he say? That Alex had been well-liked, left behind a girlfriend, played poker in the tournaments on Saturday nights, that even Cecile looked a bit sad as she drank her white wine in the Grub as the Crow cawed its fury that afternoon? Is that all a life amounts to, after the Fae folk have stolen it for their own?

Zach clears his throat. 'All right, let's change the subject. I have to tell you about days off.'

Lara looks cheered to hear that. 'So, days off are safer, obviously, because we're back in the real world.'

What's this real world you're talking about, Zach? he hears Juliet laughing. *Tell me more.*

'Belinda tells us where it's going to be with a few days' notice, then the Grub doors open at first reveille – that's nine o' clock, absolutely sparrow's fart but there you go – and we'll be on some platform of some train station somewhere, usually where there's, like, engineering works or a red signal or some bullshit like that. You've got until midnight to get yourself back on the Grub and then we leave for the next place.'

'How often do we get one?'

Zach grimaces. 'Not often enough. And we never know when they're going to be.'

'But isn't that—'

'—illegal, yes. And Belinda's usually all for the unions, but she says there's absolutely no other way the Crow will let her do it.'

Lara bends over the board and reads a few more of the dial labels.

'If you've got a special occasion – wedding, funeral, that kind of thing – just let her know. She's normally quite good about trying to get you there, sets you up in a guest cabin for the night, lets you out in the morning near wherever you're trying to get to. Better than using normal trains, anyway. And safe. Never heard of a fairy going anywhere near the guest cabins.'

'You ever meet a fairy before?' Lara asks Zach. There's a casual tone to her voice that Zach can't quite work out.

'We see a couple hundred of them every night right there,' he points out into the auditorium.

'I mean, like, outside the Grit. For a conversation, or whatever.'

Zach turns to her, alarmed. 'I must be fucking your induction right up because that is not on the cards. Listen to me, and listen good. There are no conversations with fairies. There is no, like, hanging out. If you follow the rules you won't encounter one and if you do, you run. Got it?'

Lara nods. 'Sure. Sorry.'

Zach goes back to his lighting cue sheet to hide how flustered he is. He would like this new girl to trust him, to feel safe, to feel like he told her everything she needed to know. He would like her to survive her pledge. And yes, he would like her to like him. He sneaks a look at her, frowning at the lighting desk. Not wrong, is it? To want to be liked by your closest colleague? He tucks the thought away and flips over his piece of paper.

'All right. Let me talk you through act two.'

Back in the Grub, the dining car is busy. Alina is slurping butternut squash soup and scrolling through her phone, while next to her Milly is stirring her soup listlessly. Derek is sitting with Yolanda and Lance, enthusiastically shoving lasagne into his mouth.

'You see, Yolanda,' he's saying, waving his spoon around. 'There are two things we don't take bets on, here at *The Apple and the Pearl*. The first is who Lance will be taking to his bed next, and I won't talk about the other one because I'm already persecuted for my honesty.'

Lance's knuckles whiten and his lips tighten in fury. He puts a possessive hand on Yolanda's back as Derek giggles and puts a finger to his lips.

'Derek, you need to – '

'Now I won't say any more because I can see you two would like a bit of privacy. I will just say there are a couple of young men I'm looking out for because I do believe they'd make a handsome addition to any fairy court, and a few young women I'm keeping an eye on for you, Lance. Whenever you're ready. You let me know.'

And Derek giggles, lets his spoon clatter into his bowl and gets up, adjusting his dirty black jeans as he saunters off.

Kavi knows he needs to go up to the Grit to set his ropes for tonight and make sure they're not snarled, but he sits for a minute with Alina and Milly, scrolling through his phone, eyes flicking past posts from his childhood friends – parties, holidays, jokes that you'll only get if you spend more than ten hours a day online. He sighs, then starts to type a text to his mum: *It's Jamal's birthday today, could you please tell his mum happy birthday if you see her at the shop? Love you, all good here x*

Belinda sits with her laptop at a table on her own, typing an email back to the bell smith. *Yes, two more incidents since I last saw you, that's why I'm looking to tighten things up.* She wonders if she should ask after his daughter, or his horses, or look up something from the news to make a general comment on. Really, she wants to ask him about his retirement plans, because he has looked after the bell on the Grub for forty-six years and his father looked after it for thirty-nine years before him so if he's about to drop dead or decide he'd like to devote the winter of his life to his pets she'd like to know about it. She types: *I hope your daughter is getting on well at university – any sign she'd like to join the family business?* She debates putting a little cartoon smiley face, decides against it, then presses *send.*

She scoops a spoonful of soup and eats it. Cold. She turns to the counter but Gino is already moving through the booths towards her. 'Let me give that a blast in the microwave for you,' he says, as he removes her bowl.

He hesitates a moment. 'While I've got you, Belinda, I'm getting worried about the milk.' He smiles ruefully. 'There's only so many scones I can make.'

Belinda takes off her glasses and folds them next to her

laptop. The changeling. Yet another problem to deal with. 'Maybe another supplier will be higher quality?'

'This is the fourth supplier I've tried.'

Belinda sighs. 'I will sort it, Gino. Thank you for your patience.'

He smiles and takes her bowl away as Belinda stares at her laptop screen, unseeing. How exactly will she sort it? Throw Henry out of a window in the Grit? March into the Otherworld and insist they take him? Maybe she should just level with him, say, *Look, I know what you are and what you're trying to do – and maybe you know a little bit about me too – but this is not working out and we are going to need to find a solution before somebody figures it out and takes matters into their own hands.* She takes a notepad out of her handbag and writes: *milk, changeling, ask Crow?*

Sitting on the grave of Desmond C Jones, dead in 1765 may he rest in the eternal peace of the blessed, Jean checks her emails. Her scarf is pulled tight around her throat and her hat close over her ears. She abhors being cold and this damp mist will do mischief in her lungs if she doesn't wrap herself up. Her oboe and her handbag rest safe from the damp on the grave of Desmond's wife Mary, beloved wife and mother, dead in 1782. She swipes and swipes, deleting marketing spam from websites she last used months ago – she should unsubscribe, but the extra clickthroughs feel like too much work – saving all the interesting things for reading later. A chatty catch-up message from her cousin complete with a picture of her newest grandchild; a reminder to come for a dental check-up; three invoices. She marks the ones she needs to respond to, checks the time – three twenty-five, a good time to call him – finds the number of the nursing home and calls.

There is a pause before the ringing starts and in the silence she imagines the phone like a beam of light from a torch, searching up into the sky and across the land, whatever land they're currently stopped in.

A woman answers the phone on the fourth ring. 'Good morning, Hillview Care, Kasia speaking.'

'Hello Kasia, it's Jean Petersfield here. Is Dad available and able to chat?'

'Of course! It's a good day today, Miss Petersfield. I think he'll be thrilled to hear from you.'

'Fantastic. Just cut me off if he's getting tired or agitated, I honestly won't mind.'

'I'll go and get him now.'

Jean hears the phone clunk as Kasia takes it off the hook. She hears the rustle of her trousers and the squeak of her trainers on the scrubbed linoleum tiles as she walks along the corridor to her father's room, snatches of conversation and music and TVs. A faint voice saying 'Bertie, it's for you' and the music in the room at the other end of the line – an aria from *Don Giovanni*, if she's not mistaken – cuts off mid note. A fumble, a crackle of static, a heavy breath and a cough, then:

'Albert Petersfield speaking.'

'Hello Daddy, it's Jeanie. How are you?'

'Jeanie girlie! What a treat to hear your voice!'

A warmth spreads through her despite the autumnal chill. He sounds well. Lucid, content, confident.

'It's lovely to hear you too, Dad. How are you doing?'

'Is it cold? You sound like you're somewhere cold. Are you wrapped up warm?'

'It is a little cold here but I'm fine.'

A pause. Jean tries to think of something to say. She usually describes where they're stopped but today she worries that it's a bit too close to the bone – ha ha – to tell him that today the Grub pulled up in a graveyard and she's sitting atop someone's grave. Her father is eighty-nine. There aren't too many more phone calls left.

But he cuts in before she can say anything. 'Tell me, have you lit a candle for your mother and your grandmother?'

Of course, it's All Souls'. 'Not yet, Dad. I will later, after the show.' She can stare into the flame and think about her mother and then she can light another candle for all the other dead things in her life: her dreams, her ambition, her financial stability, her chances at romance.

'Percy Montgomery used to gather all those inclined in his office and say a few words on days like this – a big C Catholic, was Percy, always said he'd have gone into the seminary if not the theatre which never made a blind bit of sense to me but Aleko and I used to go along to hear his fine tenor singing psalms – and tell me, how is Aleko, is he keeping well?'

'He's well. The same as always really.'

'Good, good. Listen, I was telling Kasia the other day – no, not Kasia, the other one, the one who sings those lovely tunes from Nigeria, her name's gone now but anyway, I was telling her about the show and she was asking what was my favourite part and I said well it has to be that bit right at the end before the wedding, you know the part that goes like...'

He starts to hum the melody of the White Suitor's solo, the same melody he sings on the phone every time she rings. She understands why it's this tune that has slipped between his decaying synapses and stuck there. It's got an eerie tone that slips between melancholy and euphoria, and the way the cello calls across the rest of the orchestra with that plaintive voice, never to be answered, it makes you think of all the things you haven't done or said.

Her father breaks off mid phrase to say, 'And tell me, the lad who dances the White Suitor, is he any good?'

'He's great, Dad, really good.' She told him the same thing when he asked her the same question last week.

'I was listening to a programme on Debussy the other day – I listen with Freddy down the way, his legs don't work anymore but he can still hold his violin – and I told him how Aleko and I used to – and how is Al, how is he keeping?'

'He's fine, Dad, you know how it is here. One day is much like the next.'

Time goes in spirals aboard the Grub. You think you're living the same day over and over again but then you look out of your cabin window one morning and you've grey hairs frizzing at your temples and mysterious aches in your knees.

'And are you looking after your reeds properly? My daughter is a musician, you know, just like her mother and I. I can get her to tell you what she does to keep her reeds dry and supple, if you like. She plays the oboe too, although she was a gifted pianist. Could have been a soloist! That's what I tell Freddy down the way. I don't think she liked the spotlight. A team player is my Jeanie, she likes the swell and roar of the orchestra and honestly who could blame her, I was a sucker for it myself.'

Jean sighs. His lucidity turns within a conversation now. Talking to him used to be like listening to a medley of greatest hits from the musicals – nothing was complete but each subject merged into the next in a way that made sense. Now his confusion is becoming a discordant jumble, staccato bits of different scores jumping in mid-phrase. Soon the melodies will begin to drop off, one instrument at a time. The silences will grow longer, stickier, the jangle of tunes harder to distinguish. She both dreads it and longs for his decline to be over.

'That sounds lovely.'

'It is! Oh it is. Proudest moment of my life, at her graduation performance when she played the solo in – ah, that's why I was talking about Debussy to Freddy, that's what I wanted to tell him – Hannah, darling, did you remember to book the piano tuner?'

Jean feels her eyes prickle with tears. He talks about her mother more than ever.

'Yes, Bertie, I did. He's coming on Wednesday.'

'Well done you. Jeanie's lesson is on Thursday, that'll be perfect.'

A silence. She imagines her father poised as if with his hands over the keys of the piano, squinting at the sheet in front of him, trying to remember where he was in the score. *See if you can take it all in with one glance, Jeanie,* he used to say when they sat down together to play duets. *See if you can breathe the notes in through your eyes.* They'd practice every morning before school, him turning the pages for her as she worked her way through the Chopin preludes. *Easy does it, Jeanie girlie, like you're stroking a cat in the dark.* She'd go and wash up her breakfast bowl, pour the orange juice her father never remembered she didn't like down the sink and grab her school bag from the kitchen table. By then he'd be playing his beloved Dvořák and she'd let the front door shut behind her with a bang, picking her way through the flowerbed growing wild with roses and honeysuckle to the window, where she'd wave goodbye at him and he would blow a kiss without missing a single note.

'I lit a candle for my late wife, Hannah, this morning. And then you know what happened? A crow came and sat on the windowsill. Not the Crow of *The Apple and the Pearl*, just an ordinary corvus, but still. Everyone said the Crow didn't have favourites but I believe Hannah proved that wrong. It saved her one night, you know. All Souls' in

1979, and there was a line of them on horseback waiting outside the stage door. All of them greedy for Hannah – it was terrifying. But then the Crow was there, spitting and cawing and hissing around Hannah's head and it grew like this black monster in the sky and we were all in the mud with the fury of it.'

A pause. 'I'm sorry, I must get off the phone. My daughter might ring at any minute and I don't want to miss her. All Souls', you know, and the Grub is never a safe place on the day of the dead. It's been lovely speaking to you.'

'Of course, I understand.' She wishes he would know her just for a moment more before she hangs up but the phone goes dead.

It's not the first time she's heard the story of her mother being rescued by the Crow, but it didn't happen on All Souls' before. She looks out over the graves towards the Grub shrouded in mist. Wouldn't it be better to have a kind of lottery system, where the Fae folk get some kind of tribute at regular intervals? At least you could prepare, say your goodbyes, make your peace with the ugliness of the loose ends of your life. She rubs the phone screen with her thumb. If she gets taken today, All Souls', when her father says the Grub is not safe, is that the kind of last conversation he can treasure for whatever remains of his life?

Quickly, she swipes through her phone to find her son's number and calls him. It rings and rings and she tries to think of something nice and loving and not at all nosy to say to his voicemail when he picks up the phone, something he could listen to with love if she is, in fact, heading off with the fairies today.

'Mum! Nice to hear you but I haven't got long. I'm just off out.'

'Sorry love, I didn't mean to disturb you, we can talk later if you want.'

'No, it's okay, I'm a bit early. How are you?'

'I'm fine but are you all right? You sound like you've got a cold.'

'Just hungover,' Sam says with a laugh. 'Went to a Halloween party last night dressed as Dracula and the lads from across the road brought a bottle of tequila. Feeling a little ropey.'

'Have you had a good breakfast? A fry-up will sort you out.'

'Done all that. Kind of helped. Listen, I was going to go and see Granddad next weekend, is that okay?'

'That's great darling, I think he'd really like to see you. He sort of drifts in and out while you're talking to him so remember what we talked about?'

'Yeah. Just go with it. I'll take my sax. He never gets confused when we're playing.'

Jean feels that prickle behind her eyes again. What exactly is she doing here messing about with creatures from the spirit realm when her family need her?

'Mum? You still there?'

'Yes, darling, I'm here.'

'It's just that – and I hate to ask – but I'm running a bit short on cash.'

There it is. That's what she's doing here. The sale of the house paid for university; half her salary goes to Hillview and the other goes to Dracula costumes and tequila shots.

'Have you spoken to your father?'

There's a silence at the other end of the line. She knows what he's going to say but she admires the way he wrestles with it. She remembers how, when he was a little boy, he'd come home on a Sunday evening after he'd spent the day with Ricky fractious and smelling of cigarette smoke and beer. When she put his dinner in front of him he'd gobble it down as if he'd not been fed all day. And she'd ask, as casually as she could, *did you have fun with Dad today?* and Sam would look up at her, mouth full and eyes wide and nod slowly. *I was very good, Mum,* he'd say, and her heart would crack a little along the fault lines his father had ripped into it. *I did exactly as I was told.*

'Dad's cheque bounced.'

That lowdown, no-good piece of shit. She cannot imagine what she was thinking. Two years of her life she spent with that neanderthal! When she saw him at Sam's end-of-year performance last year, nothing, not a single sliver of whatever had drawn her to him, remained. He was no longer sleek or lithe or gave off that wild perfume of sex and danger. He was just a middle-aged man with a paunch and a roving eye, and when she sat next to him as they listened to the jazz standards played well, if with little personality, it was as if she were sitting next to a stranger.

'Right. I'll transfer you something today. But maybe give it a rest with the fancy cocktails.'

'It wasn't *my* tequila, Mum. I only drink cheap stuff, I'm saving to get a new amp.'

Three generations of utterly broke musicians, four if you count her mother's mother who sang and danced in music halls until she gave birth in her dressing room after a show. Jean had loved that old woman. She spent every night of her childhood with her while her parents were performing, snuggled under the covers with her grandmother singing songs with the bawdy bits swapped out for nursery rhymes. She died when Jean was twelve. Then her mother a year later, of the cancer that was already curling itself around her stomach as she stood holding Jean's hand over the old woman's coffin, tears streaming down her cheeks as she tried to sing 'Daisy Bell', the song her mother had been famous for. A one-two punch, losing them both.

'Well, sweetheart, you'd better go. Lovely to speak to you.'

'You too, Mum.'

'Do you still have that emergency number I gave you?'

'Yep. On the fridge and in my phone.'

'Good boy. See you later.'

'Bye.'

Jean puts the phone on Mary Jones' gravestone and squeezes her eyes shut. She wonders if Mary minds being stuck with her husband for all eternity. What would she have done if she and Ricky had both died during those years they were still married and some idiot had buried them next to each other, lying under the ground decomposing, their cells mingling again, the worms chomping and shitting through them both? *I'd have haunted Sam mercilessly until he dug up my bones and threw them in the sea rather than stay next to Ricky,* Jean thinks.

She remembers her father on her wedding day, just about to open the car door to drive her to the registry office. The bulk of Sam wriggling under her skin, kicking at the bouquet of daffodils she'd picked from the garden. He'd stopped, looked at her over the bonnet. *Are you sure, darling? You know you don't have to go through with it. It's not too late to change your mind.*

And she'd said *yes, Dad, of course I'm sure.* And Sam had kicked and she'd huffed and puffed to get in and then out the car and of course Ricky was sleeping with at least three girls in the chorus by the time Sam was six months old, although she didn't chuck him out until Sam was almost two.

Her nose starts to stream a little with cold. She tucks the notepad back in her bag and wipes her face with her sleeve. She shuts the lid of the oboe case, the damp air's no good for the reed. She's well and truly shafted without that thing: it's her only way of keeping her menfolk alive. One more year and Sam will be leaving university and he can sort himself out, although he's determined to be a musician so who knows when she'll be able to retire and ask him for cash for a change.

She should have seen it coming but those years of

Sam's childhood were a fog of debt and exhaustion. She was working in the West End six nights a week and taking recording whenever it came up, and in the dressing room during intervals she would sit with a little book and write down everything she'd earned and everything she'd spent, watching the columns stubbornly refuse to balance. Her father had been Sam's main carer since he was four, bedtime stories, bumps and bruises and bellyaches, he was the one who did all of it. By the time she broke through the surface of the mist and gasped for air, it was too late to save him.

On her thirty-seventh birthday – Sam was nine – her father made her sit on the sofa and listen to her son play Bach, and of all the curses of all the fairy godmothers, the boy was talented.

Then it was *please Mum, I'd like to learn the sax like Dad* and her father had said, *go on Jeanie, it's well and truly in the boy, his blood sings like yours and mine.* Orchestra after school and jazz band on Saturday afternoons and her nothing more than a chauffeur and cook, never a chance to make up for those lost years. And still, only paying off interest on the credit cards and waiting for those royalty payments with her heart in her mouth and hoping the mortgage and her salary didn't sail past each other at the door to her bank account.

Once he'd started to buy that horrendous aftershave and spend hours sitting alone in his room only to thunder down the stairs whenever the phone rang it was *Mum, do you know anyone who can teach me the guitar, I'd like to get better.* A growth spurt and a dusting of hair on his chin and he was forever out, God knows where and who with but he'd smell like dirty clubs and weed on a Sunday morning, though he still sat down to play duets with his grandfather, the way she had every morning of her adolescence.

Then, *Mum, can you help me write my personal statement,* and *Mum, have you got a minute to listen to my audition pieces,* and God love the boy he was planning to be a musician like the rest of them. She must have made it look easy, all those years of scrimping and all those grey hairs of worry. She must – and she regrets this bitterly – have made it look fun.

She should never have allowed it. She should never have let her father teach him the piano and said no to the sax. She should have locked her father's LPs in the attic, got a job in a supermarket and signed him up for extra maths instead. Then he might be training to become an accountant now. Then he might stand a chance of making something of his life, building something solid that matters.

Not ending up somewhere like here, literally away with the fairies. Not ending up like her, broke and alone, and utterly dependent on a bit of cork and brass staying dry to keep body and soul together.

She shoves her laptop back in her bag and fastens one latch on the oboe case, but before she can swing her handbag over her shoulder her phone buzzes. A text. She opens the message with one swipe of her thumb.

We hope all aboard the Grub is going well and you have still not been taken to another realm!! xoxo

Toni. Jean's vision swims, her heart starts to pound.

Only the second time she's heard from them in the almost two years since they've been gone. The first time, she messaged back that she missed them desperately and there has been silence ever since. Why have they got in touch now? Today, All Souls', the day of dead things. And with such a nothing message too. No meat to it, nothing even to snack on. No acknowledgement of the long silence, nor the sweetness that filled their days before it.

On their first day the three of them had sat together in the wings on the chairs Mackie had set out for them, politely ignored by the dancers and crew. Beryl had leaned back, eyes closed, hands mimicking AJ's as she picked out the intricacies of the score and Toni had watched the comings and goings of the dancers with delight. Jean watched the show and listened to the score with an eerie sense of déjà vu. Everything was familiar to her.

After the show the three of them stood in a jumble in the corridor outside Belinda's office with their suitcases and instruments. Toni, her curly black hair tied up with a scarf and her cello-callused fingers nervously smoothing the hem of her jacket; Beryl with her long grey hair arranged in an elegant chignon.

They said the words, pricked their fingers and Belinda had got out her watch – *sync to me, please, then I'll show you to your cabins* – and they were pledge-mates forever and ever.

Afterwards, they sat in the dining car and Jean asked them how they met. She read somewhere that people thought you were a good conversationalist if you asked them questions about themselves. And she was trying to be a good conversationalist, belatedly. She was trying to see this job as an exciting new chapter, not a final failure in a long string of fuck-ups, trying not to think of herself as a drowning salmon, swimming upstream to where she had been spawned.

She had just turned forty-eight, Sam had started university and her father had moved into Hillview the week before. She had seventy-four pounds in her bank account, three maxed-out credit cards and a sheaf of bills in her suitcase.

It was in Prague, Toni had said. *We were each covering for a friend at the symphony there…*

…then she went off on a contract to Sydney for a year and I went back to London, recording and teaching…

…but we couldn't do long distance, not at our age…

…so we asked a friend if they knew anywhere we could tour together…

…but no cruises because I get seasick…

…and he gave us Belinda's number.

The pair of them smiled at her like one being and Jean felt something move in the pit of her stomach. That night she'd thought it was jealousy, to have someone to go through life with, to lean on when the wind almost blew you down, to keep the chill of loneliness at bay. Now she thinks of it as something awakening, stirring. An ember of a long-dampened fire kept smouldering in a ball of kindling, finally given air.

And what about you? Toni had asked. *How did you come to be here?*

A lie would have been so easy, so quick and clean.

I was born here, she said.

Toni's mouth fell open and Beryl's perfectly painted eyebrows shot into her hairline.

My dad was first violin, my mum was clarinet. Apparently I used to spend shows in a basket in wardrobe and my mum used to feed me during the intervals. They left when I was about a year old so I don't remember a thing.

But that wasn't strictly true. Jean did remember. Or her flesh did, that deep place inside us which music is the first to fill and the last to leave. She knew all the melodies, could hum them perfectly, knew she'd have no need of her score by the end of the week.

And how did they keep you, you know – Beryl waved her hand vaguely at the window – *safe?*

Salt scattered around me and thirteen horseshoes sewn onto the mattress. There was a picture in my parent's house when I was growing up.

It sat in a silver frame on the mantelpiece, the colours fading a little more each afternoon when the sunlight streamed in through the window. Now the photo sits on a chest of drawers in her father's room and he makes the carers dust it every single day. Sam said that he tells them the photo is of his daughter, his granddaughter or Queen Mab, depending on his mood.

Well, we're very pleased to meet someone of such distinguished pedigree. Beryl had said, and their curiosity about her was sealed. Jean basked in it, discreetly. It was the only interesting thing about her.

Her father had pledged with AJ as second violins. Just the two of them standing in the old company manager's office, their violins propped against the wall. They sat next to each other night after night, bows gliding in perfect synchrony, until her father was promoted to first violin.

Then the old conductor had been taken during the curtain call. As her father told the story, Mungo St John Fitzwilliam – cellist, conductor, pinewood-whittler, Morris-dancer and Welsh folklore enthusiast – placed his baton upon the music stand as the dancers bowed and bowed and bowed and the musicians stood in silence. And in the blink of an eye, something from the audience reached into the pit and took him. The last thing seen of him in this world was the oily shine of his patent leather shoes.

The next morning Percy Montgomery, the old company manager – dark circles under his eyes and a scent of pungent fear-sweat wafting whenever he moved – called her father and AJ into the office with the Crow glowering in a corner.

And I never knew, Jeanie girlie, if our names were already in a kind of hat for the job, if the Crow had only whispered to him that very morning, or if there were other voices he had to kowtow to, but we were there in front of him, and he said, 'Gentlemen, I would like to ask you both to sing me a song.' And I don't know what I expected but it certainly wasn't that.

He'd told her this with his soft hands in hers, just before she left him at Hillview to get the taxi to Liverpool Street station. At the time she had treasured it as a moment of lucidity, but now she understands that he had saved the story all these years for this very moment, the time she left to return to the place of her birth. So that she would understand, so that she would truly know the stakes as her father and mother had known them, surviving through multiple snatchings and attempted snatchings, a show every night with hundreds of creatures from the Otherworld in the auditorium licking their glistening lips.

So I sang 'The Skye Boat Song', he said, his gaze somewhere over her shoulder. *I don't know why, it was just the first thing that popped into my head, and Aleko sang* 'Greensleeves' *and old Percy Montgomery just looked at the Crow and then at Aleko and said, 'Congratulations, you are the ninetieth conductor of* The Apple and the Pearl.*' And of course I was disappointed, though I hadn't ever thought of conducting before, but a month later your mother told me she was carrying you.*

She flicks the other latch on the oboe case and puts her handbag over her shoulder. She remembers AJ smiling at her on the morning after her pledge, his delicately veined hands folded over three copies of the score as she sat with Toni and Beryl in the musician's green room. *Warmest of welcomes to you all.* And then he'd turned to Jean and searched her face for traces of his old friends, her parents. *And welcome back to you, Jeanie.*

She walks a little stiffly up the main avenue, bordered

by mausoleums, towards the Grit. The drizzle thickens and she pulls up her hood.

It started only a few weeks later. They shared a bottle of wine in the dining car after the show and Beryl bought two more. *It's a celebration!* she'd said. Toni had leaned forwards like a conspirator: *Would you like to come back to our cabin to finish this off?* And something in her belly had answered, like a hibernating snake opening one yellow eye to the spring, something shocking but unmistakeable. It had been so long, and it had never been a woman, let alone two.

The oyster taste of pussy, the softness of limbs in the bed, the way flesh yielded under the gentlest of pressure from her fingertips. The laughter, the languid stretch of skin, the sneaking back to her single cabin in the early hours, holding onto the dark windows to steady herself against the swaying of the carriage, her skin fizzing like seafoam, salty with sweat, slick with longing.

The memory of it makes her dizzy; the shock of it gone winds her. She stops, staggers a little like when her blood was still going topsy-turvy with menopause. She leans against the cool pink marble of a crypt, shivery and flushed.

Her body had opened to them like those seeds that lie dormant in the desert for forty years and then sprout and bloom within a week. She was greedy for them both – the long, elegant curve of Beryl's waist, the weight of Toni's breast in her hand. She had no idea if anyone else knew. Once or twice she'd thought there was something leering and knowing in Lance's eyes, but now she thinks he's just that sort of man, the sort Ricky used to be. A tomcat prowling alleyways, yowling for sex.

She pushes herself off the pillar, grips her oboe case and carries on up the avenue of the dead towards the Grit. She keeps her eyes on the theatre. It looks like a haunted house today, the spires piercing the grey clouds like swords. You could never accuse it of failing to dress for the occasion.

She was born in her parents' cabin aboard the Grub. Percy Montgomery, the old company manager had found a midwife – how, she'd never quite figured out – and two replacement musicians, and given her father two weeks' paternity leave and her mother three months on full pay. *That's why you pay your union subs, Jeanie girlie, so that they see you as a living, breathing human first and a music-maker second,* her father had said. Born during the Crow's second act solo, cord cut as the curtain came down, taken to the caboose to be presented to the Crow just before the midnight bells. *Has this ever happened before?* her father reportedly asked old Montgomery. *Any legends about this or what it might mean? Not that I know of,* Montgomery said. *Your girl there is one of a kind.* What bullshit. She's turned out to be as ordinary as a drop of rain in April, entirely failed to live up to anything spectacular her birth might have foretold.

The stage door opens and Mackie shuffles out, rummaging in the capacious pockets of his cargo trousers.

He nods hello, makes a wry, slightly embarrassed face at the slim silver bar in his fingers. 'Gave up years ago, couldn't afford it. Couldn't get them regularly when I came to work here, and you know what Belinda would say if you were trying to stash weeks' worth of fags in your cabin. But I still like stepping out for a break every now and then, you know? Gives you something to do with your hands while you have a little think.'

Jean smiles. 'Don't mind me.' She's always liked Mackie. She should have married a man like that. Kind, slightly shy, competent enough under his bumbling. Too late now, of course. She can't sleep with a man again, even if a candidate did present himself.

A caw catches their attention. The Crow is perched on the stone balustrade, which is chipped and mossy and moody today. The huge bird gleams although the afternoon light is sludgey. It gives another caw and Mackie chuckles.

'All right. All right. We heard you.' He walks over and carefully places the vape in front of it. 'Bad for me anyway.' He smiles at Jean again, tips his head in a little nod and disappears back inside the Grit, letting the stage door slam behind him.

Another caw, an indignant nudge. Jean reaches into her pocket and pulls out the crust of toast she always saves from breakfast for encounters like this and a two-penny coin. She lays them both on the ground and the Crow hops down onto the bottom step to peck at the crust. Jean watches.

'Should I write back, do you think? Is there any point? I'm stuck here anyway.'

It flies back to the balustrade, picks up the vape in its claws and hops back down to the crust of bread.

'You're not going to tell me, are you? You don't give a shit.'

The Crow stops pecking and looks at her with a long, cool stare that Jean returns, although her eyes start to itch.

'Of course I won't break my pledge.' She wants to look away but she feels the need to meet this challenge, to live up to whatever it was the Crow liked about her mother. 'I spoke to my father today. He was talking about you. He thinks of you often. Thank you for saving my mother, by the way.'

The bird's gaze softens and Jean cannot bear that flicker of tenderness. She looks away. 'Fine,' she says. 'I can see your point.' It gobbles down the crust and then grabs the coin in its beak, the vape in its claws and with two tugs of its great black wings, flies away over the graves, back to the warm shelter of the Grub.

She starts to climb the steps of the Grit, her boots echoing on each stone stair. She thinks of climbing these steps with Toni and Beryl, arm in arm, the three of them batty old women giggling at clouds, only she knowing the sweet ache of being pressed against their bodies.

But as quickly as it began, it was done. They only stayed for one pledge. They didn't even tell her they weren't going to pledge again. She found out like everyone else, when Belinda put the notice on the board. It was as if all those nights in their cabin had never happened, like they'd been some kind of sad, erotic dream. They said goodbye with a kiss on each cheek in front of everyone and she had to smile and wave as they walked off the Grub at Edinburgh

Waverley, like they had been nothing but two other sounds in the orchestra, two other beating hearts to keep safe with salt and iron.

She pushes the stage door open and the stuffy, warm air of the Grit hits her. It smells like hairspray, sawdust and stale tomato soup as always, no matter how it's rearranged its corridors overnight. She unzips her coat as she glances at the noticeboard by the door to the stage, scanning it for anything interesting or important. Tonight's casting, a handwritten note from Mackie inviting everyone to drinks tonight to celebrate his new pledge, a sign from one of the dancers asking if anyone's seen a certain green coat. Nothing for her.

The door to the stage opens and Derek emerges, whistling the tune to the orchard dance in a faintly menacing way. Jean stares at the noticeboard, hoping he will glide on past her.

'Good afternoon, Miss Jean.' No such luck. She pretends to look very closely at the sign advertising the fire safety procedures.

'Hi, Derek.'

'Lighting a candle for anyone today?'

The cheek of the man. As if she'd discuss something as intimate as her own dead with this troll. *I will never let him near me again!* Toni muttered, horrified, after he cornered her in the Grub one night and asked her if she'd ever had a boyfriend.

'No one in particular. They went into the Pearl a long time ago.'

'My condolences.' Derek simpers and bows as he backs away. 'May their memories live long.'

Oh fuck off, Derek, she thinks as she grabs the handrail to climb the stairs to the green room, suddenly weary. Sometimes she lies in her narrow single bed in her single cabin and thinks about Toni asking her to come with them. *We'll get a small flat, pool our money, teach and record. We'll stop touring forever, we're all getting too old for it.* She thinks about packing up her cabin and walking off the Grub at Liverpool Street again, maybe Marylebone, wherever they'd have wanted. Walking out into the train station, ignoring the way all the other passengers' eyes slide off the iron of the Grub lingering on the platform, pretending she can't see it either as she walks away into a – another – new life. She thinks about having her father's piano delivered, sitting at it each morning – *See if you can breathe the notes in through your eyes, Jeanie* – having Sam round each Sunday to feed him, listen to him play, hear stories about what he's been up to.

As she touches the door handle of the musician's green room it twists under her hands and opens. Michael is standing on the other side, his satchel over one shoulder and his jumper baggy around his chest. She feels that twinge of pity that the sorry sight of him always provokes in her these days.

'Did you know there's phone signal today?' Jean says. She tells him more to be polite than anything else. Like everyone else, she struggles to know what to say to Michael since Evelyn left. The miasma of misery that floats around him almost stinks of something rotting, and although she wants to be kind it's been months now, and still he goes around with those plugs in his ears for whatever the Crow's doing to him, and still his second act solo is making the tannoys weep, and still she has not seen him smile, not even once.

He looks back at her blankly. 'Yes. I know that.'

He pauses on the threshold of the doorway before he passes her, his face in shadow.

'How's your dad?'

A flicker of the old Michael, the gently charming young man who strung his heart with his violin.

'He's well, thank you. Quite lucid today, actually.'

And Michael nods, pleased to hear it and strides past Jean towards the stage. On the tannoy she can hear Cecile clapping her hands. '*Alors, mesdames et messieurs*!' she cries. 'Break time is over!'

Wilf, Steve and Jasper are playing cards in a corner and give Jean a cheery wave as she passes them. She nods a brisk hello to Henry the second violin, but he ignores her the way he ignores everyone, and she sits in an armchair to pull her phone from her pocket.

Henry's practising a small section of the Red Suitor's solo, playing the same couple of bars over and over again, but he's getting it wrong each time with a discordant note in the middle of the phrase that he can't seem to hear to correct. She types: *How lovely to hear from you. We are stopped in a graveyard – yes, I know it's All Souls', you know what the Grub is like with a metaphor –*

She stops. Henry plays that discordant note and makes a growl of frustration. She deletes the message. She types: *I have been thinking of you both endlessly. I am heartsick and soulsore and no one cares because Michael goes about like he's condemned–*

She can hear where he's going wrong. She should tell him, she can't bear to listen to this all afternoon but really it's Lance's job to make sure everyone's score is correct. And what has Michael been doing, sitting in front of him night after night while he gets this bit wrong? She deletes the last sentence. *I have been thinking of you both endlessly. Spoke to my father and Sam today, they're both all right–*

She stops. She puts her phone in her lap and sighs.

'It's F sharp,' Jean says quietly.

'Sorry?' Henry startles.

'It goes, *da da di da da di da* F sharp.'

He looks at the score in front of him. 'It says E in here.'

Jean shrugs. 'It's F sharp.'

He frowns, pulls his violin to his chin and plays the bars again. The notes trip perfectly from his beautiful instrument. 'Of course.' He murmurs. 'I remember now.'

And there is such a curious look of longing in Henry's face as he plays that phrase properly that Jean cannot breathe for a moment. Her heart caught in her mouth, she has a bright flash of understanding. Henry's fixed gaze on Michael each night as AJ comes into the pit; the way you hardly see Michael without this handsome face hovering somewhere nearby; the way Henry has refused all other overtures. There's something charmingly old-fashioned about his constancy. She doesn't know when or how it started or if Michael has ever given him any reason to hope, but the sadness of it all swamps her as Henry plays the Red Suitor's melody with his eyes half shut. Words rise desperately in her throat: *You know, I also love someone – two someones – who don't love me back. I am also paralysed by grief, I am also leaden with a useless secret, I am also stuck here without any hope of loving anyone else ever again.*

On the tannoy, Cecile calls, 'Tonight's cast of the hunting dance, *s'il vous plaît*!' and the toilet flushes next door and Sandra comes into the room, phone squeezed between her ear and her shoulder, wiping her hands on her jumper. Jean smiles at her and she mimes hello back.

She wants to grab Michael's face and squeeze his grey cheeks between her palms and snarl, *Listen! Everything you think you know about love is wrong. You think you would have loved Evelyn forever the way you did these past months but you're full of shit and she knew it. It always falls apart, like everything, like the whole damn universe will if you leave it spinning for long enough. Your love will tear over the tiny sleeping bodies of your babies, the piled-up bills, the exhaustion, the endless conversations about plumbing. And then you'll look at each other and you'll just see someone that you used to love, someone you know better than anything by now but maybe you don't even like anymore and it'll be like being inside your own head, itchy, annoying, you'll do anything to get out of there. So she left you to keep you loving her and you're too stupid to see it.*

But what right has she got to lecture anyone on real love? She, with a few sterile relationships in her twenties, a failed marriage to an idiot, almost two decades of resigned celibacy before a late, glorious flush of passion refracted like a rainbow through two bodies, abandoned because… well, she's still not sure why it ended, and isn't that what hurts the most? She, who sits here typing and deleting and typing and deleting a message to the women she loves, unable even to say she loves them, even to herself?

Jean picks up her phone again as Henry starts the Red Suitor's solo from the top. She types: *How lovely to hear from you both. Hope you're well and thriving in the real world. We are stopped in a graveyard, which is slightly obvious of the Grub but you know what it's like. All fine here, you know how it is. Thinking of you both.* And she presses send before she can change her mind.

She puts the phone at the very bottom of her handbag and pulls out her laptop. While it whirrs itself into sentience, she opens the lid of her oboe case again and rummages for her glasses. She logs into her bank account, sends Sam some money, pays the other three invoices. She looks at the photo of her cousin's grandchild; there is something of Sam as an infant about the little one's chubby face and she starts to type an email to her cousin to tell her so when her phone buzzes at the bottom of her handbag.

She shuts her eyes. She'll look at the message, of course she will but first she'll sit here for a moment, wallowing in the beauty of that message's boundless possibilities because before she swipes her thumb across the screen and sees its words it could say anything, anything at all. *We've got a place by the sea, we want you to come and live with us.* Or, *we are very happy, we are living with a lovely young lady called Veronica and she does us the power of good.* Or, *fuck the money, we'll help you, you're ours.* She told the Crow she wouldn't break her pledge and she meant it but how will she stay here for another two and a half months if they're calling her, how will she open her oboe case each morning knowing that they are waiting for her, how will she deal with the danger in the auditorium each night knowing that there are those who love her out there in the world?

She opens her eyes, closes her laptop and reaches into her bag.

In the stage right wing, Bella is lying under the props table with her foot stretched over her head, listening to the piano gurgle the tune of the third act hunting dance. She's using the underside of the table as an anchor for her foot and sewing a ribbon onto the heel of a brand new pointe shoe.

The piano stops mid-phrase – there's been a lot of that – and Cecile shouts at Luke, who has become redder and redder each time she's stopped him. Now he looks like a tomato about to go splat under a heel.

'*Non*!' She claps her hands and the piano stops mid-bar. 'I said the arms go through *la seconde* on the way to the fifth, I need accuracy! Again!'

From where she's lying she can hear Michael's soft, weary sigh as he plays the opening notes of the hunting dance again. Most of the dancers have been spared the agony of watching Luke rehearse this role very slowly and very publicly, but Cecile has said they're going to run through the Pearl waltz next and so she has to wait, ready to jump up at a moment's notice, for however long it takes for Cecile to get bored of poking and prodding at that poor boy and decide to move on.

She checks her watch – four seventeen, there's still over an hour to go until Cecile is obliged by the union to let them go – and pushes the needle through the canvas lining of the pointe shoe. She could do without rehearsing the bloody Pearl waltz again – she knows four parts inside out and could do the other four with a quick walk through – but she'd rather die than grumble. You've got to show willing. You've got to be up Cecile's arse and keep in her favour so when it's time for someone new to learn a principal role you're right there, smiling and reliable. You've also got to know what you're doing and do it well, something that's a little far from poor Luke right now.

Mind you, she's been a model member of *The Apple and the Pearl* for two and a half years now and there's not been so much as a sniff of her learning a principal role. Some days she thinks she's close, when Cecile walks past her during a *frappé* exercise and pauses before walking by without a word. She imagines explaining her pride in that to anyone else, can picture their baffled pity. *No, you don't understand,* she'd say. *Silence is praise, usually.*

At night she lies in her cabin massaging out her calves, daydreaming about the day when Cecile will beckon to her during that caesura in ballet class between the last *grands battements* at the barre and the first *adage* in the centre. When, instead of changing her pointe shoes from the hard ones she's breaking in to the softer ones, she'll obediently trot to the front of the stage, skin prickling with the curious eyes of the other dancers as they wonder if she is in favour or disgrace. Cecile will quietly tell her to make sure she's watching one of the Princesses – she thinks it will be the White Princess, because the solo is full of quick little jumps and tricky beats and she's got the power and stamina for it. The daydream skips a couple of months, past all the costume fittings, the well-meaning advice from Mara and Stephanie and Stuart, past Josh's inevitable sneers, past Cecile's theatrical screeching during the interminable rehearsals to the moment when the curtain goes up on the first act on her first show, the dazzle in her face, the audience hungry for her and she for them, her first chance to be truly–

A shadow falls across her, blocking the light to see her sewing by. She bends her leg back into her chest and rolls out from under the props table to see Kavi the fly operator looking down at her with a half-smile playing about his mouth.

'I thought it was you,' he says. 'You're the only one with those orange leggings.'

Well now, isn't that interesting. He's been noticing her legs. She is kneeling at his feet, her fingertips almost touching his steel-capped black boots and there is a flutter low in her belly. She stands, kicks the half-sewn pointe shoe back under the props table and leans against the edge. She fights the urge to brush the dust from her hair. She is attempting a seduction, and aren't you supposed to pretend like you don't care? Like if they can't or won't just take you as you are, a pale-faced, orange legwarmer-clad, dusty-haired idiot, then it's nothing to you.

'I just came to check something for Charlie,' he says, but he doesn't move, just keeps staring at her with that smile like he knows a secret.

The silence between them stretches like strings of glue, ensnaring any clever thoughts she might have had. The truth is she's out of practice. Alina the wardrobe mistress, warming to her favourite theme: *Yes I use the word CLOISTERED ladies because although there are technically men employed here I see NO relationship material and NO ONE I would willingly fuck.* And although all the girls in the dressing room giggle when she gets going on this topic, there is something of the maiden aunt in the titter, something desperate that none of them will acknowledge. Jessica, a bit drunk at pledge party: *I just want to feel a man's hands on me, you know? On my actual skin, not on the bodice of my sodding costume.*

Bella did know. It's been literally years since she's been to bed with anyone and this is the first time there's been even a hint that someone wants her. All right, yes there was Lance the trumpet player who'd sidled up to her in the dining car in her third week to compliment her hair, and of course she'd been flattered at first, then aroused, even though she had already heard that Lance was that kind of guy. But then she'd caught sight of Mara's stony face over Lance's shoulder and skittered away, feeling queasy at the thought of causing romantic uproar in her very first month.

Mara, in the dressing room before ballet class the next morning: *I'm fucking sick of it, it's gone beyond sexual incontinence, now he's just being a dick because no one will stop him.* She'd pointed at Bella with a mascara wand. *You seem like a smart girl so let me tell you this for free – you'll be happier here if you find someone other than Casanova with his cornet to get your kicks with.*

But Alina is right, there is no one else to get your kicks with. Henry the second violin looks like an underwear model but he doesn't seem to take an interest in anyone but Michael, which is a shame because Michael definitely plays for the other team. Luke the new boy has the sex appeal of a slice of cucumber. Alex had been lovely but firmly Anita's and now he's gone she can't even talk about him, let alone move on. Zach the lighting guy is kind but sort of shambling and awkward. Max the second violin has some mysterious girlfriend out in the real world and the new harp David is old. Like, at least forty. And then there's Derek. Last week he caught her at the noticeboard by the stage with the back of her Pearl waltz costume undone and whistled. *That's a good show for a fairy prince.* Bella had cringed helplessly. Jessica said she should report him to Belinda, but Bella has the feeling even Belinda's powers are limited when it comes to Derek.

So it's surprising that there hasn't been more of a stampede for Kavi. He's not exactly handsome, but there's nothing offensive about his face. A slim build, clean, no indication of being a dickhead. What is she missing?

It's been two months now since they first locked gazes in the dining car after the show and there've since been: seven long looks accompanied by shy smiles; eleven *hello-how-are-yous*; three occasions where they've been sitting with a larger group in the Grub, swapping stories about when Belinda's told them off; and one time when he happened to be leaving the Grit at the same time as her after ballet class and they walked along a windy clifftop and talked about the sea. And now. The two of them, alone in the semi-darkness, with Cecile's increasingly furious counting echoing out into the auditorium and a silence elongating into a cringe. She doesn't know if she actually finds him attractive or if he's the only chance for her to get laid this decade and she doesn't care anymore. She wants to get there before any of the others, and right now he's standing in front of her and her orange legwarmers, and she needs to say something intelligent before he walks away thinking she's a moron.

'Are ballet mistresses always like this?' he asks, gesturing to the stage.

Oh thank God, he spoke first. The table is digging into her hip so she pulls herself up to sit on it. 'Mostly. Some of them pretend to be nice, but actually they play favourites and smack you down behind your back.'

She swings her legs. She's trying to look insouciant and flirtatious but maybe she just looks like a kid. 'Cecile doesn't do that, she's a bitch to everyone. I appreciate that about her.'

Kavi laughs. 'I don't think Cecile knows who I am and I'm fine with that.'

'Oh, she knows who you are; she knows everything. She just doesn't care.'

He hooks his thumbs into the pockets of his jeans and leans back on the table.

'Have you worked in ballet before?' she asks. It's a stupid, small-talky thing to say but it follows on from what he said.

'I've done two other ballets,' he says. 'Both were like this, set in a kind of mythical past, with kings and queens and magic and fake medieval costumes. I like it. I get to watch the show from the flies, and it's really beautiful.'

She thinks about him watching her dance from above, her spinning, leaping, darting head moving around the stage.

'I guess Cecile might be a dragon and kind of old-fashioned in her methods,' he continues, 'but she keeps the show spick and span.'

From the stage comes a stream of French swear words, the bang of a stool falling over and a particularly Gallic sound of disgust.

Kavi smirks and she holds back a snort of laughter.

'Fair enough. The show would be a mess without Cecile keeping us in line. And she's also a great teacher, you know. Her classes are excellent.'

He nods a little. 'That's important in ballet, isn't it.'

'Oh yeah. Ballet is all about lineage, you can't learn it from a book. You have to show up in front of a teacher who apprenticed themselves to someone else and to the art itself, and yes, that's elitist and unfair but that's how it is. There's no democracy in ballet, no negotiation; there's only the form. And then you've got to kind of kneel in front of this ideal, like, you sacrifice yourself on the altar of what ballet is even though you'll never attain it. No one will. It doesn't live in this realm.'

She waves her arm vaguely in the direction of the as yet empty auditorium. 'That's why *they* come to the show, you know? Because they're drawn to the beauty of human bodies striving and yearning for that ideal. They feed on that space in between the dancer and the dance.'

She takes a breath and shoves her hands under her thighs to sit on them. He's frowning, but in a go-on-tell-me-more way, so she keeps going.

'So when you do an *arabesque*,' she says, 'you're doing your own version of an *arabesque*, a version which aims for the ur-*arabesque* but will inevitably fall short. Your leg will be a little too low, or a little turned in, or your back will fall too far forwards and spoil the line. Maybe it'll be your foot spoiling the line with a sickle at the ankle. You'll place your arm just as the choreography says, one arm draped behind you and the other guiding your gaze forwards, with your chin lifted to match but something about the picture will not be quite good enough. Cecile will correct you, and after you do what she says your *arabesque* will be better, but there'll still be something in the pose that'll fall from the ideal in some way and you'll hardly ever be able to say what it is.'

What a wanker she sounds. What made her say all that? She's gabbing on like bloody Derek the follow spot. Watch him excuse himself now, mumble something about how he must be going, doesn't want to get her in trouble with Cecile. Soon she'll see him in the Grub with Jessica, or Anita and the next time a young, half-decent straight man pledges here Kavi will take him aside and say *yeah, she's fit you know but she's kind of intense.*

'That's nothing like poetry,' he says.

'How do you mean?' she says, and her stomach does a one-two bounce-then-dive. Of course he's a poet. That's the way this place works. The Crow hates her. Who else would it give her as a boyfriend?

'Well, when you write a poem you've got nothing but the words in your head, right? And you don't know if it's good or not and that becomes an obsession. How can you know if it's good? Why do some people think it's good and some think it's bad and some are totally indifferent to it?'

He's looking at her like he wants her to answer, but she's still trying to figure out if she is more or less interested in sleeping with him now, so she shrugs apologetically and he carries on.

'That's because there's no such thing as an ur-poem, no ideal poem that all the other poems are trying to live up to. It's just a jumble of words that have to be persuaded into poem shape after they've done their day job in lists and love letters and lullabies.'

She smiles. 'Words have day jobs?'

'Of course.' He leans in to her, conspiratorially. She knows they've been noticed by now. One of the girls waiting in the other wing will have seen their heads drawing together in the darkness as Cecile's counting drones on and the news will be drifting among the rest of the dancers by the half-hour call tonight.

'Some words, like... Okay, I've thought of some: *exquisite* and *caress* and *gleam* – well, you don't have to ask them twice. They love being written into poetry and they jump right into the lines, snuggle down between the commas and coo. Other words, like *mud* and *water* and *baby* have to be, like, cajoled and teased and tickled. But–'

He holds out a finger to her and she tries not to be impressed because she is still – *still* – trying to figure out if this poetry thing is good or bad.

'If you can settle them there, tuck them inside a metaphor or something, let them get comfy. Well, then they'll sing the sweetest song you'll ever hear.'

She cocks her head, not sure if she can tease him yet. 'Is that one of your poems?'

He laughs. 'The Crow isn't keen on me writing. I've lost every single notebook I've ever written in, the notes app on my phone crashes constantly and any time I ask to borrow Mackie's laptop he says yes but it never works out.'

She winces in sympathy. 'It does that sort of shit, doesn't it?'

She's just about to tell him how the Crow used to trick her in the first month after her pledge, moving her cabin up and down the corridor after the show, until she got fed up and went to sit in the caboose one day after ballet class. She waited with a five pound note in her fist until the Crow showed up and put the money in front of it, told it to stop dicking about, she loved the show, the other dancers were complimentary about the way she'd covered for some injuries and Belinda had just put in an order for fifty pairs of pointe shoes for her so give it up, she was staying, when Kavi speaks first.

'So what about music?'

'What about it?'

'Does it strive for perfection or is it a jumble like poetry?'

She considers that for a few moments. 'Music is like ballet,' she says. 'More like ballet than like poetry. There's the note, the precise pitch of the sound that was created along with everything else in the instant of the Big Bang, but any time you make a noise it falls short of that perfection, which only just exists, like the way a quark or whatever is kind of there and not there at the same time.'

'You know, I don't think so,' he says. 'Music is more like poetry because we make sounds all the time, we're constantly hitting things and moving air and causing vibrations to ricochet everywhere but only some of those sounds are music. The rest is just Belinda arguing with Mackie and the curfew bell and, like, Zach farting.'

'Fine.' She laughs. 'Music is like poetry and dance is a world apart from everything. You win.'

'Or you win. Your art is further from the mundane and closer to the impossible than any other art.'

She grins. 'You're right. I win.' She slides off the props table with one fluid movement, and as she moves she catches sight of a wolfish hunger in his eyes and her skin fizzes with pleasure.

'*Alors, les filles*!' Cecile calls from her stool at the front of the stage. A quick mark through of the Pearl waltz for spacing, please!'

He smiles at her. 'See you later.'

She lifts a hand lamely to wave as she hears the patter of too-hard pointe shoes on the stage behind her. Does he mean see you later as in, *Bye, probably won't chat to you again until we next bump into each other*, or does he mean it as in, *If you're in the dining car after the show tonight let's get a drink together*? The logistics of this seduction suddenly escape her. How exactly is she meant to seal this? Just knock on his cabin door after curfew and hop into his bed?

No time to figure it out. She mumbles 'see you later' and trots on to the stage to take her place among the ten girls dressed in their woollen leggings and baggy jumpers. Cecile counts them in and when she passes the prop table a few moments later, her limbs moving automatically through the choreography to Cecile's croaks of *and a one and a two and a three* to keep them all in time, she glances into the wings to see if he's still there, watching her as she swoops and bends and stretches, but he's gone.

In the stage left wing Zach and Lara stand on either side of a small flight case marked *PEARL*.

'The thing to remember is never to touch it. Mackie and Belinda are the only ones allowed and really, I'm only supposed to show you because Mackie thinks new people should see it at rest, so to speak, on their first day so they don't come over all funny during the show.'

'What happens if I do touch it?'

Zach sighs. 'Belinda fines you three days salary.'

'Three days?'

Zach grins and flicks open the latches. 'I told you she's harsh.'

They lean over it, faces illuminated by its fluorescent glow. It's about as big as a beach ball, teardrop shaped, with a smooth and glossy surface. It smells a little like the acrid smoke of singed plastic and Lara rears away from it. She's never wanted to touch anything less in her entire life.

'Can you imagine the size of the oyster that made that thing?' she murmurs as Zach shuts the case. He shrugs.

'Makes sense that monsters live in the sea. It's the monsters that share the land with us that keep me up at night.' Zach wheels the flight case over to the wall next to the props table and shoves his hands in his pockets, shifting from foot to foot.

'All right. I need to visit the – uh – little boy's room and then we can get something to eat. You be okay here for a minute?'

'Sure.'

He smiles shyly. 'You're doing really well. I'm impressed. You're hard to freak out. I guess your psychic auntie is really doing you a favour now.'

She slumps into a chair and shuts her eyes. Her mind is a whirl of faces and names and her face aches from holding it in a pleasant, neutral expression no matter what crazy thing Zach has just said, no matter who has just introduced themselves with an instantly forgettable name. No wonder no one's ever heard of this show, no wonder Belinda was cagey during her interview, no wonder the pay is double the starting salary for a lighting technician. Fairies and magic trains and crows who can see into your soul. What would Mum and Auntie Doreen make of this?

On stage, Cecile shouts, 'Have a moment to compose yourselves then we'll run it one more time.' There is a murmur of relief and a patter of light footsteps.

She opens her eyes to find a young man right beside her, drinking from a water bottle set on the props table. A dancer, lithe and hairless, dressed in a maroon leotard thing and some black fleecy trousers that don't leave much to the imagination. The remnants of acne spot his forehead, a prominent Adam's apple bobs as he gulps at a bottle of water and damp locks of mousey blond hair cling to his flushed neck. She offers a tentative smile and he smiles back with something like relief.

'Are you the new LX assistant?'

She nods. He hesitates, then holds out a hand for her to shake, which she does though it seems too formal, like they're playing at being grown up.

'I'm Luke. I was the newest one before you.'

'Nice to meet you. I'm Lara.'

So here's the poor bugger who's replaced the poker-playing ballet prodigy no one will talk about. He doesn't look like he's stepping up to the job. He looks pale and cowed. There's something tender about him, something a little too raw that makes you want to look away.

'Do you like it here?' she says. 'I feel like people are really kind and friendly.'

Immediately she sees that she's said the wrong thing. His face crumples, and he has a long glug of his water to hide some kind of disappointment.

'I wouldn't say Cecile is exactly friendly.' he says, his voice a little lowered. 'Everyone else knows the show inside out, so I've got a lot of catching up to do.' *Too kind*, Lara thinks. *Too nice*. Didn't anyone ever tell him that the human world chews you up and spits you out if you're too good, let alone the fairy world? Lara baulks a little at the thought. Should she be, like, preparing to be snatched? Should she have a plan? Should she be learning what she can about the fairy creatures, just in case? Is Zach going to make that uncomfortable, squirmy face if she asks him this question?

On stage Cecile shouts, '*Alors*, we go back to the hunting dance one more time and then I will release myself from this torture for today.'

Luke screws his eyes shut, lifts his chin and peels the fleecy trousers off his legs. 'That's me. Wish me luck.'

He appears on stage and Cecile's face darkens at the sight of him. Poor boy. Lara watches as the ghost of a mean-looking old lady stands in the wings and glares at Luke with a scowl on her face. Hounded by the living and the dead. Maybe that's why he looks like a cringing dog waiting for someone to kick him. Maybe without that old woman's spirit following him around he would be able to flourish. She could help him, perhaps, offer to release him from whoever she is – a grandmother, probably. That would be kind. A good deed. A way to start off here on the right foot.

But here's the thing, it's never easy to tell what the right foot is when you're dealing with the dead. She started off getting it wrong when she was only a child – insistently telling her year three teacher that a baby wanted her to cuddle him, that he was crying for her, that he was right there on her desk, couldn't she hear? – and then she blacked out on the playground after a long, hot lunchtime of dodging the ghosts her school friends lugged around. Mum, after the teachers called her in for a meeting after school: *Doreen, get down here, you need to teach the kid to keep her bloody mouth shut.*

At first, Mum and Doreen had been thrilled. They'd

gone hell for leather on the multi-generational medium angle, making posters advertising the psychic child prodigy, dressing her up in frilly dresses for the double-price seances but Lara had pretended the ability left her on the morning she found a rust-coloured stain on her bedsheets. That was the sort of thing Doreen, Nana and Mum went in for so they believed her.

It had been her who had persuaded Granddad to stop knocking the teapot over and hurling pictures off the wall. She'd sat in the airing cupboard of the new house for hours, colouring in and chatting to him. After he'd disappeared gracefully into the boiler pipes she realised that it wasn't so simple, this ancient dance between the living and the dead.

Now the spirits are like birds in the sky, almost always harmless and hardly ever out to get her. Or anyone else. She's learned the dead don't always have a reason to hang around. Sometimes they just linger and there's nothing you can do about them. That's why she doesn't offer to intercede unless she is a hundred per cent sure there is something she can do, and that something will be welcome. It was all right for Auntie Doreen, because when someone's paid a hundred quid to come to a seance you can reasonably expect that they're all right about getting messages from their husband, mother, friend, son.

But what is Lara going to do here on *The Apple and the Pearl*, a show so surprisingly filled with ghosts she is struggling to pay attention to the living rather than the shadows they're carting around? What might she do about the little blond-headed boy sitting cross-legged next to Cecile, for instance; or the woman wearing a cape of goose feathers standing next to Belinda; or that old lady who right now is thumping her cane at Luke's feet in time to the music?

A shadow falls over her and she opens her eyes. A man is standing over her, another crew member by the look of his black jeans and black sweatshirt. He's balding, with a few wisps of straw-coloured hair combed over the top of his head, and his jowly cheeks are covered in grey stubble. Behind him, stretching the whole depth of the stage, is a long line of animals – cats and foxes and toads and stoats.

'Lara, isn't it?' She nods. She'd like to stand so she doesn't have to look up at him but he's too close to her. 'I'm Derek the follow spot.'

'Nice to meet you.' He doesn't hold out his hand and she's glad.

Derek giggles, a strangely girlish sound for a balding man with a paunch. 'What's your boyfriend's name?'

She glances at the parade of animal souls behind him and when she meets his eyes again she sees his expression has tightened in glee. Who or what is this man? 'I don't have a boyfriend.'

'Girlfriend?'

Lara presses her lips together and shakes her head. Will she get in trouble if she tells his man and his shadowy zoo to fuck off on her very first day? Maybe this is a test, and if she takes a hard line with this creep today then he'll leave her alone. She glances over Derek's shoulder to the door to the corridor. Where is Zach?

Derek smiles. 'Our Zachary will be pleased. Don't you go breaking his heart now. We don't need any more miserable men here on *The Apple and the Pearl*.'

Lara frowns. She's not sure what he's talking about but she doesn't want to ask him, she wants him to go away. She looks back at the stage where Cecile is furiously counting the music over the pianist and poor Luke is pink with embarrassment, but Derek crouches so that his face is right next to hers.

'I bet you Zachary won't have told you about the Crow.' His breath is hot and sour and his clothes stink of old cigarette smoke. She leans away, keeping her gaze on the dancers. Nana's voice in her head: *If anyone messes with you, you just kick him in the balls.*

'He did, actually.'

'Well, let Derek tell you a bit more.' He leans closer and she gets another blast of his fetid breath. 'See, the Crow is old. She came from a people who are long gone now, a people who ruled Faerie before all the poncy earls and queens we see out there. And Crow is kind, like all her sisters out in the world. She brings souls from one world to another, makes sure they don't get stuck in between. And Crow sees. She knows all your little sad and dirty and shameful thoughts. You can't hide from her. Don't even try.'

Derek smiles. 'But a clever girl like you probably knows all about that, don't you? It being All Souls', and all.'

He's staring at her, one side of his mouth curled in a sneering smile, and she is unable to look away even though the animals behind him are getting agitated, with little mews and growls, even though she has the feeling he is seeing a little too much of her, even though –

'Everything okay?' Zach's voice is too loud, a little confrontational. Derek rises immediately and gives Zach a mocking salute. Zach glares at him, then turns to Lara as Derek slinks away, whistling quietly as he strolls through the wing and crosses the stage behind the safety backdrop. 'You ready to get some dinner?'

Lara nods and stands quickly, wiping her damp palms over her thighs.

'Was Derek being a dick?'

'Kind of.' She follows Zach into the corridor and past the noticeboard.

'What did he say?'

'He told me some stuff about the Crow.' How can she explain that sense of unease he brought with him, the odd gleam in his eye, the menagerie of souls?

Zach holds the stage door open for her and a blast of cold air hits her face.

Zach grimaces. 'I'm sorry. He's so weird. I try to avoid him as much as I can. You can report him to Belinda, you know.'

'I bet Belinda's got a whole drawerful of complaints.' Lara looks down at their boots as they trot along the avenue between the mausoleums, footsteps out of sync with Zach's long stride. There is a gravity between their bodies now, something charged between them. She is hyper-aware of the presence of his living, breathing body and the absence of any ghosts trailing him. The relief she felt as Zach appeared behind Derek, the repressed fury on his face, the way the sheer bulk of him shoved Derek away.

Don't get involved with a man who has ghosts, girl, Auntie Doreen had told her. *You want someone clean, someone unencumbered by their dead. Only invite the living into your bed, take it from me.*

She looks up at Zach. 'Have you ever met the Crow?'

He looks surprised. 'Not really. I mean, I've seen it from a distance and heard it and stuff. I tend to think if it wants me, then it knows where to find me.'

Lara watches the pale shapes flitting around the graves as they come closer to the Grub. *A clever girl like you,* she thinks. Oh dear. She will have to watch out for Derek.

Taking her foot off the sewing machine pedal, Milly drags her chair over to the tannoy and climbs on it. She turns the dial on the speaker right down so that Cecile's voice becomes nothing more than a faint mutter, her tuneless, toneless counting just too quiet to hear. She drags her chair back to the machine, brushes the dust from the soles of her trainers off the seat and positions herself over the seam again. She lets her foot hover over the pedal and adjusts the white tulle. The needle starts to *click click clack*

clack and she guides the pinned seam through the needle, her expert fingers smoothing the tulle to keep it straight. She likes the sound of the machine, its busy humming and whirring, the sounds of making something out of nothing, the music of the tiny twisted threads binding themselves together into beauty.

A wave of burning nausea swells up her chest and she takes her foot off the pedal, shuts her eyes and rubs the heels of her hands into her cheeks. She turns away from the half-made costume in case she vomits on it and leans right forwards, her hair dangling into her face. *Fuck,* she thinks. *Fuck fuck fuck.*

Since this began – sixteen days ago and counting – the only thing she's found that works to stop herself from throwing up is to lie flat on the floor. She lays on her back and stares at the speckled ceiling. The grey linoleum is cool and smells of the fabric sprays they spritz onto the Suitor's costumes that can't go in the washing machine. Surprisingly, the scent eases her stomach so she turns her cheek to the cold surface and takes a long sniff.

She reaches up to the table with the sewing machine to get her phone and rolls onto her side. She calls up the calendar with her thumb, scrolls up to September, counts the weeks, and the days. It's still the same as it was half an hour ago when she last checked.

She has to tell Danny. And she will, as soon as she's decided what to tell him.

But, realistically, what else can she say? *Big news, but I think it'll be okay, we're having a baby!* And he'll be shocked and he'll stare at her with his green eyes wide and she'll have to grab his hand to stop him from floating away into the sky the way men do when you say these things to them. Especially without a ring on your finger and a piece of paper with his name on it tucked away.

And he'll say, *But we were so careful!* And she'll say, *Well yes, we were a little bit careful but let's be honest we didn't do all that we could,* and he'll frown a little and she might joke – depending on the vibe – *Well, you know what they call a couple who pull out!*

And his frown will deepen, a little reproachfully, and he'll say something like, *Just give me a minute, I'm still getting used to this.* And she will squeeze his hand a little harder, to tether him, to anchor the sturdy ship of him here with her, in the port, not out there on the high seas where any rough, rogue wind can blow him off course, and she'll say, *It's okay my love, we'll be okay. You know what they say, the show must go on.*

They'll go to Belinda's office after the show to tell her, and she'll sigh and look at them over her spectacles. *Will you leave at the end of your pledges or are you asking for me to arrange parental leave?* And she'll probably have to hold him again, to steady him. *We'll leave at the end of our pledges, thank you.* And Belinda will nod. *You'll always have references and our good will here.*

They'll go to stay with her parents in Leeds while they find a place of their own and Danny gets a job. Near enough to his parents in Doncaster, too. And she'll set up a room in their house as a sewing room, get her machine out of her parents' loft and put some of her savings towards some silk to make some outfits on spec to show off what she can do. Wedding dresses and curtains, maybe set herself up with an Etsy shop. And the show won't go on, not exactly, but something will and that will be the point, that will be the whole story of it. It'll be a good little life. No shows, no magic, no glamour. But a good life nonetheless.

The nausea starts to recede so she gets up, goes to the door where she keeps her bag and rummages for the sandwich she tucked away earlier. She tears off a dry crust and chews it. It helps, for a minute or so. On the tannoy she can hear Cecile's faint voice dismissing the dancers from rehearsal with that same perpetual note of disappointment. Milly feels sorry for the dancers really, not because of Cecile exactly but because nothing they do can ever be enough. When she makes a costume, she knows she can make it perfectly. It doesn't always come out perfect, but she can unpick and redo it. The dancers never get that chance. The show goes on whether they are perfect or not and they know it. The knowledge of it gnaws at them, fucks them up. They stand in front of the mirror in fittings, gazing miserably at their lithe, muscled bodies, frowning at the bits they say Milly's made look fat. Or short, or long, or whatever. She remembers Alina glancing at her and rolling her eyes as they dressed one of the corps de ballet girls on Milly's first day. *Can you imagine looking like that and being so fucking miserable about it all the time?*

Milly has a swig of water and it's cool and soothing on her throat. She chews another crust of bread. The only person she's looking forward to telling is Gino. As the bump grows over the next five months until her pledge is up he'll slip her cups of cardamom and cinnamon-spiced milk, and little light cakes and the sticky, burnt bits of rice at the bottom of the pan – the kind of thick, pale food the creature inside her craves. She yawns and looks at the clock. Hours and hours to go yet until the show's over but it feels like night already. She could fall asleep in that hard plastic chair right now and not wake up until curtain down.

She sits back down at the sewing machine and finishes the seam on the tulle. She holds it up, examines the line of it. Looks good. She positions the other seam at the machine and hovers her foot on the pedal. She could tell Danny tonight. She could wait for him in their cabin after she and Alina have packed up the costume trunks, and when he comes in to change and shower she could tell him. If she times it right, he might even mention marriage. By this time tomorrow they could have told Belinda and in forty-eight hours, tops, she'll be having cream in her porridge and perfect little slivers of ripe pear, whatever it is she fancies right at that moment, and this roiling sickness in her will be sated.

She picks up her phone from where she left it on the floor and types *how to stop morning sickness.* She reads the top results: dry crackers, sour things, keeping hydrated. Some herbal supplement that looks a bit dodgy. Some experimental drug you can only get abroad. She gets up, has another sip of water from the bottle by the door, heaves and swallows bile, lies down on the floor again, her phone cradled in her hand.

Would you just stop it, little one? she thinks. *Would you just let your mum keep her lunch down, just for today?*

She imagines the little being inside her, growing by the second. Now an arm, now a kidney, now ten tiny little fingernails. Soon, she'll get one of those apps that tells her what bits of its body it's getting week by week, comparing its size to a piece of fruit. She imagines it floating around in its salt water home. She read somewhere that the salinity of amniotic fluid is the same as the sea, but a few days ago when they last had signal she looked that up and discovered she was wrong. It was a myth, one of those things that feels right and good but is too glib and simple to possibly be true. She found out that amniotic fluid is salty, yes, but seeing as seawater varies in salinity across oceans and depths, there's no way to say it's the same concentration. Still, it's the sort of thing she might tell Danny, once he's got used to the idea. He'd like that. He'd start talking excitedly about how everything is connected and there's a master plan – he might even suggest they watch one of those videos about pyramids and aliens together and Christ alive, she's that tired that she might just say yes – and some of that excitement might spill over into the baby.

Poor thing. It could do with someone being excited about its presence.

Although it would be wrong to say she isn't excited.

There is something of a flutter about how she feels about this new creature. She didn't invite it into her body, was stunned to feel it make its home in her but now – look what's happened – she wants it. Perhaps she even loves it already, in a blurry, animal way she can't quite grasp. She feels stupid calling this love, this odd, old, savage certainty that she would die for this being inside her that is wreaking so much havoc because right now it's nothing but a tight waistband and this constant rising bile. But there you go, she loves it, it's the only word she's got for it.

They say a mother loves her children no matter what – but what will she do, how will she love her baby in her nice little post-Apple and Pearl life if it comes out scaled or winged? Violet-eyed and black-haired; cunning and sly? Well, the show will go on. Danny will leave, of course, even if she can explain to him the truth and she will struggle for money despite her savings. The child will grow and she'll – do what with it? Send it to school for maths lessons and PE, make angel wings from wire and tinsel for the nativity play? Ignore all the other mums when they ask which grand-parent has those eyes. Keep it away from birthday parties after incidents with chocolate biscuits and fizzy pop. Wait up all night while it sneaks off to thickets of hawthorn and elder, following the far-off drums and pipe music from its other people, its other kin?

She rolls onto her back, lays a hand on that low part of her belly that aches in the mornings. Maybe she's being dramatic, thinking the worst, *catastrophising again*, as Alina would say. It's probably Danny's. The simplest explanation is usually the right one. The Grub had stopped by a long, placid lake and Danny had been for a swim with Mackie and Charlie the deputy stage manager that afternoon. After they'd packed up the Grit they'd gone straight to their cabin for once, brushed their teeth with companionable chatter about their respective days and curled up in their bed, fingers entwined, mouths finding each other's in the darkness, kind and familiar bodies soft to each other as the Grub began to rock.

Only three days later it was the autumn equinox and the Grub had stopped in a dense woodland of oak and hornbeam still in the full leaf of summer. Belinda was on edge all day, even writing a sign for the noticeboard: *Be careful please, I will not be mounting any rescues for anyone who fancies a jaunt into the greenwood tonight.*

But honestly, what could she have done? It wasn't her fault, she wasn't at all seduced by the dappled light. It was a forest, so what? They stopped in them all the time. She's replayed the moments before he appeared so many times, rewinding and playing again in her head. It was not yet fully dark, as they were loading the Grub after a show, and Alina pushed a trunk of costumes to her to get onto the ramp up into a carriage and it veered off into the trees. She had to run to catch it as it slid downhill, gathering speed along the way, trying to get ahead of it although it seemed it had a mind of its own.

The trunk caught on an exposed root and she lunged

for it to grab the handle. She grunted as she wrenched it back towards her and there he was, on the other side of the trunk, black shirt slashed to the navel, slightly damp black curls tumbling into his violet eyes. She swallowed as she felt the glamour washing over her, a cold tide of dumb dread. A slow grin slid across his face and she saw a hint of his teeth, pointed and gleaming white. She knew exactly what was going to happen next.

And yes, okay, she was raped, that's how it was, she knows it. She imagines going to the police. *Hello, yes, I was raped, no you won't find him, he's a fairy, no I mean a literal fairy, one of the fair folk, lives in the court under the hill. No I don't know his name.*

She can't even tell anyone here in the show. Alina would look away, tears in her eyes, then give her a brusque, squeezing hug and never mention it again. Belinda would pull her spectacles off, rub her eyes and ask her to write up an incident form. Mackie would blink and say nothing for a long time, longer than she would be able to bear standing in silence and Danny would… well, she doesn't really know what Danny would do and that's how she's going to keep it for she's not going to tell anyone. Ever. The show will go on and that's all anyone needs to know.

Three days. That's all there is in it. She opens her phone, types: *how do you know when you've ovulated* and reads a couple of articles she's read before, articles that haven't helped her before and don't now. She opens a new tab and types: *can a human and a fairy conceive a baby?* She swipes away the page without looking at any of the results. She isn't sure she really wants to know.

She sits up. Takes another sip of water. Yawns. It really would be better not to know.

She sits back at the machine and pulls the mannequin towards her. She checks the folder with the dancers' measurements again, makes sure she's got the bust and waist set to Bella's measurements – she better not go and have a post-show encounter with a Fae prince now or Milly will have to start all over again – and pulls the half-finished costume over the mannequin's body. She fills her mouth with pins and starts tucking in the next seam.

She will teach the baby how to sew. Girl, boy or fairy child of the Otherworld. She'll show them how to thread a needle and stitch a neat seam, darning socks and repairing buttons. Life skills, like cooking yourself some dinner and knowing how to pay your taxes. When they're old enough she'll get out her knitting needles and show them knit and purl and how to follow a pattern and they can sit together on winter nights when Danny's working and listen to music – all right, this vision does work better if the baby's a girl but she doesn't want to be that kind of mother, the woman that dresses her baby girl in pink things she can barely move in and lets her baby boy run riot. No pink, no blue, not for her baby. She thinks the baby will be born around midsummer – something she tries not to think too hard about – so the first thing she'll make can be a light crocheted blanket for swaddling, white and cotton to keep them cool and not show the milk stains. She'll knit jumpers in sunflower yellow and scarlet and emerald for the winter and for their first birthday she'll run up little summer dungarees in rainbow prints of dragons and tigers and trees. In fact, she'll start now.

She spits the pins onto the table and grabs her phone. She calls up her favourite haberdashery site and starts adding yarn and fabric to a new order as if it will disappear as soon as she's seen it, a virtual supermarket sweep, each item weighting her into this new life for herself and the baby – and Danny, as soon as he knows about it – each ball of wool and roll of cotton something that will tether her and her little family to the human world. There's a sale on for Halloween-themed fabrics – little grinning pumpkins, skeletons and ghosts – but she doesn't choose any of it. No need to provoke the baby into anything supernatural, it'll have enough problems as it is.

The tumble dryer beeps and Milly presses *buy now* on her phone. A sweeping wave of contentment washes over her, mingling with the nausea to leave her light-headed. She leaves her phone on the table and just as she crouches in front of the machine it pings with the email confirmation.

She empties the contents of the tumble dryer into two baskets, men's and women's. The men's basket is a jewel-bright nest of Lycra, the women's a tangle of pink tights and flesh-coloured polyester croptops. She sits cross-legged on the floor to separate each item and roll each thing into a ball to pack it neatly into the basket again. The laundry smells clean, chemically fresh in a way that soothes Milly's churning stomach and gives her a feeling of peace. The smell of the detergent that Alina orders in bulk is the smell of *The Apple and the Pearl* for her, the smell of a job well done, dancers with clean and beautiful things to wear, the smell of the show going on as it always must, beginning all over again for another night.

Behind her, the other machine rumbles away. This is the slightly temperamental one, the one adorned with the laminated sign-up sheet for the cast and crew to do personal washing. The one that occasionally prompts Alina to furiously scribble a note for the noticeboard by the stage: *JUST BECAUSE THE PERSONAL WASHING MACHINE IS LOCATED IN WARDROBE DOES NOT MEAN I AM ANYONE'S LAUNDRY SERVANT.* It rumbles away with someone's things inside, a dancer's by the look of it, one of the younger men by the way the whites are all mixed up with the colours. She'll make sure her baby will never do anything like that. She won't have them walking around with pink streaks on white shirts, giving them away as someone who doesn't know how to look after themselves.

She glances at the clock. Five fifteen, almost time to start setting costumes for the show. Two long clothes rails line the room, one for men and one for women. Milly looks at the long velvet sleeves of the pages' costumes, the sequins dripping from the Pearl waltz dresses, the thick, black brocade of the Crow's cloak. In a few minutes, she'll have to take one of the copies of the casting that Alina keeps pinned to the back of the door and distribute these costumes among the dancers, tutus draped over one arm, the basket of washing balanced on a hip, up and down the stairs until everyone has all their underwear and all their headdresses and no one can blame her if they go on stage looking anything less than spectacular. She slumps back in the chair, her eyelids heavy. Exhaustion sweeps over her. She can't do it. She's too tired.

Listlessly, she removes the bobbin from the sewing machine and winds more white cotton around it. She threads the machine again, takes the tulle skirt from the mannequin and lines up the seam. She screws her eyes shut against the tide of nausea. How will she do this for the next five months? How does anyone carry on their lives while cooking another being like this? She feels pathetic. There are women out there running marathons, running companies, running countries, and she can't even manage to put a few knickers away.

She closes her eyes and swallows a heave of bile. How can there be so many humans crawling all over the planet when this is the misery they bring to their mothers?

Five thirty, and Alina flings the door open. 'Didn't see you in the Grub, thought you might be hiding in here.' She sees the bodice of the new White Princess' costume on the mannequin and the layers of tulle half threaded through the sewing machine. She frowns.

'I don't think that's a priority, you know.' She puts her

reusable cup down on the designated food and drink table near the door and shrugs off her coat. 'Cecile only told us to start thinking about it.'

She opens the cup and the smell of rich black coffee wafts out into the room. Milly swallows, saliva pooling under her tongue. She is going to be sick. She swallows again and again, trying to keep her lunch down. She breathes through her teeth.

'Oh sorry, are you hungry? Did you want me to bring you something?'

'No, no. I'm okay. I ate earlier.' She joins Alina at the door and has a swig from her water bottle. It eases the roiling in her belly for the moments it's held in her mouth and as it's slipping down her throat, but the relief soon fades.

Another waft of coffee makes her heave. 'Are you drinking that black?' Milly asks. 'At this time of the day?'

Alina makes a face. 'Something wrong with the milk again. Tastes fucking awful.'

Milly turns back to the sewing machine, nausea tinged with panic. When did it start, these complaints about soured milk? She thinks back to what she read online a few days ago when they last had signal: *folklore about changelings spoiling milk and curdling butter is consistent between cultures.*

'Mackie's hosting in the Grub tonight, did you see?' Alina continues. 'It's his pledge day. And there's someone on probation too, blonde LX girl.'

Milly makes a non-committal noise as she sips her water but inside her chest something folds in upon itself. There will be drinking until long after the midnight bells, a long night of lager-swilling, whisky-gulping drunkenness and Danny will be there until the end with the rest of them. She won't get a chance to tell him tonight and tomorrow he'll be too hungover. It'll have to be the day after. But it doesn't really matter. She can wait. She's planning to take some secrets to her grave: she can carry this for forty-eight more hours.

'Great.' Milly says. 'Hope the new girl pledges, we could do with a bit less testosterone around.'

Alina snorts as she drains the dregs of her coffee. 'Won't change anything round here. One more woman on the crew isn't going to make your man and the rest of them magically teetotal.' Alina presses the pedal bin with her foot and dumps the empty coffee cup inside. 'She may, however, have a good effect on Zach, who seems to be half in love with her already.'

Milly shrugs. 'As long as he doesn't do a Michael when she rejects him.'

Danny won't drink so much in their new life, she knows it. The others won't be there to goad him on, the booze won't be subsidised, they'll spend evenings when he's not working curled up in front of the telly or chatting about this and that. She lets her lips part and tries to breathe through her mouth. Easily led, is Danny. She'll have to make sure it's her who leads him, when they're back out in the world.

Alina takes off her coat and hangs it on the peg next to the door. She bends forwards, shakes her long black hair into a ponytail and gathers it with one of the hairbands she keeps on her wrists.

'Guys or girls?' Alina asks, pointing at the two waiting washing baskets.

'Girls,' Milly says immediately, thinking of the stink of cheap aftershave, feet and unwashed dancewear in the men's dressing room, never freshened, no matter how many times Alina throws the windows open, no matter where the Grit sets itself up.

'White Princess costume looks good, by the way.' Alina says as she plucks one of the casting sheets from the back of the door and clamps it between her teeth. Milly follows her with the other sheet of paper balanced on the stack of underwear in the washing basket. She's surprised to find tears prickling at the back of her eyes. She is so pathetically grateful to Alina for saying exactly what she needs to hear. No one else will notice where she's taken care not to sew any sequins or gems around the bodice so the dancer can be partnered easily about her waist, no one else will see how precisely she's matched the pattern on the seams of the tulle, no one else could appreciate how she's cut the hem at the most flattering point of the leg. They'd only sniff accusingly if she got it wrong. Not that she does this job for thanks or applause, you'd be waiting a long time if you were. The show goes on, because it's the most important thing, the only important thing. It's like motherhood, she thinks as she trudges down the stairs to the women's dressing room. You pour your heart and soul into making a body for another to inhabit, and if you do it right you'll always be invisible. A silent wind carrying your child over mountains and oceans, a weightless shield against every storm.

Before she opens the door to the dressing room she stops, puts the washing basket down and wipes her eyes. *Pull yourself together*, she tells herself sternly. *And get on with your job.* She stands up and feels sick. She puts a hand on the doorknob and feels sick. She tightens her grip on the plastic rim of the basket and swallows. The show must go on.

Six o' clock, and the technicians fill every booth of the dining car, scraping the last smears of Gino's lasagne onto their forks and into their mouths. Lara sits with Zach and Mackie, eating lasagne with one hand while the other is paging through the black ringbinder she's been carrying around all day.

'Can I just ask about this bit here in the contract' – she flips through the binder on her lap – 'where it says about a forfeit if I break my pledge?'

Mackie sighs. 'Breaking your pledge incurs a penalty. It's decided by the Crow, with Belinda fighting your corner. It's a bugger, but though Belinda and the unions have been busting a gut over the years, you just can't know what your forfeit will be until it's asked. It could be simple like a bit of your stuff. Hairbrush or pair of shoes or something. Could be a limb or seven years' service.'

Lara looks down at the contract in her lap. Zach sees

a quick flash of fear cross her face like lightning, just like anyone he's ever seen sitting with a contract in their lap. *A limb?* he can hear the girl thinking. *Is he fucking joking?*

A few tables away, Derek finishes his meal, belches, and passes by Kavi on his way to the counter. He slaps him on the back and says in a stage whisper so loud the entire crew can hear him, 'You wanna be quick mate if you're to have a chance with the new girl. Seems like Zach is mooning after her too.'

Kavi reddens as he gets up from the table, Zach chokes on a piece of roasted pepper and Charlie says firmly, 'See you up in the Grit, Derek.'

Danny stands before Derek has a chance to turn to him, still chewing his pasta, and returns his tray to Gino. He follows Kavi out of the dining car and jumps down beside him onto the dark earth.

A shriek in the stillness, followed by an answering howl.

Kavi starts, stumbles into him. 'What was that?'

'An owl, mate.' Danny kindly, firmly, rights him, gives him a pat on the shoulder. 'Get your torch out and let's get up to the Grit. Quick, before Derek catches us.'

Ten past six, and the graveyard that lies between the Grub and the Grit is fully dark, the thick cloud obscuring any light from moon or stars. Belinda stands at the open window of her office, elbows on the sill, staring out over the black graves towards the Grub. An updated list of things to do – the new LX girl's contract, check October's payroll, write out a notice for the next day off, get a plumber for that dodgy shower in the Grub – runs through her mind but she stays still, breathing deeply of the loam-rot smell wafting into the Grit. Winter is her favourite season on *The Apple and the Pearl*. Safer, statistically speaking, and easier to manage. The Otherworld contracts to a cosy radius around the theatre and the train; the cast, crew and orchestra nestle inside that circle, waiting for spring.

All Souls', and they're stopped in this place to share earth with the restless dead. Already November, and only one snatching all year. She thinks of that poor lad's parents, perhaps spending today at the freshly turned earth of his grave. His father on the phone, voice cracked in shock. The Crow sitting in her office in the Grub, glowering as it listened to her stutter apologies to the boy's parents. *Does the Crow punish you after we lose somebody?* Mackie had asked, falteringly, one night after a bottle of wine. And she had said, *Of course not, it's not a monster,* because the truth was too complicated and too humiliating even for Mackie's wise tenderness. Percy Montgomery, cleaning his glasses so as not to have to look her in the eye: *Each snatching adds a full cycle of the moon to your service here. No, I didn't tell you that and I deeply regret it. The Crow would never have let me go otherwise.*

They all think they're safer after a snatching. They think it works like some kind of pressure cooker, that after the thing's blown it has to build up in tension again before someone else will disappear. Belinda tries to disabuse the company of these silly notions: she is merciless about the fines and the curfews and the rules, passing on the Crow's punishments to the rest of them because why should she be the only one to suffer indentured servitude?

She shuts the window and pulls down the blind. All Souls'. Still uncomfortably close to All Hallow's Eve, hoof-prints near a grave and too much mist to see much beyond your hand. She opens her laptop and reads the newest email from the bell smith.

Yes, my daughter is very much enjoying university and somewhat interested in casting, though she doesn't quite understand the full extent of the work yet. I will see you at Didcot Parkway on the 12th and I'm very much looking forward to it.

Six twenty-five, and the door to the musician's green room opens. There's a commotion outside. Henry checks his slightly late watch – it says six twenty-three – and reaches into his bag for the extra roll he filled with a slice of cheese at lunch. A long stream of musicians wander in, lugging their instruments, brushing rain off their jackets, exhaling garlic fumes of Gino's lasagne. There's Jean, urgently typing a message on her phone. Max, the second violin listening intently to Ellie the viola, nodding and making little sounds of agreement. Steve roars something at Lance, who grins and goes to join the three fat musketeers, dragging David the harp along with him.

Henry takes a bite of the sandwich – it's good cheese,

he reluctantly decides, some kind of soft, herby, creamy thing – and watches Michael as he slumps in the corner among the tuxedos and evening dresses. Across the room, a conversation is beginning on a favoured topic – what the music of *The Apple and the Pearl* would have sounded like five hundred years ago, a thousand, fifteen hundred. Lance thinks the melodies would have been the same with only the arrangements following the musical fashions of the times, while Wilf the cellist has always maintained that while the basic story has been similar, there might not have even been music in other eras, let alone something recognisable as the score they play nightly. Henry takes another bite of his sandwich. He should have made himself another one. He's hungrier than he thought.

Twenty-five minutes to seven and down on the stage a broom goes *swish swish* across the floor, tiny motes of dust flying from the brush into the air. A pile of splinters and dirt gathers near the footlights, awaiting the attentions of the woman clad all in black who hunches over her broom. She stops, bends slowly to peer at something she finds on the floor. She picks it up between a thumb and a forefinger and puts it in her pocket.

Light a candle for the departed on All Souls', the Crow thinks, *light a whole fucking bonfire for your dead whether you've seen them into the Pearl or not, but if your loved one went to sing and dance in the Otherworld then there's no candle for you, no body to bury, no name to speak aloud either. The poor lass whose fella got took a moon ago. Sad but she can't show it and it breaks Crow's heart, yes it does; and if the gates of Faerie weren't locked to the Crow she would swoop in, yes she would, she would get the dancer lad and the French horn and any of the others taken, if still they dance and sing there. You don't want the Crow for an enemy, sweethearts, yes, that's what the Belinda woman tells you as she pricks your little fingers for the Grub, but who does the Crow hate among the mortals? Well that's not a fair question, the Crow saves her bile for Fae creatures, the bastards and pledge-breaking ninnies like the fiddler. Put his heart in a stew and ate it, plopped it right in the soup the cook gave and slurped it up, now he's bound tighter and how does he like that?*

But Crow takes no pleasure in pledge-breakers, no, Crow wants to keep the artistes happy, yes she does. Tried so hard with the angel-fingered harp woman but all she wanted was to get back into a world which had never loved her, certainly not so well as Crow and the fiddler do. The Grub needs a King and the Grit needs a Queen and no, the dancers playing dress-up each night are not enough, though the Mara girl and the Gregory man will play their parts tonight as well as any others Crow has ever seen.

But to have a King and a Queen back again! A pair like Albert the fiddler and Hannah the piper who gave the nest a chick at long last – and kept The Apple and the Pearl *safe with the blessing of a baby. The midwife brought the meat of the afterbirth to Crow that night and down it went, all that bright blood into Crow's belly to keep Faerie at bay a little longer. Only two snatchings in the whole decade after the Jeanie girlie's birth!*

Percy Montgomery had danced himself a jig but of course they got slack and Faerie got hungry. Magic got up and ran out the door, just like magic always does.

Who next to play King and Queen and give the Crow a chick? The seamstress has a changeling in her belly, more's the pity – Crow should warn Belinda – and the dancer lad who had a noble bearing is gone. All Souls', and Crow will let her beloved men and women of the theatre be with their dead for tonight. Tomorrow will dawn as tomorrow always does and then Crow will set about finding another belly to hatch a chick for The Apple and the Pearl.

The wings are silent. The house lights throw a drab, murky light across the stage and the auditorium. A caw in the direction of the lighting box and the house lights brighten a little. The woman comes right to the front of the stage, and squints out at the auditorium. Her gaze roves over each row of seats, each gilded carving and piece of stucco. Satisfied, she caws again, softly. She stows her broom away behind the prompt desk and with a flurry of feathers, the black serge of her dress becomes wings and the Crow flies across the auditorium, through the open doors into the foyer and out into the night.

Twenty minutes to seven and all the dancers are in their dressing rooms, faces illuminated by picture frames of lightbulbs to stare into the depth of their pores, wondering how they will do it all over again and if their ankles, shoulders and hips will hold up for another three acts.

Luke is smoothing his hair with a little bit of gel and going over the orchard dance, trying not to hum the melody too loudly. Greg is carefully taping his knees – King tonight, again, because he can't do any other part any more – and next to him Josh is smearing thick black make-up over his face, neck and chest.

In the women's dressing room, Stephanie is sewing a ribbon on to a pointe shoe and listening to her affirmations. Zuleika is texting her brother. Mara is scrolling through the news on her phone, reading aloud an article about two celebrity actors getting a divorce to the interested parties of the dressing room.

Anita is writing a card for Harriet, who is making her debut as the Red Princess tonight. She writes out the little rhyme, *three sisters never to be seen*, but she has to stop when she gets to the last line about the Crow who sings in her nest, because her eyes are filling with tears and she doesn't want to smudge her writing. Alex wrote her a card before her first Red Princess with this rhyme in and she still has it, although you're supposed to give everything left behind to Belinda so she can destroy it. She gave Belinda the toothbrush he kept in her cabin and a couple of pairs of socks, then wrapped everything else – all the letters, the cards, the presents, the photos – in a package and sent it to her mum's house.

Milly and Alina are moving between the dressing rooms and wardrobe, each with a cast sheet clamped between their teeth and arms full of costumes on hangers. Cecile is in her office, working on tomorrow night's casting. AJ is in his dressing room, humming through the orchestral arrangement for Glazunov's *Raymonda*, which he does not think much of as a score but finds relaxing in a mind-numbing way before a show.

Charlie the deputy stage manager arrives at the prompt desk and settles himself in his chair. He checks he has everything he needs: headset charged, score all correct, lighting and set cues all there. He takes a swig of water, checks his watch, waits for the minute hand to catch up.

Outside the Grit it is raining. A mizzling kind of rain that leaves everything glistening wet and dampens all sounds. The bell, when it comes, is muffled and sluggish. It rings once, twice, three times, then pauses as if fatigued. Once, twice, three times again and the Grub shudders with the vibrations. Once, twice, three times again and the mist clears a little around the Grub, the droplets of water juddering as they meet the iron. Nine more peals sound solemnly into the night and the last takes a while to fade completely, still echoing on the mossy gravestones as Gino shuts and bolts the window of his kitchen, turns on his extractor fan and starts chopping carrots.

Five minutes to seven, and on stage inside the Grit Zach is showing Lara how to angle the downstage lights on the act one backdrop.

'And of course the folder with the lighting cues is the most important thing to follow but you never know what's going to happen on this show so Juliet always used to tell me to rely on the rhyme the dancers say.'

'What rhyme?' Lara cocks her head.

'Okay, it's stupid but it does help.' Zach clears his throat. 'King, queen, sisters never to be seen – I don't know what that's about, maybe they've just got to stay inside, you know what fairytales are like – orchard, sea, suitors in a dream – because the princesses go to rescue the princes, right, that's kind of interesting, I guess? And then orchard, quest, the Crow in its nest.'

Just downstage of them, Danny mutters to Kavi up in the flies as he lowers the safety curtain along the line of the proscenium arch. Belinda stands behind them, droplets of rain dripping from the hem of her black coat. Charlie watches the sheet of iron as it touches the stage and presses the call button. The light that tells him he is broadcasting to the whole company shines scarlet. A crackle of static, a whistle of his breath echoing throughout the backstage area.

'Ladies and gentlemen of *The Apple and the Pearl*, this is your half-hour call. Thirty minutes, please.'

'House is open, Mackenzie,' Belinda calls from the stage. He looks up from the image of the lighting rig on his laptop screen.

'And everyone in?' he answers, as he does every night. Belinda nods tightly, as she does every night, and walks away across the stage, her shoes squeaking a little on the vinyl dance floor.

You're told on your first day here about the curfews,

the bells before the show and the bells at midnight. But Mackie knows that not everyone really understands the consequences of being outside either the iron walls of the Grub or the salt-sprinkled stage of the Grit by the time Charlie comes on the tannoy until they've experienced what Belinda calls *an incident*.

When Alex the dancer lad disappeared a month or so ago, they were not what Belinda would call tight. There were too many new pledges who hadn't seen the aftermath of a snatching, hadn't been locked in dressing rooms or cabins until Belinda could count everyone, hadn't witnessed the Crow shrieking as it wheeled around the Grub, hadn't felt the leaden weight of the now-forbidden name on the tongue. After Bobby the French horn tripped over a tree root on the way back to the Grub after a show and fell into the Otherworld last September, there had been a flurry of new pledges. The new harp; the new flute; three new violins; a new French horn; a new cello; Kavi – though he had no worries about him, sharp as a tack; and three or four new dancers looking pretty wet about the ears.

Then Alex didn't turn up to rehearsals, the Grub and the Grit were locked for a couple of hours, the Crow keened. And those new pledges went about with a dazed look for a week or so, their induction into the world of *The Apple and the Pearl* truly complete.

On the upside, safest place after a lightning bolt is under the storm-struck tree, Derek had said the next evening in the dining car.

What the fuck is wrong with you? Danny had snarled and Milly had put a restraining hand on his arm.

Alina had drained her gin and tonic and slammed it onto the table. She put her clenched fist over her mouth as if stopping herself from saying more and strode out of the dining car. It has always been the most egregious insult on *The Apple and the Pearl* to wish a snatching on someone, and Mackie was grateful to Alina for holding herself back and saving him from the inevitable – and in this case, unfair – disciplinary procedure.

Mackie looks up from his laptop screen again to see Derek fiddling with a wing flat on the other side of the stage, a power drill tucked between his knees and Danny beside him, violently pointing at the frame. He sighs. Where in any of the available worlds did Belinda find Derek?

He knows that every snatching makes Belinda publicly furious and privately heartbroken. She makes him, AJ or Cecile fill out those blasted forms, she gets a bottle of wine from Gino to take back to her cabin and she hires someone new. After the dancer lad had been taken, Belinda had been red-eyed for days. *I had to tell his parents that he'd fallen from a tree,* she'd said to Mackie a few days later. *The Crow will get me some kind of body to send them for a funeral.* Mackie always feel intensely sorry for her on those occasions. He brings her a drink after the midnight bells and tries to gauge if she wants company as she drowns her guilt or if she wants to rage in solitude. After Alex's snatching, Belinda had sat in her coat with the open ledger in front of her for a good half an hour before Mackie had been able to persuade her to get the whisky down. *And the worst of it is that I'm not surprised, not at all. Good-looking, talented. They take the best of us and leave the oafs here to rot.*

To be fair, not every snatching makes her cry. She really hadn't seemed to care much about Bobby the French horn. He'd been a shambling, musty kind of bloke whose face was set in a permanent sneer.

Zach bounds over, trailed by the new lighting assistant, a blonde girl whose name Mackie knew this morning but has now forgotten. 'Any joy on that upstage light?' he asks.

'I'm thinking leave it off for tonight and reposition the ones next it.'

He turns to the blonde girl and smiles. 'How's your day been? Has Zach explained how things work around here?'

She looks uncertainly at Zach, who nods at her encouragingly. 'He's told me quite a lot, yeah.'

'Has he let you know about our audience? How to stay safe?'

The new girl glances at Zach and nods. Zach shuffles and shoves his hands in his pockets.

'Well, it's my pledge today too, so hopefully I'll see you in the Grub later.' He looks back at his laptop, and Zach, who does at least know when his presence is no longer required, withdraws, holding out his hand to float protectively behind the new girl's back like he's leading her across a ballroom floor. Mackie sighs. He could do without Zach falling in love, to be honest.

His nineteenth pledge. How did that happen so fast? He's done all the jobs on the technical team except anything in wardrobe – you wouldn't trust him with a needle and scissors – but this is his seventh pledge as the boss. He knows the show better than anyone, even better than Cecile and AJ. They're blinkered by their devotions to the dance and the music, but Mackie can't afford that. He can't play any instrument, but he can hum the whole score and he knows each one of the dancers' cues, although you'd not want him anywhere near a pair of tights.

He pulls up his internet browser. He's got almost nothing done today because of the distraction of it, those three little lines lit up on his screen beckoning him to check on the outside world. He reads the news – still a shitshow out there, like it was this morning and last Wednesday when they last had signal – then he clicks onto one of the social sites he lurks on whenever there's enough signal. He's lost count of how many times he's seen that blue screen today. It gives him no nourishment at all, yet he finds himself returning again and again to take little sips of this slow acting poison, nosy envy that dissolves a little more of whatever pride he used to take in this job every time he drinks.

There's a steady parade of photos from the lives of people he used to know but hasn't seen in years: the beach holiday of his second cousin; the puppy of one of the set builders from his first job; eleven albums of photos of *The Apple and the Pearl*'s last assistant stage manager's house renovation. The photos are sunny, smiley, carefully edited to show nothing but contentment. They make him feel a kind of panicked uselessness. What can he post from here? How would he describe this life to those who have never lived it, or even the peculiarities of this show to those who do know what it is to dedicate your youth to the darkness behind a stage? The constantly refreshing feed is filled with pictures of blokes he used to know who now alternate their winters between panto and *Nutcrackers*, spending summers working festivals or on Asian tours with ageing rock stars, playing the same circuits over and over again with nothing changing but the songs and the pain in their backs when they lay down in their beds. A part of him wishes he was doing that too. Or that he could have got a job in a regional producing theatre, something with holiday pay and a pension, bought a house to live in all year round and pottered in the garden on Sundays. Perhaps it's not too late to do that. Pledge day comes around so quickly, you never get enough time to really consider if this is what you want to spend another journey round the sun doing.

'We're ready for curtain check, Mackie.' Charlie hovers by a wing flat, headset already in place. The stage behind him is empty but for Belinda waiting at the bottom of the ladder side of the tallescope, clipboard in hand, kicking one toe absently at the braked wheels. The rest of the crew are loitering in the wings as they always do at this time, carefully busying themselves with minor tasks or chatter, so they don't watch him and wonder too hard what exactly is in that curtain that stinks of the sea. He knows some of them think this is some kind of magic spell that got solemnly handed to him when he made his first pledge as the boss, but that tongue-twisty-tying thing the Crow does makes him unable to explain that all you have to do is feel along the line of stitches near the top of the curtain for the rough little grains of salt in there and check there're no gaps. He'll have to tell one of them one day – if he had to take a bet on it right now he'd say it would be Charlie – and perhaps there'll be a little puff of disappointment in his heart that it's no more complicated or arcane than that.

The first time he'd had to get up on the tallescope ladder to check the salt lining himself he'd felt a little dizzy and it was nothing to do with the height. He was terrified of missing something, leaving a hole in the protections that a rogue imp could slip through and run amok through the cast and crew. *This is management now,* Belinda had huffed as she waited at the bottom. *You've got to take responsibility for all these souls.*

And as he climbs each rung now, hoping his trousers don't split at the groin and give Belinda something to cackle about, he thinks of Juliet saying, *You listen to your elders and betters when they tell you what to do to get the show on, and when it comes time for it you tell the young ones what you were told and anything else you've learned in the meantime. It's a chain, Mackie, right back to some poor bastard packing a wagon with a load of pipes and harps and drums.*

Belinda nudges the brakes off and starts to push the tallescope along the stage, as Mackie reaches for the curtain, groping for gaps in the salt. His fingers do this now without him thinking about it – like most things here, it's best not to think too much about it – and he deftly rearranges it. Every few weeks he takes a carton of table salt from Gino and pours a little more inside the lining. He's got no idea why it needs replacing, he does it because seven years ago Juliet told him he should – she hadn't ever done it herself, she was just the most senior member of the crew left when Bill the old technical manager lost himself in the greenwood one June afternoon. That one had hurt Belinda. Now, whenever they're stopped in a forest with dappled green light and softly scented air, she puts a notice on the board, demanding everyone *be careful*. As if that will change anything, as if Belinda's stern words could be worth as much protection as all this salt and iron.

On the day Bill disappeared, it was chaos. The locked dressing rooms, the furious Crow, Belinda rubbing her temples later that night in her office, Mackie's hastily repeated pledge as the new technical manager and Juliet at his shoulder every day for a month, *Absolutely not, I'd never want to be the boss, me and the Crow see eye to eye on that at least, but I've watched old Bill for ten years or more and I'll help you find your feet.* The show was a shambles for a couple of weeks before Mackie got everything under control. Including the curtain.

Mackie grew up in fairgrounds and carnivals. He's always known about doorways sprinkled with salt and iron horseshoes and a shirt worn inside out on Mayday. He remembers parking the van at a stopping place near Nottingham one summer and sleeping out in a field wild with cow parsley and buttercups. His father made a fire and his mother tuned her fiddle and his uncles sat around smoking and playing cards while the children played in the hedgerows and the aunties pulled food out of baskets and cold boxes. And all the while Mackie could hear the swifts shrieking and he could see the air hazing at the edges of the field where they were visited by creatures attracted to the music and the fire and the laughter and the sense of freedom under the sky. They kept their distance, adding only a quiet song to the swifts' cries that spoke to Mackie of that sweet melancholy of late summer, the sensation of everything ripened to such a fullness that the only way for them to grow was into rot and ruin.

But in the morning the camp was surrounded by men with glittering eyes carrying bats and spades and a taut, gleeful threat of violence. His father had looked at them for a long moment and given the signal to move on. In minutes they were on the road, leaving nothing but flattened grass and the itch of a fight left to dissipate into the air rather than pound into bones.

Listen, his father said later that day, smoking his cigarette after they'd set up the dodgems and the helter-skelter. *There's been argy-bargy between travelling and settled folk since the time someone first scattered some seed in a field and stuck about to watch it grow. They're frit of us because we're closer to the fair folk than they. They think we step between worlds, and they love us and hate us for it.*

'Done.' He calls down to Belinda, and Zach strides onto the stage, new girl scurrying behind him, to wheel the tallescope away upstage to fix his light. As he climbs down the ladder he hears Charlie muttering into his headset, asking Kavi to drop the curtain and raise the safety. He hurries back to his abandoned laptop in the wings to get another little shot of poison from that seductive, destructive screen just as Charlie says, 'Ladies and gentlemen of *The Apple and the Pearl*, this is your quarter-of-an-hour call, you have fifteen minutes, please.'

The feed has refreshed itself again, innocently churning out more saccharine photos of people from his past. The first thing he sees when he opens his laptop is the face he's loved for decades, a face he still sees in dreams when the Crow is particularly restless, a face he once hoped to look at for the rest of his life. He clicks on the image to make it bigger. Helen, twenty years older than the woman who shows up in his dreams, with lines around her mouth and eyes and speckles of grey in her glossy black hair. She's got her arms around two teenage girls with eyes exactly her shade of green, like the dappled light in an oak canopy. He scrolls down to read the comment. *My beautiful girls on my birthday, it's been the privilege of my life to be your mother! xxx*

She never used to be so sappy, he knows it's the necessity of gilding your life for this monstrous thing that's made her write something like that. He scrolls down to more comments; *Best mum ever! xxxx* and *Gorgeous as always mum! xoxo* and thumbs-up and hearts and smiley faces and because it is hurting him somewhere high up in his ribs to see this, he clicks on Helen's name to see more pictures of her. At the beach, on a clifftop, holding a cake filled with candles, lounging in a garden among sunflowers, dressed in a ski suit, over and over Helen's face which torments him like a million tiny poison pinpricks. *This is what you gave up to sit in a black box with a pocketful of salt*, he thinks.

He clicks back to the picture of her with her daughters. He tries to see the girls' father in their faces, to unpick the mix he made with Helen and edit his own face onto theirs, to make the young women he might have had with Helen if only he'd been able to stay put. The daughters he might have cradled and sung to and ridden a bike with and stood helplessly by as they cried over a boy or a girl or a piece of homework and there is such a pain in his chest now, such a bright flash of agony that he clamps his mouth shut to stop himself making a keening noise. *I can't be on my own anymore, Mackie,* she'd said as she pulled his ring off her finger and laid it on the path between them. *You belong to the theatre, not to me. I want to love a man who lives in my house without itching to be out of it.*

And he could have said, *No, put your ring back on, I'll only go back into work to give in my notice, I'll stay here with you and get a settled job.*

Instead he had turned away, left the ring on the ground and done another three months on that musical, he can't even remember what it was called now, it was shit anyway, telling himself she had already made her choice. When he'd woken too many times with beer-stink vomit down his front and an empty ache in his belly, he realised enough was enough and sat in the greenroom of the Alhambra in Bradford with a copy of *The Stage* and a pen. He rang the number on the ad for a stage hand on a touring ballet, spoken to a curt woman who turned out to be Belinda, and found himself at Leeds station at dinnertime on a Tuesday. Change clinked in his pocket and he used it to call his father from one of those old payphones that linger like archaeological artefacts in public places no one can be bothered to renovate.

Well, I'm off away on a new show, Pa, a touring one so I won't be around for a bit. His father had made a noise of approval: he agreed with the travelling life even if it wasn't done in the traditional ways, thought it unnatural to stay in one place. *You've two legs for a reason, boy,* he used to say. *You ain't a tree.*

Whereabouts are you playing then? his father had asked, and Mackie had swelled a little with the satisfaction of saying, *Well the show's called* The Apple and the Pearl*, Pa, so we'll be playing in all sorts of places.*

He could imagine the expression on the old man's face, a glow of pride and not a little jealousy, and when the old man had said, *I never knew you had it in you boy, you go on there with my grace,* Mackie had felt released from his father's long grip at last. He knew the old man thought there was nothing more he could tell or teach him and never expected to see him again, and he left that life behind scoured of guilt, every scrap of longing for his father to see and hold him gone. *He thinks the fair folk have got me now,* he told Belinda in one of their moments of quiet understanding. *And he was glad and proud. He's old-fashioned like that.*

There has been no one else, all these years. No one

unless you count Juliet, which he doesn't, because when Juliet beckoned you to her cabin and took you to her bed you did as you were told and were pleased about it. It wasn't love, it was barely lust, it was something else, some kind of tribute to an ancient queen, a tithe, a toll paid on this long, ancient road the Grub chuntered along.

He pulls the cursor to hover over the thumbs-up icon. He presses it. He imagines Helen opening up her blue screen of dissatisfaction in a few minutes or a few hours or a few days and seeing that he, Mackie, that man she used to love, has given his thumbs-up to the picture of her and her daughters and he imagines that she will know he was thinking of her, that he was regretting her, that he was acknowledging all the years that lie between now and the time in which they loved each other, the only force of nature not even the Fae can escape no matter how long they delay it. That he was saying – clumsily, with a garbled language of cartoon pictures – how much he wished it had been him who had put those babies in her belly and watched them grow beside her.

'Mackie!' Shirley the assistant stage manager, calling him with something approaching panic in her voice, although that doesn't mean much, she's a bit highly strung and that's just how she sounds. 'Could you just come and have a look at this on the act one backdrop please?'

He quits the screen with the photos and shuts his laptop. The show is about to start and for the next few hours he won't have time to sit and moon over a woman who probably hasn't thought of him in years, he'll be rushing from wing to wing, headset hot on his ears, the familiar tides and eddies of the score flowing around him. Then, as soon as the curtain hits the stage for the third time, he'll lead the swarm of his crew all over it, dismantling the gear and the set, ready to pack in the Grub again, and of course he has to go to Belinda's office to do his pledge again. And his life here will continue the way it always has, the way it has to be because he's the one, the only one, who knows how to check the salt grains in the curtain.

'Coming.'

Twenty-five past seven and Charlie calls beginners on the tannoy. The orchestra is all assembled in the pit. They are only waiting for Max, one of the second violins, to slip past the tuba, dodge the forest of woodwind pipes and plonk himself on his seat behind Michael. *I need the adrenaline rush*, he says every time Jean complains that he puts her on edge.

Once Max is settled, they all reach for their handfuls of salt and scatter them on the ground. AJ enters the pit, the pockets of his jet-black jacket reliably weighted with salt, and the musicians get to their feet. A normal audience applauds the conductor, but this audience don't care. A conductor is just another mortal nobody to them and so they continue their languid conversations. Everyone in the orchestra is used to that now. It's the smallest of the odd things about this show.

He nods to Jean, who raises her oboe to her lips and plays

an A. Michael tunes to her, head cocked to grip his violin under his chin, one hand on the peg and the other on his bow, this wordless, discordant song they sing each and every night. Then the woodwind and brass join to match them both, their hot breath blowing a hurricane through the pit to make a tendril of AJ's silver hair quiver. Finally the strings take their bows to their instruments and the Grit is a glorious roar of perfectly jarring notes that roll and tumble over and around each other until each instrument falls off and the cacophony fades into a silence as beautifully tense as an arched bow ready to loose its weapon.

Up on stage, the sound of the orchestra tuning sets the dancers to a fever. The show is about to start and although they are all buttoned and zipped up in their costumes and everyone who performs in the first act is present on stage, they still wish for a few more minutes, a couple more practices of that tricky pirouette, a moment longer just to retie the ribbon on this pointe shoe. The wings thrum with last-minute action: a checking of the props table; a spanner on a bolt of a boom; a whispered question on a headset to Zach up in his salt-strewn lighting box.

AJ, the ninetieth conductor of *The Apple and the Pearl*, raises his baton and there is finally a hush from the auditorium. Jean puts her mouth to her reed, AJ brings his baton down and the Grit fills with the unearthly sound of her instrument, a note that sounds like a seed awakening in the earth at the beginning of spring, unfurling towards the gathering light.

Charlie says, 'Curtain', and the plush red velvet curtains that look so soft but would crush you dead if you stood beneath them, lift away from each other to frame the proscenium like plump, stained lips that would suck the meat from your bones and kiss your skeleton later.

As he hears that first sinuous note of the oboe, Romero is in his dressing room pulling on the white tights of his costume. The mirror before him is speckled with droplets of hair gel and it's refracting his image slightly. The tights fuzz and blur as he moves them over the soft brown hairs on his thighs and up over his buttocks to his waist. He tucks them into the thick band of his jockstrap and reaches for his boots before he can look too hard at the tiny ledge of displaced flesh around his waist.

On the table behind him is a bowl of three still-warm arancini with molten mozzarella at their cores. Gino sent them over from the Grub with Charlie, nestled with a napkin in a little warming tray and a dish over the top to keep the heat in and the hairspray out. He's nibbled half of one; he's saving the other half for the first interval. He'll eat another half at the second interval and another half just before the third act wedding dance for a little kick of energy, which leaves him a whole arancino to look forward to as he's wiping his make-up off and getting changed after the show.

The subtle fragrance of saffron lingers in the air, mingled with sweat, lightbulb-singed towels and the spray cleaner Alina uses on their beaded jackets that can't be spun in the washing machines. Romero swallows, just to taste the pollen of it on his tongue again. The dish is carefully crafted just for him. Gino only uses ingredients he knows Romero can bear and only in combinations he knows will sing a sweet music together. Saffron, to feel the sun on your face on the first days of spring. Sticky rice, for the feeling of lying down to sleep, sated and happy. Breadcrumbs rolled in olive oil, for the crunch of warm boots in fresh snow. Mozzarella, for the gentle nuzzling into a baby's soft neck.

Tonight he's dancing the Blue Suitor. As he manipulates the soles of the boots to warm the leather, he pedals through his feet slowly to stretch the tendons under his arches and warm them through. He imagines his muscles stretching like the mozzarella, soft and elastic and filled with milky sweetness. He pulls on the black leather boots with the soft sole and fits them over his toes. He is uncomfortable, as always. The seam of the tights makes an awkward ridge under his foot and he dreads putting on the itchy jacket. Costumes make everything worse. He'd be a better dancer if he didn't have to wear this sequinned crap while trying to move.

He's worn almost every costume by now. He started off a page, where everyone starts, and now, in the four years he's been with the company, Romero has danced every single male part except the King and the Crow. He's been every Page, and now every Suitor, and he's done the orchard dance and the hunting dance and the wedding over and over again. Some dancers find it boring, doing the same show every night – those are the ones who leave after a pledge or two. But Romero's never minded. There's a comfort in life here, a certainty to the flow of each day. He does class, rehearsal, the show. Looks at the casting for the morrow as he leaves the theatre, he eats dinner, he helps Gino tidy up, he goes to sleep, he does it all over again.

He arranges the dance boots over his calves. He's got these ones perfectly broken in now, moulded to his feet and comfortable to wear, but it won't last. Three more weeks, he estimates, before the leather starts to wear through at the big toes and he has to start all over again with the blisters and callouses of new boots.

He pulls on the sequinned jacket of the Blue Suitor with an itchy squirm and does up the hooks squinting in the mirror. He covers his arancini with a napkin and leaves the dressing room, shutting the door carefully behind him.

The door to the women's dressing room next door is framed by a row of battered pointe shoes propped up on their toes. The ribbons are spilling everywhere, the smell of hot glue and sweat wafting along the corridor. He nudges the ribbons out of his path with one leather-tipped toe, and when one shoe tumbles onto its side he quickly props it back up again. Moving someone's shoes would be like eating the food Gino made only for him. You learn quickly what's communal and what's someone else's territory here, and if you take a while to get it right then Cecile's shouting and the passive-aggressive sneers of the other dancers will usually see to it that you learn how to rub along.

Romero had been determined to rub along. There was no other option, he had nowhere else to go. He'd been cut in the first few rounds of every other audition he'd been to; *The Apple and the Pearl* had been his only chance at employment as a dancer. He'd watched class, rehearsals and the show on his first day, taken his pledge that evening and tried his best to disappear into background and give no one an opportunity to take against him. He wasn't sure if anyone other than Michael the violinist, his pledge-mate, noticed he was even alive for the first three weeks and he was fine with that, until the chef – he didn't know his name yet – caught him in the corridor just before the midnight bell.

Okay, Gino had said, blocking his way through the corridor. He'd only just finished up for the night and his forehead was beaded with sweat from his ovens and his white jacket was covered in splashes of sticky scarlet sauce, but he was intent. Whatever he wanted to say was bursting out of him. *I've given you long enough, now you need to tell me why you don't eat.*

Romero was skewered like a chicken for the spit.

I do eat. He remembers the panicked shame fizzing in his chest as he glanced over the chef's shoulder to the door that led towards the cabins. His feet itched, he wanted to run.

Gino had clasped his turmeric-stained fingers and raised his eyebrows.

What exactly is it that you eat? Grass? Flakes of paint from the set? Air?

I eat things I have in my cabin.

Gino had grimaced, a look of physical pain like Romero had punched him. *Things? You eat shit from a packet instead of my food? No wonder there's nothing of you.*

He'd looked away from Gino, into the dark window to see his own face, pale from the residue of his stage make-up and the ever-gnawing hunger in his belly. *One day,* he thought, *this chewing, chomping monster that lives inside me and feeds only on crackers, dried apple rings and secrecy will consume me completely.*

But what does your mother say about this skin and bone? Gino had softened his voice and leaned towards him. *And don't tell me all you dancers are skinny. I've been cooking for these people for twenty-two years and I can tell the skinny from the starved.*

He looked back to Gino. *My mother's dead.*

Your father then, what does he say about what you're doing to yourself?

Romero gave a wry, bitter grin.

Right. I see. Well, I understand this thing can be hard when you're suffering but you need help. Come to the dining carriage after the show tomorrow night and I'll show you what beauty there can be in a plate. And if you don't come I'll show up at your cabin and drag you here.

After the show, Romero went to the dining car shaking, his palms clammy. The man would shove food into his face, he would sit him down and spoon revolting things into his mouth, and if he refused and clamped his lips shut like a baby he'd find himself in front of Cecile and Belinda, their disappointed stares boring craters of shame in his skin.

He stood in the gangway avoiding the gaze of anyone who'd been friendly to him so far, trying to breathe through his mouth. Already the smells were disturbing him, making it difficult to think. Onions to make his toenails smart; pepper to make him think of drownings at sea; anchovies to make his stomach swoop at the thought of falling from a great height.

Later, he realised that more people than Gino had noticed that he didn't eat. Belinda, for certain, probably Cecile, maybe someone like Mara, Stuart or Greg. Your misery is everyone's else's here. Just look at the way Michael is making everyone suffer.

Gino had seen him hovering by the gangway that night and smiled, flicking a wave of silvered hair out of his eyes. It was impossible for Romero not to notice the way his beard petered into silver as it covered his neck, the way his green eyes crinkled at the corners when he smiled, the way his shoulders filled his white chef's coat making him think of the boulders on the shoreline that never wavered, even with the sea crashing against them all day and all night. It added an extra layer of humiliation, to be reduced to wreckage by this thing that squatted inside him in front of a man like this.

Come here. He took Romero by the shoulders and guided him through the serving hatch and into his kitchen to deposit him in front of three small chopping boards, each with a pile of fresh herbs lying on it. Romero wanted to gag, so close to these fresh things all spewing scents like some primordial soup. The monster started to agitate.

Gino pointed to the one on the left.

Crush the leaves between your fingers and tell me what your senses say.

Romero took a coriander leaf and squeezed it. He put a finger to the tip of his tongue and tried not to shudder. He could just about bear the assault of the smells – he was used to blocking his sinuses and leaving his lips a little agape to breathe – but to taste this thing the chef had given him made him want to cry. He shut his eyes to stop the tears spilling over his eyelashes. He would have to break his pledge and leave, no matter Belinda's dire warnings. The monster was pounding at him, roaring to get away, there was no way he could bear this.

What do you taste?

There had been nothing else to say. The monster raved in his belly but a small voice, a surprising voice of mercy that he now recognises as the Crow's whispered, *Just tell him the truth.*

Jealousy, he said, and opened his eyes.

Gino frowned and looked down at the tiny flecks of green on the chopping board. He picked up the slim stem of a chive and handed it to Romero who nibbled on the end.

The feeling of being so drunk you can't feel your legs and you're not sure if you're standing up or not.

Gino folded his arms and leaned against the counter.

How long have you experienced food like this?

All my life.

And it's worse here?

Romero nodded. Since taking his pledge it was as if the dial had been pushed past the maximum. He found himself weeping with terror from the smell of a pinch of cinnamon in a bowl of porridge, or trying to hide a painfully swift erection from a single sip of orange juice.

Okay, said Gino. *Is there anything that doesn't make you feel bad when you eat it?*

Crackers and apple rings.

Gino suppressed a shudder. *Anything else? Any real food?*

Romero had shrugged. The monster made it too difficult to try.

Right. This is what we'll do. I'll make something just for you every day after the show, something simple, not too fancy, and you tell me how it makes you feel. And if it upsets you I'll remember and I won't make it again.

Romero felt a sudden stab of what he assumed was hunger, something he hadn't felt for years and years, at least since he'd lived with his aunt and the monster had started to nibble at him. *But why would you do that?*

Gino turned away and busied himself with tidying the herbs he'd set out. *Did you make a pledge on your first day here?*

Yes.

Well, everyone's pledge is different, and this is mine. He held open the door to the kitchen. *Come back tomorrow night and I'll have something ready for you.*

His costume is driving him mad, itching the tender skin over his ribs and he stops by the noticeboard to scratch and adjust it. He holds the door to the stage open for Milly who is jogging towards him with a threaded needle in one hand and the other on her chest.

'Ta,' she pants as she passes him, and he follows her into the blackness of the wings.

The temperature on stage is balmy, the lights exuding heat in all directions. Shirley the assistant stage manager is sweating as she wraps Benji in the red cloak of the Suitor. Romero goes to stand next to him, ready for Shirley to fuss around him with the blue cloak next.

'Good luck, mate,' Romero whispers to Benji as Shirley trots back to the props table. 'You'll be great. Just keep breathing.'

Benji gives him a wan smile. 'Cecile told me this morning that she should have given me an extra week to rehearse. She said it like she was telling me someone had died.'

Romero rolls his eyes. 'That's the sort of thing she says when she has full confidence in you. Honestly, you'll be great.'

The Pages march off stage and for a moment Shirley is distracted by gathering up their decorative swords and shields and placing them carefully within their marked-out places on the prop table.

On stage, Greg and Mara are sweeping around each other in the mock courtly dance of the King and the Queen. They're Romero's favourite couple to watch in these roles – the command in the breadth of Greg's shoulders and the aristocratic way Mara holds her head. They're his favourite dancers to watch in almost any role. Theirs is the kind of charisma you simply don't have at the beginning of your career, no matter how easily you turn five pirouettes, no matter how fresh the line of your *arabesque.* It's as if every time you step on stage you accrue a little more magnetism, until your knees are shot and your hips creak and your back is crooked but no one can take their eyes off you. Romero can feel it happening to him, a slow build-up of glamour that glitters on the skin under the glare of the stage lights. It makes him feel powerful, but it's not without its dangers. He's noticed the haze that rises from the auditorium during curtain calls lingers for a fraction of a second around Greg and Mara – and Stephanie and Stuart too – no matter what roles they're dancing, even if they're only in the corps de ballet that night. It's dangerous, in a thrilling and glamorous way. Charlotte used to have the little speckles of light in the haze dancing around her head for a full minute before they were drawn to the back of the stage and into the Pearl on its podium, and look what happened to her.

Shirley returns to his blue cloak – which she pleads for them not to attempt to wrap on their own as Alina is very insistent on how they should fold and drape – and Stuart, dressed in the glittering cream jacket of the White Suitor, appears by his side with a waft of aftershave.

Stuart slaps Benji on the shoulder. 'Here we go, mate. The three that lie in a dream. We'll be looking out for you, just enjoy yourself.'

Benji looks a little green. Romero remembers the first time he danced one of the Suitors – it was the Red one, which is the easiest although it's tricky on the stamina going straight from the solo to the *pas de deux* – he had thought he was going to throw up. Gino had made him a sweet potato curry spiced with lemongrass for courage and cardamom for spring in his feet and Cecile had told him that he'd be a passable Suitor if he learned to land his *tours* cleanly.

The trumpet blares, loudly pulling his attention back to the show currently in progress, announcing the entrance of the Crow. Romero leans to one side to see Josh saunter out onto the stage with his black cape billowing behind him and the sleek black feathers of the headdress gleaming under the lights. A familiar stab of envy twists his stomach. He'd love to dance the Crow one day but he's afraid of that headdress. He knows it will itch him on the soft places behind his ears and under his jaw. He's seen the way the others groan when they take it off in the wings, their hair dripping with sweat, their foreheads dented by the rim. He imagines the glue melting into his face as he starts to sweat, the heat releasing the intimate odours of everyone else who has ever worn it: their skin, their hair, their teeth. It makes his stomach roil. He both longs for and dreads Cecile beckoning him with one red-tipped finger to tell him to start learning the part. He hasn't decided yet if he'll tell her he doesn't want to or if he'll try and wheedle a new headdress out of Alina. Maybe he'll try that first. If Alina says no, which he can imagine her doing, with that sardonic so-you-think-you're-better-than-anyone-else-who's-worn-this-monstrosity eyebrow, he'll ask Gino to have a word with her. He doesn't do that often, throw his weight around as the beloved of the most important person in the whole company, but when he does it works. There is no peace for you on board the Grub if Gino is not happy with you. Maybe that's why Cecile is such a bitch. Gino won't talk about their long-running feud. *Our pledges are opposed to each other*, is all he'll say. *Just another of the Crow's tricks.*

Romero doesn't have a favourite dancer as the Crow: everyone who performs the role teases out something different. Stephanie is the most birdlike – the way she cocks her head and preens the feathers on the costume, she sometimes seems uncannily like a real, giant bird. Mara is cold and glamorous and fierce – she could be on a catwalk. Stuart is an alpha, dancing it like the kind of bird that would piss all over your lunch and laugh about it. Greg doesn't dance the Crow anymore because his knees are giving up on him but when he did he played it for laughs, hamming up the leering at the Princesses and cavorting like a kind of gremlin. Josh, on stage now, gives the Crow something wistful and haunted, like he's flown a hundred leagues to be here and has seen things you can't imagine.

It's the only part Romero can think of in any classical repertoire that can be performed by a man or a woman. The rest of ballet is so rigidly gender-defined, so stiflingly segregated that just the fact that the role exists thrills him and goes a long way to healing the bruising from all those jobs he didn't get, all those directors who looked past him as if he was invisible. He has to get Alina to make him a new headdress. He can't retire without dancing that role.

Josh finishes his solo, standing with his back to the audience, with one hand held out towards the wing where the three Suitors wait. A rolling arpeggio of the harp and the cellos start the Suitors' theme, slow and steady and noble. Romero holds onto his cape with one hand and places the other on Stuart's sequinned shoulder. Benji's trembling hand lands on his, and they all walk out of the wing together, chins held high, a carefully neutral expression on each of their faces because they're supposed to be a vision the Crow has conjured for the court.

He always finds it hard to tell when he's no longer in the wings and is now on stage. Since his first show that border space has fascinated him. A tiny tear in the fabric of time and space, a liminal moment between being hidden in the blackness and being bared, exposed for all the audience to see. Just a step, a small shuffle from dark to light. He wonders if there has ever been anyone who has fallen inside that gap between the wings the way you can fall into the gap between tolls of the midnight bell.

The Suitors' first dance is solemn and proud. Swathed in those carefully draped cloaks, they parade slowly around the Princesses. Benji's doing well, his steps perfectly in time with the music and matched to him and Stuart. He no longer looks nervous; he looks like a prince. Romero can sense a couple of particles of that charismatic glitter alight on his skin.

The three Suitors stop at the back of the stage, poised in perfect stillness gazing out across the auditorium. He remembers the first time he'd looked out there, on his second week with the company. He'd been a Page escorting the Blue Princess and as he took Stephanie's warm hand and stepped into the light, the force of the fair folk's combined glamour hit him like a brick wall. He'd stumbled and Stephanie had gripped his hand to keep him upright. *You're okay, just push through it and don't look too closely, it happens to everyone,* she'd whispered as they paraded around the stage, her regal smile fixed as Romero pulled himself together.

Now, as Josh cavorts around them, Romero looks determinedly at the gilding of the balcony and counts the round bobbles there to distract himself. He feels Benji's shoulder stiffen under his hand and he gives him a squeeze, to reassure him, to keep his attention here on stage and not out there in the horrors of the auditorium. He thinks of the lunch Gino made him, still lining his belly. Avocado, for the feeling of stretching arms and legs in bed on a lazy morning when you don't have to set an alarm, mashed with sun-dried tomatoes for thirst slaked, and basil for a message from a long-lost friend. All spread on a slice of brown toast, for the feeling of unexpectedly hearing the first few bars of a favourite song. He thinks of the two and a half arancini waiting for him in the dressing room. He thinks of Gino, chopping and frying and stirring and mashing, alone in the Grub, pledged to keep each one of them here fed and watered until their own pledges are over.

The violins start. Greg and Mara lead the court in a slow, mournful dance around the three still Suitors in the middle of the stage and the danger is past. Now he lets himself watch the other dancers moving past him. Harriet is doing well in her first show as the Red Princess, confident and calm. The scarlet of the costume suits her. Luke, the newest pledge, fluffs a lift, tripping over his own feet and Romero hears Zuleika the Blue Princess hiss *Sort yourself out*. Another crime on Luke's rap sheet, which, judging by the way Cecile shrieked at him this morning in rehearsals, is getting longer and longer. Now he's pissed Zuleika off and she'll be tense and nervous – even more tense and nervous than usual – for their *pas de deux*.

The court exits stage right and the three Suitors pause in a tableau of low *arabesques*, still joined hand to shoulder, until Josh banishes them with a flick of his cape. Romero follows Stuart into the stage right wing as Josh walks to the back of the stage and breathes deep into his belly. The first solo is a killer on the lungs, they all say.

The wing is busy with Shirley buzzing around Greg and Mara to remove their crowns for safekeeping, Danny hauling the second act set into place and Anita marking the Crow's solo with one eye on Josh to prepare for her first show in the role, whenever Cecile decides she's ready. Romero tries not to be jealous of her, getting to dance the Crow before him. She'll be good at it. She's got a strong jump.

Zuleika grabs Luke by the sequinned jacket and pulls him away from the stage.

'That was not fucking acceptable,' Zuleika whispers as Josh begins his solo, standing on her toes to bring her face close to his. Luke is looking stricken, opening and closing his mouth like a goldfish. 'You were late, you were off the music and you didn't know what you were doing.'

'I'm sorry,' Luke says, his chin wobbling as if he is trying to hold back tears. 'I won't do it again.'

'I know you fucking won't.' Zuleika lets go of his jacket with a little shove, opens the door to the corridor with a graceful, silent fury. Romero slips behind her, already easing the itchy jacket off his shoulders. He doesn't want to get involved. Let her burn off a bit of steam, let her feel above someone. That should calm her down.

In the dressing room, Romero hangs up his jacket and sinks into his chair. He stretches to one side, then the other. The second act is the big one for the Blue Suitor but he's ready. He isn't nervous, but he'll make a little show of warming up and practising a few turns and lifts with Zuleika when Charlie announces act two beginners. She likes to get worked up, Romero's realised, after being her main partner for a few months now. It masks her nerves. And she's been even more on edge since Michael's girlfriend left him and the violin solo in the Blue *pas de deux* has turned into a dirge that sends the Grit's tannoys wild with weeping and makes everyone quiet and glum. *What do you think of, when Michael gets going during our* pas de deux*?* she asked him a couple of months ago, when it became apparent that Michael's grief wasn't going anywhere. He likes Zuleika, but he wasn't about to tell anyone, not even Gino, what memories really force themselves into his mind – his father's fists, his mother's screams, the fat, groping hands of his uncle under the duvet – so he made something up. *My mum's funeral*, he'd said with a sad little smile, hoping this conversation was going to be short. *What about you?* he'd asked and her face had darkened in a way that made him think he was going to regret asking. *The week my dad came out of prison.*

You're his pledge-mate, aren't you? Greg had said to Romero the week after this tannoy business started. *Can't you have a word, try to cheer him up a bit?* And Romero had genuinely tried, sitting with him for breakfast, bringing him tasty little tidbits from Gino, chatting about nothing as they walked through the pleasant summer landscapes the Grub stopped in, but three months ago Romero had gone to Belinda to renew his pledge and Michael had not been there. *Isn't Michael coming?* He'd asked, stupidly, and Belinda's lips had tightened. *I'm dealing with it, Romero. I appreciate you've been trying to help.*

Josh, a week later during the second interval as he stepped in the puddle under the tannoy in his socks: *I honestly believe Michael's life would be better in a fairy court.*

Mate! Stuart had said at the same time as Greg tutted *Josh!* Josh had thrown his wet socks on the floor defensively. *I'm not saying anything you're not thinking.*

Behind him, Luke clears his throat. Romero winces. He hopes the new boy isn't going to start confiding all his woes, which must be legion, the way Cecile treats him. If he can't help Michael then there's not going to be much he can do for Luke.

'It's hard to learn all the choreography at once,' Luke says with an embarrassed little smile. 'But at least the music is nice.'

Romero makes a little *hmmm* noise and watches Luke

peel off the tights from the page costume in the mirror. He suppresses a twinge of guilt. He can't be bothered right now to play agony uncle, let-me-give-you-a-pep-talk mentor. Right now he's eating, and besides, no one did that for him. Greg and Stuart had been pleasant but fair enough, they were pleasant guys, Josh had been outright hostile and Charlotte had stood in the wings and laughed while Alina sewed him into the hunting dance costume he was too skinny for. He had certainly not mourned Charlotte when she was taken, though of course you're not supposed to say that.

Romero watches as Luke picks up his phone and scrolls aimlessly, the guilty feeling spreading across his skin. Zuleika didn't need to speak to him like that. The thing is, everyone's still missing Alex, who had been genuinely popular among the cast and crew. Tall, good-looking, a good partner to dance with, a founding member of the Saturday night poker sessions – which are on indefinite hiatus now – replaced with someone shy and spotty, straight out of school. *Where the fuck did Belinda find this kid?* Josh had grumbled at the end of his first week. *She couldn't come up with someone who can learn the choreography?* And Greg had touched Josh's arm as a gentle rebuke but no one had said anything in Luke's defence.

Romero looks at the plate of arancini. Now they're going to taste like the feeling of wanting to do the right thing but not being sure what that is. A nightmare scenario: because everyone ignores him, Luke is snatched in the next week or so, which casts a pall of guilt over the whole company. Cecile will scream at Belinda, *You didn't let me have a proper audition! What do you expect?* Mara will tell Josh that he's a rotten excuse for a human being. And Romero will not be able to eat arancini again.

He turns around. 'You're missing a little spacing trick in the wedding dance. You know the bit before the *chassé arabesque*?' Luke nods. 'You need to travel the two *assemblés* before that so you're in front of the King by the time you turn downstage.'

So small, such a piece of nothing, but Luke looks pathetically grateful. 'Thanks. I know exactly what you mean. I'll do that tonight.'

Romero goes back to his arancini. He puts a jumper over his lap so he doesn't spill crumbs on his tights and annoy Alina. He turns off the hot lightbulbs that ring his mirror, puts his feet up on the table and takes the other half of the first arancino between his forefinger and his thumb.

He spent his second month going straight to the dining car after the show to help Gino serve and clear up. In that time he learned he could stand to eat carrots if they were braised in olive oil, potatoes only if they were roasted, raw green peppers, cous cous, lamb's lettuce, courgettes if they were steamed, lentils any and all ways, cream, mozzarella, sunflower seeds, chickpeas if they were whizzed into houmous, and salmon baked in the oven with a drizzle of lemon. Gino prodded him gently in the stomach one night. *You're making me very happy,* he'd said. *You're getting fatter by the day.*

A bolt of electricity passed between them. It was late,

past midnight, and the dining car was empty, lurching with the Grub as it passed on wherever it was going. Romero drew back, but something, perhaps his contented bellyful of dhal, made him bold. He put out his hand and laid it on Gino's chest. No spark now, just a warmth that spread from his fingertips and through Gino's shirt and onto his skin, and he'd felt Gino melting towards him like butter on a slow, tender flame.

I'm too old for you, Gino had whispered, his voice thick and rough, but he had not pulled away. His beard was prickly on the soft skin of Romero's neck. *I could be your father. Go and find a boy your own age.*

Romero takes the last bite of the first arancino and chews it slowly, deliberately, as he places the napkin back over the plate. Saffron, to feel the sun on your face on the first days of spring. Sticky rice, for the feeling of lying down to sleep, sated and happy. Breadcrumbs rolled in olive oil, for the crunch of warm boots in fresh snow. Mozzarella, for the gentle nuzzling into a baby's soft neck.

The Crow's solo is ending, the last, plaintive note of the oboe fading away into that curious silence that ends each act of this show, and Romero imagines Josh standing with his back to the audience as the curtain falls, back arched and arms raised as if calling rain. Slowly, deliberately, Romero licks each fingertip clean of the film of oil that coats his skin and lets a couple of stray crumbs dissolve on his tongue.

The orchestra wait for Jean to take her oboe from her lips, take a breath and swallow, then they all stand up as silently as they can and leave the pit, not daring, never daring to look back into the auditorium. They go straight to their green room where Wilf, Steve and Jasper tuck into their usual first interval snack – a bag of salted nuts each. Sandra the clarinet goes to the loo where she uses the last of the toilet paper, and she means to replace it but forgets as soon as she's finished washing her hands. Max the second violin and David the new harp are talking about the football, Max swiping through his phone and reading out recent scores. Jean sits near them, silently sipping coffee from a Thermos. Her phone buzzes and a small smile creeps onto her lips as she picks it up. Lance strokes Yolanda's black-silk-clad thigh but he is thinking about the smooth skin on Mara's back as she stood in the corridor in the Queen costume, waiting for Alina to fasten the hooks. Michael sits tuning his violin, staring into space as he plucks at his E string. Henry sits just behind him, pretending to read something on his phone. A knock on the green room door and AJ opens it, standing awkwardly on the threshold.

'May I speak with Henry a moment please?' He smiles. 'Nothing at all bad, I promise.'

Belinda drops her handbag on the floor and presses her temples. After a moment's hesitation, she locks the door. Sitting at her desk is a wizened old woman wearing a bin bag covered with tiny black sequins.

'Thank you for coming.' Belinda says. 'We have some

personnel issues to deal with this evening.' She pulls her notepad out of her handbag and flicks to her to-do list.

'All right, I've got here: Is the new LX girl suitable; can we think of something to help the new dancer settle in; we have to do something about the changeling; can Anita dance the Crow; can Bella dance the White Princess; Wilf the cellist needs another formal warning about the booze; and last of all – what did you do with Michael's heart?'

Upstairs on the dancers' floor, Milly and Alina are in the women's dressing room wrestling with Jessica's Pearl waltz costume which has spontaneously lost a sleeve.

'I didn't do anything!' Jessica looks stricken, standing with one pointe shoe on and one bare foot, her arm stretched high above her head. 'I promise, I just put it on as usual!'

'Fuck fuck fuck,' whispers Alina through a mouthful of safety pins as she and Milly sew the sleeve back on, their needles diving through the seam like kingfishers in a brook. 'This fucking show, these fucking tricks, I'm fucking sick of them.'

On stage the crew are moving scenery. Danny mutters to Kavi through his headset as he guides the seascape backdrop down onto the stage, painted blue and green with waves and clouds and small silvery flashes of what could be fish.

'Your hands all right?' Danny asks as the backdrop shudders a little. He winces and steps further out of the way, shielding his eyes from the lights as he squints up into the flies.

'Fine, mate. The rope's just a bit sticky.'

'Well, mind my head please.'

Zach crouches by an upstage lighting boom, pointing at something while Lara leans over him and frowns.

'Is there any way to predict how the stage will be different tomorrow?' Lara is saying. 'Like, does the Grit have a pattern or anything?'

In a little pool of light downstage, just in front of the curtain, Zuleika practices the tricky pirouettes in her solo. Cecile watches her from the darkness of the wings. She checks her watch: eight twenty-six. Zuleika does the turn perfectly once, twice, three times to be sure, pulls her legwarmers down her thighs, balls them up and tosses them into the wings.

Mackie sits on a bench hunched over his laptop. Shirley presses a strip of masking tape onto the props table and labels it *King – Crown*. Charlie presses his little red button, leans towards his microphone and says, 'Act two beginners please, act two beginners.'

As the first, shy notes of the violins creep over the tannoy, Cecile sits in her office with two sheets of paper on the desk in front of her – the casting of the performance that is currently underway and a blank version for tomorrow night. She's done most of the corps de ballet and she's working her way up to the soloists and principals, but she's distracted, keeps checking the silent screen of her phone, glancing over her shoulder, seeking out her reflection in the square of mirror above the desk.

She pulls the paper towards her and stares at it. She needs to finish this casting before the end of the act. She stretches, hands clasped above her head, and tries to get comfortable in her chair. It's an ergonomic office chair, ordered in one of Belinda's fits of health and safety paranoia, but she's never sat on anything so uncomfortable in all her life. The only thing she likes about it is the way you can swivel. She can turn away from these blasted blank sheets of paper with a single touch of her toes on the floor.

On stage, the surge of the overture subsides, the clarinets begin their looping, swooping song for the Princess's dance and Cecile picks up her pencil to write Zuleika's name in the column next to the words *Blue Princess*. She puts Greg's name next to the word *King* and Romero's next to *Blue Suitor*. She writes Harriet and Benji in for the Red Princess and Suitor, to give them another shot to get comfortable in the roles, and gives Stephanie the Queen.

She puts Josh's name next to the White Suitor, even though it's not his best role, which means it should be Sarah for the White Princess. That leaves Mara for the Crow, and she'll put Stuart in one of the gaps in the hunting dance, just to keep him humble. There are no stars on *The Apple and the Pearl*.

She flings the pen down and glances at her watch. Eight thirty-six. Not much time left now. This morning Gino had cheerfully told AJ, *Phone and internet signal should you want it!* while he slid her customary espresso across the counter without making eye contact. She would quite like to make it up with Gino and sometimes she rehearses what she might say in apology. *I should not have tried to interfere with your menu choices, of course our dancers should be well nourished, forgive me.* Or, *I was just trying to make my mark on the company, trying to be in charge by doing what the ballet mistresses of my youth had done.* Or, *Please understand, Gino, when* I *was performing I ate two apples and drank four coffees a day and no one cared about my health at all.* But with every passing pledge it feels more and more impossible. She no longer cares if the dancers of *The Apple and the Pearl* are fat or thin – and she's seen that the audience do not care either – but now she's walled up behind her own stern mask and Gino exclusively communicates with her through AJ, though he still knows to buy that Sancerre she loves.

She looks at her watch again: eight forty. Might she have missed him? It's never happened before; normally he's like any three-year-old in that you can't miss him. He jiggles and jangles at your elbow, insistently demanding your attention. But she did not want to take it for granted. All day, she's been looking for him in the shadows and folds of things, behind graves and in between the dark ridges of the bark of the yews. Waiting for something, anything. His imperious little voice in her ear, a glimpse of his golden little head. Even a compulsion to place a gentle hand on a sleeping chest. She'd taught class like it was any other day of the year, ignored Michael's abject attempts at an apology, allowed herself to get worked up thinking about him thinking he's the only one with any kind of grief, then made herself feel calmer with a bit of shouting at the new pledge in rehearsals. Luke is objectively disappointing but Cecile has to admit that it is not his fault that Belinda went rogue in hiring him, nor that Alex was so talented and likeable. *He has no family in the world, Cecile,* Belinda had said reproachfully, *he'll do fine for the corps de ballet.* Cecile had had to do some deep belly breathing to avoid shouting right here in her office. *This is not a home for waifs and strays, Belinda, this is a ballet company. And I am not anyone's mother.*

And how it hurt to say that! Especially in October, her favourite month of the year, counting down with every fallen leaf to this day, All Souls', when she will get to remember that she was once, indeed, someone's mother.

Her son appears to her differently each year. That first time it was a scent that followed her around all day, the smell of the talc she used to sprinkle onto his mottled newborn skin. In the years after it was a glimpse of him standing next to AJ on the conductor's podium during the White Princess's solo, a long conversation about teddy bears with his disembodied voice in her cabin just before reveille, a vision of him swinging from the curfew bell as she left the Grub after lunch.

At first she thought she was mad. Then she wished she were madder so she might have more of him. Was he following the Grub every day of the year but it was only on this day, All Souls', that he was able to break through that so-called veil between worlds?

The Pearl waltz ends with the clatter of pointe shoes as the girls skitter off stage. There is a silence as Romero as the

Blue Suitor walks on to the stage, and Cecile imagines AJ watching him, baton raised, ready for Wilf's cello to sound and Romero's jump to land at exactly the same moment.

She has never told AJ about Antoine, not in all these years. Not that he was born, not that he died, not that he comes back to her every year on this day. She thinks of that time seven years ago when AJ almost – but not quite – asked her to marry him. She would have told him about Antoine, but the moment passed. She thinks of AJ's handsome profile, the way he draws a score in the air with his long fingers, the way he touched the keys on the electronic piano when he used to play for ballet class, like he was stroking the tender skin of a newborn baby. In another life she could have loved him. They could have lived together in a small house with roses climbing around the front door, books lining the walls and a grand piano. Children. Grandchildren. Glasses of cognac in front of a fire, with his beloved Rachmaninov on the record player and a–

'*Sur le pont d'Avignon…*' Oh, here he is, at last! She can hear the sound of splashing and a child singing gleefully out of tune.

She used to sing this song to Antoine as she bathed him, throwing the rubber toys into the water. Cecile had read that music was good for brain development so she sang anything she could remember, all the time. Nursery rhymes, Charles Trenet, poorly pronounced Beatles songs. She had no idea how to raise a child. She had grown up with only a father, unmothered, unmoored by that continuing presence in your life. She was making it up as she went along and singing to her son drowned out the insistent feeling of you're-a-failure in her mind.

She kicks her shoes off and leans back in her chair. She squeezes her eyes tightly shut, listening to him burbling rhythmically to himself. She can hear the sound of something bashing against porcelain and his little voice has an echoey feel, like it's bouncing off tiles.

'*Maman*!' he calls, and she almost feels his breath move the air between them but she doesn't look round because she knows Antoine will not be there; she only gets to see him, or hear him or feel him. Not all at once. After twenty-two years she has learned this. '*Chante*!'

She smiles.

'*Et les belles dames font comme ça*,' she croons, and she imagines her little boy laughing, a rubber bath toy in each fat fist, raising them above his head to plop them into the water.

'*Et les beaux messieurs font comme ça,*' Antoine sings back and she remembers the way people used to smile indulgently to see the two of them sitting together on the bus, devoted Madonna and child, singing an old-fashioned nursery rhyme, dipping their heads in mock courtly bows.

She hears him take a deep breath to shout the long *ohhhhhhh* before the next verse and she joins in, their voices rising together to a tuneless pitch before crashing into an airless gasp.

He collapses into giggles and she drinks in the sound, lets it pour into her lungs like cool, crisp mountain air, lets it drive out all the dust of days on end spent in the dark box of the Grit. She will eke it out all through the dark of winter, the blush of spring and the blaze of summer, surviving until next year.

A knock at the door. Cecile operates a not-exactly-explicit closed-door policy, letting it be known yet unspoken that, unless you're AJ, you'd better have a really good reason for knocking on this door. But before she can turn to Antoine's voice and tell him to be quiet, he shouts '*Entrez*!' with the glee of a beloved game about to begin, the same way he used to when she'd call him her little prince and pretend to be giving him a royal buffet for him to enjoy in his bath.

Cecile hears the door creak open and she spins around on the ergonomic desk chair. Her eyes fly open to see Greg, dressed in his King costume and hand-knitted purple socks with MONDAY stitched on them, staring at the wall.

Cecile feels something like ice water drip down her neck as Greg lifts one hand and waves, a shy and dopey smile on his lips.

'Can you… you can see him?'

Greg nods.

Cecile swallows a sob. 'Tell me what he looks like.'

'Little blonde head, brown eyes. Playing with a rubber snail. Chubby. Looks like a baby, really.'

Idiot. He was almost three, not a baby at all.

'*On y dansé, on y dansé*,' yells Antoine but she notices with a bubble of panic that his voice sounds muffled now. She needs to get rid of Greg, he's ruining everything.

'Greg.'

He turns to her, with difficulty, and a dim part of her notes with pleasure that it is as difficult for him as it is for her to tear his gaze away from the spirit.

'Get out.'

Greg nods. He opens his mouth to say something, thinks better of it, then shuts the door gently behind him.

But the click of the door has disturbed her son's spirit because the singing stops and he calls

'*Maman*?' and there is a tremor of petulance in his voice that used to make her panic, the prelude to a tantrum that would have him beating his fists on the floor, throwing his head from side to side and screaming until he gasped for air, all while she sat next to him, trying to hold him, wondering what she had done wrong to induce such rage into such a little body, wondering if there was something monstrous writhing inside him trying to get out.

'I'm here,' she says, and she sings again, slightly desperately. '*Sur le pont...*'

'*Maman*!' he cries again and now there is the echo of a scream behind his voice, the flump of a soft flesh on metal, a screech of tyres. It gets louder and louder in her mind, drowning out Antoine's singing, and now she can't sing back, her throat is ashes. This is how it always goes. First there is the beauty of him, back again, then there is the cruelty of reliving what took him away.

She calls out to him but his voice gets more agitated. She realises he can't hear her anymore, he's leaving her. Again.

He's been with her no more than ten minutes, interrupted by that dolt, but she has never been sure what time means to Antoine, to anyone on the other side. A few years ago she read that the physicists no longer reckon time as one straight line but rather a looping river of eddies and pools, and as soon as she saw the words she knew that's where she is, stuck in one of time's eddies, drifting around this tiny corner of the universe, waiting for something, anything of her dead son to appear to her.

He's gone. There is only the sway of the cello of the Blue Suitor's solo and the soft thump of Romero's *jetés* landing on the stage floor. She reaches into her desk drawer and pulls out the bottle of cognac and a glass. She pours herself a couple of fingers and downs it.

Greg is a kind and gentle man, and truly a talented dancer, but she will never forgive him for this. These past couple of years his body has reminded her of a beloved old labrador, blind and limping with farts that stink of death, but pity has held her back.

The last time she tried to sack someone for being too old it was Charlotte, and not even a week later she was snatched before ballet class. Mara, tear-stained in Belinda's office, her accusing, sharp gaze. *She just disappeared, went into the cobbled path like it was water!*

Now she thinks she would enjoy seeing that happen to Greg. She should call him back, do what she hasn't done for fear of the fairy creatures – tell him his days here are over and that he has to leave at his next pledge. Then she can wait for one of those creatures to notice that he's slow and old and leaving the show, and let it take him. She would have to have a meeting with Belinda and fill out those ridiculous forms but he would be gone. For good. Before he has the chance to whisper about what he's seen to Josh, who will tell all the other dancers, who will tell the wardrobe mistresses, who will tell the stage hands, who will tell the drunken musicians, who will tell AJ.

She pours herself another slug of cognac and tips it down her throat. The walls of her office blur pleasantly.

Why was he knocking on her door? Why the fuck would any of the dancers, let alone one who has known her for so long, do that? What could be so important that tonight of all nights Greg had to climb the stairs to her office, a place she cannot recall him ever even walking past, to speak with her?

She hears the violins start for the Blue *pas de deux* and the tannoy begins to crackle. It starts to drip salt water onto the floor and she groans. She does not want to know of Michael's grief; tonight of all nights she might succumb to it. She has asked AJ to do something about him over and over again but he's always demurred, saying the Crow is dealing with him in its own way. But every night, all throughout the theatre at this point in the show, the tannoys start to weep and the keening of Michael's violin dredges everyone's memories and lovingly serves them their deepest, saddest heartbreaks. She pushes aside the completed casting, puts her head on the desk and squeezes her eyes shut against the unbidden memories.

The screeching tyres of the lorry lurching across the road, the flump of his soft body on steel, her scream, the sirens, the beeping in the hospital, the silence of the funeral parlour, the spade slicing through frosted earth. The tinkling of the piano on her first class for three years, her hot tears of shame as she looked at herself in a leotard and tights, the pouch under the navel, the heavy thighs, the drooping breasts. A mother's body with no child to show for it. Her scream, the sirens, the silence.

The *drip drip drip* of salt water stops with the last note of the Blue *pas de deux* and there is a pause before the timpani starts up the first wild rhythms of the Crow's solo. Cecile lifts her head off the desk, wipes at her face with the heels of her hands and sniffs. She tucks the completed casting into her handbag and stands up, slipping her feet into her shoes.

All Souls' and Antoine has been and gone and she is a whole year away from having him back again. All Souls', the day of the dead, and once more that much-discussed veil between worlds has drifted closed again, obscuring him from her. There is always this moment of black despair every year when she knows she must endure a whole year's worth of filling in this piece of paper in ever-different ways until she can have him again. But it is getting worse. Her grief is as fiercely edged as ever, the platitudes are wrong and time has done nothing to blunt it.

She wonders if it's the modern world of antibiotics and sanitation that's done this to her. Her ancestors would have thought nothing of losing a single child. They swam in death, they were intimate with all its faces. Death on a cough, a sneeze, a dirty fingernail. Death lurking inside a wildly multiplying cell, death hiding inside the irregular tick-tock of a stuttering heart. Death in deep water, death in a mug of dirty water. Death in the empty belly, death in the fall, the trip, the stone-struck skull. Death at birth, death a couple of minutes after birth, death as your only companion, your only solace through all the brief moments of life.

Her feet have brought her to the noticeboard at the side of the stage. There is no one about and she is glad. She feels exposed, like the tender underbelly of her is bared to the whole world. What if Greg went straight back to the dressing room to tell the others? *You will never guess what was in her office tonight. No, honestly. Turns out there* is *something she cares about.*

She could do it now. Call him out of the dressing room, tell him in the corridor, claim it's because of his weakening body, because he can no longer perform half the roles in the show and doesn't justify his salary. Of course, AJ would tell her not to be vengeful, but he always is the better part of her. He would ask her to consider that perhaps Greg, too, has yearly multi-sensory hallucinations of someone he's loved and lost and that's why he's sticking it out here in this half-world, even while his knees beg him to retire.

She takes four golden pins from the cork and holds them lightly in her palm. She'd like just to post and go but something heavy has infected her limbs and keeps her stuck to the spot. She looks at her own handwriting scrawled over the paper and the letters swim as her eyes film over with tears.

Just like it does every night, the signal that the casting's up travels through the theatre like the mysterious scent that draws the dung beetle to a fresh pat of cow shit in a meadow. Before she's even turned away from the board, she can sense bodies hovering behind her. Three corps de ballet girls lurk at the bottom of the stairs, already dressed in their orchard dance costumes, trying not to catch her eye as she walks away. The dancers are obsessed with the casting: they treat it like the entrails of a goat that can divine the future. Idiots. She posts it as late as she can just to fuck with them. It's one of the few pleasures she can count on all year round.

She grips her handbag as she makes her way back up the four flights of stairs to her office to wait for AJ who usually comes to see her in the second interval to share a thimbleful of cognac, *Just enough to keep the chill of the curtain call out of our ageing bones.*

As she opens her office door, she hears Charlie saying 'standby' on the tannoy and she sits down heavily at her desk. She takes another glass out of the desk drawer and pours out two cognacs. She downs one, pours another and turns her ergonomic chair to face the wall, squinting at it, trying to see something there. Some kind of ghostly residue, an imprint of his soul in the chilly air, any scrap of comfort that some part of him was really here. There is nothing. Only the timpani, Josh's soft landing on the stage floor and the swishing of his cloak. She hated dancing the Crow, hates rehearsing it now. Nasty birds. Death in their beaks, their wings and their caws. Just like her.

On the tannoy, the last, hectic timpani beats of the Crow's solo crash and Charlie's quiet voice says 'tabs'. She imagines the scarlet curtains falling to the stage like the blood rain of a sacrifice, all that iron tumbling into the soil, keeping all the monsters of the realm hidden from view. She closes her eyes, a little drunk now – and thank God for that, she cannot deal with the rest of the night sober – and sways a little on her ergonomic chair, waiting for AJ's gentle knock.

As soon as the weighted hem of the curtain hits the stage, Mackie is out of the wings, murmuring to Kavi through the headset to guide the act three backdrop down. Against a pale blue background there is an image of a huge half-apple, cut horizontally across to show a star where the pips nestle. The fruit flesh is a pale pink, rimmed by red skin.

Lara nods appreciatively as the backdrop comes down. 'That's beautiful,' she murmurs to Zach. 'One of those things you know, isn't it, that apples have that secret star inside them, but you still hold it the boring way and eat around the outside.'

She glances at him, suddenly unsure. 'Is this one all right to touch?'

Zach grins. 'This one's just fireproof canvas with a pretty picture on it. Tonight, anyway.'

Derek wheels a black flight case marked *PEARL* across the stage as the backdrop lands on the stage and Mackie starts to push a tall white podium into place, snug against the backdrop.

'Almost there,' Derek says as he fusses with the case so the latches are facing Mackie. 'Almost ready for the money shot.'

Mackie ignores him as he opens the flight case and pulls aside the plastic covering. Why Derek has to make everything sound so grubby he really will never know. He flicks the brakes on the podium and reaches for the Pearl, which is always light and delicate in his arms at this point in the show. A few years ago he and Belinda got drunk on New Year's Eve and he had said, *I never set foot in a schoolroom, Belinda, so I ain't got a clue but riddle me this. Why is the Pearl so light in the second interval but I can hardly grasp the bugger in my arms at the end of the show? What's the physics behind the magic of that?* She shook her head long and slow and gulped at her wine. *Mackie, Mackenzie,* she'd said. *They don't teach you that in school. You don't want to know where I spent half my childhood, but I'll tell you something, I didn't learn about the Pearl there either.* Mackie resists the urge to rub it a little with his sleeve. He places it on its little stand and listens for the little click and sigh. Almost there.

In the prompt corner, Charlie takes off his headphones for a moment and rubs his temples. He hates the pressure of the headset against his skull but he can't afford to keep adjusting the gear and miss a cue while the show's on. In the stage left wing Shirley is folding up the Crow's cloak and Danny is re-taping the edge of the dance floor where one of the corps de ballet girls tripped and dislodged it after the Pearl waltz.

Things are subdued in the ladies' dressing room. Everyone is recovering from Michael's solo in the Blue *pas de deux*. Milly furtively swishes a gulp of water around her mouth as she gathers the sweaty Pearl waltz dresses to take them down to wardrobe for steaming. Mara is fastening the bodice of Bella's orchard costume and wondering who she should resign to first, Belinda or Cecile. Bella in turn is fastening Jessica's, who is wondering if she should ask Bella to stop so she can go for a wee before they head down to the stage for beginners. Stephanie is choosing which shoes will be best for the third act, staring into space as she rises onto pointe in each pair before grimacing and taking them off. Harriet is calmly pinning her headdress, giving her head a little shake to test how firmly it's attached, listening with half her attention to the ongoing conversation about the various merits of getting online shopping delivered to Belinda's PO box or your parents' house. Anita would quite like to tell everyone about the time Alex bought her a birthday present from John Lewis and had it delivered to a store in time for him to collect it on a day off, but she can't, even if the story is relevant to the current conversation. She ties her pointe shoe ribbon around her left ankle and wonders how many fairy queens Alex has had to sleep with and whether he liked it.

There is a pointed silence in the men's dressing room. Stuart cried during Michael's solo and everyone is pretending not to have noticed. Luke left the boots from his page costume on the floor and Benji skidded on them as he came back from the bathroom. Josh lost his temper and told

Luke that if he carried on fucking up left, right and centre he would personally see to it that the Crow hauled him out of his bed by his balls after the curfew bell and left him where no one would ever be able to rescue him. There was a sticky moment when Josh looked to Greg to back him up but Greg was staring into space and missed the cue. Romero is eating the second half of his second arancino with his feet up on the dressing table, ignoring both those sulking in humiliation and those nodding righteously to themselves.

A knock at the door and Alina comes in with an adjusted belt for Benji and helps him fasten it. *What died in here?* she wants to ask but she keeps her mouth shut because it's a funny old day today, everyone's a little on edge and besides, it's always a bit dicey making jokes with the boys. Too many of them take themselves a bit too seriously and the rest don't take anything seriously at all. She gives Benji's waist a pat, wishes him good luck for his solo and shuts the door on the silence.

Downstairs, the musician's green room by the stage is filling with a gathering relief that another show is almost done. Sandra the clarinet is telling David the new harp about her aunt's Royal Dalton china collection. Lance is absorbed in his phone, and when Jasper calls across the room to ask which piece of skirt he's lining up for his day off, careless of the fact that Yolanda is sitting by the window, Jean rolls her eyes, Max snorts and Ellie the viola tuts. She woke up in Lance's cabin one frosty morning a year ago and has been noticeably less tolerant of the jokes ever since. Michael is in the bathroom, sitting on the toilet with his head resting in his hands, listening to Wilf's rumbling voice as he makes jokes about Lance's harem. He has gone about everything in the worst possible way, he sees that now. If he'd made a plan with Evelyn, if he'd listened to her, if he'd gone to Belinda for advice, if he'd confided in AJ before he packed up to leave the Grub and broke his pledge, if he'd begged the Crow for mercy, he might still have something left of a life to live.

Cecile sits in her office listening to the pleasant hum of AJ's voice talking about a performance of *Aïda* he saw many years ago. She is sipping at her cognac and gliding just over drunkenness, thinking about when she will sack Greg, tomorrow before class or after rehearsals.

The dancers are beginning to trickle down to the stage now, the little patter of shoes on the concrete steps, the swish of dresses. Belinda walks past Cecile's office door and hears AJ murmuring within. Good, she thinks. Cecile should not be alone today. She notices a puddle beneath a tannoy and, sighing, pulls a tissue out of her handbag and bends to mop it up. No matter what the Crow says, she will have to think about what can be done about Michael.

She passes the noticeboard and pulls open the door to the stage, holding it open for the boy coming up behind her, the newest of the dancers whose name escapes her just now. As she arrives in the stage right wing she sees Zach and the probation LX girl at the prompt desk, Zach spinning a roll of tape on his broad wrists and muttering intently. Looks like that's working out. One less thing to worry about. Charlie leans forwards, presses the button on the prompt desk and murmurs, 'Act three beginners please, act three beginners.'

By the stage right prompt desk, Luke hovers behind Zach's huge bulk, holding his elbows and trying not to shiver. He sniffs, swallows a little mucus and feels a scratch in his throat. Blast. He'll have to suffer through whatever's making its home in him and suffer the indignities of blame for being patient zero of whatever virus is multiplying in his sinuses right now. Better pull himself together. Belinda doesn't sign off on sick days unless she's come to your cabin to inspect your evacuated fluids and pronounced you dying.

He wraps his arms around his torso. He could go back to the dressing room to fetch a jumper or a pair of tracksuit bottoms but he's afraid he'll forget he's wearing them and wander onto the stage with them still on. No one would tell him, they'd all think it a great trick. He'd never live it down.

He can't seem to do anything right. Any attempts to be friendly are rebuffed. Not a single word in support of him this afternoon during the rehearsal where Cecile seemed determined to reduce him to a gibbering mess. The new LX girl had seemed more comfortable here on her probation day than Luke has in six weeks. *Everyone's so friendly here, don't you think?* He looks at her now, leaning close to Zach, who's murmuring to her intently, pointing at the downstage lighting boom. No, he doesn't think people are friendly here. He thinks people are waiting for him to get taken by something from another world so they don't have to vicariously squirm at his mistakes. Romero looked more interested in his snack when he tried to make conversation in the dressing room earlier in the show – but he did offer that little tip for the wedding dance, so maybe not all is lost – and Josh's open contempt after his simple mistake with the boots made that place at the bridge of his nose ache. *No,* he'd pleaded with himself as the silence in the dressing room got tighter and tighter. *Don't cry. That'll be the end.*

Charlie calls beginners and Luke stretches his back a little, pads through his feet. He thinks of the guy he replaced here, someone he knows nothing about except his name – Alex, seen on a bundle of unwashed dancewear he found under the bed in his cabin – and that he had a longer torso than Luke. He's wearing Alex's old costume now, the top of the tunic scratching at his thighs. Alina had wrinkled her nose during his fittings. *I'll give the hem a bit of a tuck and it'll do.* That's Luke all over. He'll do. Barely. In a pinch.

He runs through the notes Cecile gave him – screamed at him – earlier. *Arms go through first,* tour *lands facing front then off into the* scissonne, *eyes up to follow the line in the* arabesque. He's aiming to be completely ignored by her tomorrow. If she doesn't say a word or look at him all day, he'll know he did it all right.

In his lighter moments, on days where he has simply been ignored rather than shouted or sneered at, Luke can allow that the company's cumulative grief might have something to do with the way he's struggling. To lose a friend so suddenly, so finally, without warning or goodbye and have him replaced four days later with a spotty kid on his first job out of ballet school isn't a recipe for a warm welcome. Still, he feels a strange kinship with the disappeared Alex. A bond opposite to that of pledge-mates, perhaps: its inversion. He threw the dancewear into a bin outside Crewe train station on his first day off, but that didn't help him fill the blank space Alex left behind. Here Luke stands in a brocade-and-sequin jacket impregnated with Alex's sweat, he sleeps in a cabin that still now sometimes smells a little like a sandalwood aftershave he must have used, he dances all his roles in the corps de ballet. Sometimes, at night when he's lying in his cabin waiting for the curfew bell, he asks the imagined Alex questions. *Was it you who broke the hinge on the cupboard in our cabin? Did you also find that bit of the orchard dance with the* entrelassé *landing in* arabesque *difficult? Did you leave behind a girlfriend or a boyfriend? In the moments before they took you, did you regret it, working here on this show?*

He feels the heat of a gaze on him and looks around, worried Cecile's down in the wings already, wanting to hiss one last correction he won't be able to remember just before he goes on stage, but Cecile's not there. Instead, he catches the eye of Derek the follow spot operator and turns away very quickly. *Fuck*. He knows Derek's seen him, he always does. Having to talk to Derek would make a very shit day even worse.

Zach and the new LX girl start to climb up the ladder to the lighting box. Luke knows he has to move quickly or he's going to get caught, perhaps trying to get into the other wing or just out into the corridor, but then he feels a tap on his elbow and a scream bubbles up in his throat. He's trapped.

'All right mate,' Derek says, his hot breath uncomfortably close. He smells of engine oil and grease from the bottom of the pan and Luke leans away from him, trying to be as far away from him as he can without moving his feet.

'Happy All Souls'. You got any plans?' Derek laughs in that girlish, giggling way of his that makes Luke's stomach curdle.

'No, no plans.' He smiles weakly. 'Ha ha.'

The first time Derek cornered him in the wings like this it was his first week. Standing in the wings trying to learn all the men's parts in the wedding dance, Derek came too close and stood next to him, the diesel-and-chip-fat smell of him pungent in Luke's nostrils. That first time, he gave him a warm smile because he was desperately lonely and he wanted to show he was friendly.

So what'll do it for you? Derek had whispered with a suggestive leer and for a long moment Luke hadn't had a clue what he was talking about. *Excuse me?* He'd looked politely away from the stage although he really didn't want to – he didn't want to be caught talking in the wings. His teachers at ballet school had been firm in saying that was Not Allowed, but there he was, stuck between the rules of theatre and the rules of life, a place he's not been able to escape since. *Are you for todgers or tits?* Derek had said gleefully and Danny, passing with an armful of act one props, rolled his eyes and said, *Give him a chance, Derek mate, he's not been here five minutes.* Luke had felt his face burn in the dark. *Both, I suppose,* he'd said quietly, feeling the floor swoop beneath him. Why did he say that? What on earth possessed him?

But Derek had nodded. *Respect that,* he'd said. *Backing both horses, fair enough,* and smirked before he moved away. And as Luke watched him go he realised Derek had not expected him to answer. The idea had been humiliation and by answering – truthfully – Luke had willingly lain on the ground in front of a predator with belly and throat exposed.

Not that Derek was much of a predator. By the end of the week, Luke had realised Derek was one of those scavengers who goes around squeezing shame and humiliation and resentment out of people and lapping at the puddles. By the end of the next week he'd realised everyone else on *The Apple and the Pearl* already knew that and not a single one of them had warned him.

By now, a month later, he's understood that the rest of the cast and crew see something similar in him and Derek, something kindred in their lonely awkwardness. A part of him was offended and another part – perhaps a bigger part – wonders if they are all right and he should just give in to it. But knowing you might one day become irredeemable isn't the same thing as being already irredeemable so he still tries to avoid Derek. Except now it is too late. He is stuck until he can escape on to the stage at the beginning of the hunting dance.

Derek nods up the ladder to where Zach had disappeared.

'He'll be wearing deodorant tomorrow,' Derek mutters, with a meaningful look at Luke as though they're conspirators. 'Deferring to the sensibilities of the fairer sex, as if I haven't had to put up with his stink all these years.'

Luke is saved from having to dredge up some kind of response to this by the dimming of the house lights. He hears AJ's baton rap three times on the lectern and there is a hush. Even Derek is quiet. This is Luke's favourite part of the show, this suspension before each act when everything in all the worlds that the Grub and Grit straddle is suspended in the delicate web held between AJ's upturned palms, Charlie's red light and all the molecules of salt in all the pockets.

Charlie says, 'Tabs,' and there is a swish of curtains as the violins begin.

Derek moves closer. 'Had a good show?'

'Ok, thanks.' He should just walk away, he knows it; it's what everyone else does.

Derek leans in further and Luke sees that it's pointless to try to avoid it: this is just a penance he must perform for some unknown sin. Derek's got something to say and he's decided he's going to say it to him.

'You ever wondered how we manage to have a full house every night?' Derek asks. He's got his hands thrust deep into his pockets and is swinging back and forth on his heels. 'You'd think every elf, goblin, imp and sprite from John o' Groats to Land's End has seen this bloody show by now, wouldn't you?'

'I guess so.' He's found the best thing to do is just to let him talk, give him no encouragement and wait for it to end.

'It's just logic.'

Luke shrugs, despite himself. 'What about this show is logical?'

'It makes sense to me.' Derek lowers his voice and Luke stares at the stage where Harriet is stepping into the *arabesque penchée* that all the girls dread. Derek's whisper merges with the violins and Luke has the strange sensation of his mind splitting, like one half of him can hear Derek and the music and the other half is watching Harriet as she wobbles a little.

'Every tree, every rock, every pool of peat bog, every piddling little hill has at least a sprite, maybe even a whole Fae court attached to it. How many can the Grit seat – four, maybe five hundred? Tiny, really. And you know what, once upon a time you'd know the names of every single one of them like they was your family. Every single thing in the world would have had its name and its soul, and when they came here to watch the show the dancers and the musicians and the dogsbody likes of us would have said *Hello, how are you, hope you enjoy the show*. A kind of worship, you know?'

It takes Luke a moment to register that Derek has finished, and two halves of him slam together. He blinks and glances at Derek who is rocking on the soles of his boots in triumph, like he's figured something out of extreme importance.

'Right,' says Luke, feeling a buzzing behind his right ear that is probably another symptom of whatever virus is multiplying in his sinuses. He has no idea what on earth to say to Derek, he never does. 'Right.'

But he is saved by the sight of Cecile in the wings, fingering the beads of pink salt at her neck, watching Harriet on stage. She glances at them, her mouth tightens at the sight of Derek – or maybe him, he can't be sure – then looks back at the stage. *At least she's seen me,* Luke thinks. He tries not to cower. *At least she's registered I'm trying.*

Derek follows Luke's gaze.

'Ah, I see. The queen demands silence, I get it. Don't want to land you in it, mate.' Derek mimes drawing a zip across his lips and Luke wishes there really were jagged bits of metal he could shove into his mouth to shut him up. Then he is conspicuously, blessedly silent.

Harriet finishes her sequence of *fouettés* on one bended knee, her arms open in supplication to the flies, and then she is surrounded by Jessica, Bella and Anita wearing the green dresses of the orchard dance. They each smile brightly at her and Luke can see their smiles are genuinely delighted, their eyes full of encouragement, and Harriet looks back at each of them in turn, tearfully grateful. Luke swallows a cough that has become a lump of disappointment in his throat. *The Apple and the Pearl* is not a harsh, dog-eat-dog world. There is kindness and support and laughter here. Just not for him.

Pull yourself together, he thinks, the voice in his head belonging to his grandmother. *I cannot abide snivelling.* The trumpet sounds a trill and Dan leaps onto the stage, runs to Anita and takes her waist to lift her. Another trumpet trill and Solomon leaps, runs to Bella and lifts her. The third trumpet brings Ritchie on to grab Jessica, and Luke creeps forward, craning his neck to see. This is why he hangs about in the wings every night to risk getting ensnared in Derek's personality disorder; he has to learn this dance, and since nobody will teach it to him at the pace he needs he's going to have to keep showing up and watching it from different angles until he's got it.

Tonight he's focusing on the part Ritchie's dancing. He almost knows it, although he's never done any of the partner work or lifts, and Cecile will inevitably shout at him when he gets the spacing wrong. He's hoping Cecile will call a rehearsal for him to practice, though that might be a little optimistic. He needs one of the girls to guide him through it but the thought of going to one of them to ask if they could spare half an hour to help him makes him feel sweaty. He imagines Zuleika curling her lip. *Ten minutes, new boy. I'm busy.*

Ritchie flings Jessica up into the air and catches her in *arabesque* in his arms. Luke leans to see how his left arm is holding her but they're spinning and he can't see, and by the time they're facing him again Jessica is starting the sequence of *pique pirouettes* away from him. Shit, he's missed it again.

The three couples of the orchard dance run off stage hand in hand as Benji walks on and stands in the stage left corner to begin his solo. Luke wants to creep forward again so he's as close as he can be without actually being on stage but he's afraid people in the wings will think he's trying to learn the Red Suitor too. *Sort yourself out in the corps before you get ideas,* he can imagine Josh sneering.

He will probably never dance the Red Suitor. He's simply

not talented enough, and although that thought used to smart, he's accepted it now. Since he first arrived at ballet school and found that he was merely a mediocre dancer, pleasant enough to watch, he's been taking out that knowledge from the shameful part of himself where he hides it and examining it from different angles, until it no longer hurts.

Benji is what you'd call talented. His lines are clean and he moves like water. Technically accomplished, but not prodigious, he has a way of moving his head and shoulders that makes you sigh a little, like you're watching something beautiful that will soon fade – a sunset or the blooming of a flower. He finishes his solo and Harriet comes on stage. They smile at each other, a private acknowledgement of all the hours of rehearsal that have led them here, and Harriet drops into a deep curtsey to begin their *pas de deux*.

Luke's heard the supposedly inspirational quotes about talent being only a tiny fraction of anything, but nothing in his life has ever suggested they're right. Everything suggests the most important factor in your success is whatever the fairies doled out to you at birth. Perfectly arched feet, a supple back and hips, an easy jump. An attractive face, finding maths easy, perfect pitch, the ability to make strangers laugh. None of which he has. He's not sure if any fairies turned up to his birth at all. He could put a sign up outside the Grit one night before the show – *WANTED: fairies who gave me my talents.* He'd be waiting a long time.

When he puts it like that, he should feel lucky to have this job, any job at all. And he tries to be grateful, really he does. He knows all about how thanking something for the fact that you woke up this morning is good for your brain, but some days – like today – he'd just like a little something more to be grateful for than the fact that he's still alive.

Twenty years and three months old and his life stretches ahead of him like an endless, featureless road, cobbled and potholed for maximum discomfort. Everything he owns could fit in his backpack. Everyone he knows either dead or having to think for a moment to remember him at the mention of his name.

He has nowhere else to go. He remembers watching the show on his probation day, standing between Belinda with her clipboard clamped to her chest and Charlie at the prompt desk, knowing he would dance this show no matter what horrors it contained. He saw it then – that he was not the only lost and lonely soul here. He saw that all of them – even the really cocky ones – were here because they had for whatever reason snipped themselves – or been snipped – out of the web of obligation that tethered you out in the real world and were now floating, free.

Silence as Benji and Harriet finish their *pas de deux*, her perched high above Benji's head. Luke watches Benji as he walks slowly off stage bearing his Princess, sweat beading on his face and neck. Of all the strange things about *The Apple and the Pearl*, perhaps it's the silence that greets each dance that's the hardest to get used to. The idea that all that effort is not acknowledged. Whoever choreographed the show – and Luke's not actually sure if anyone actually knows who did – didn't take that into account. They made the ballet as if it were going to be presented to ordinary audiences in an ordinary theatre. But, he has to admit, there are some parts of the show that emerge as powerful when they happen in silence, like this part, the end of the Red *pas de deux* as the Red Suitor carries the Red Princess off stage with slow, deliberate steps, both of them staring off into the distance.

As soon as Benji and Harriet are in the wings, AJ raises his baton and calls the trumpets. Here we go, he thinks, his chance to redeem himself after the fiasco he made of the first act. Zuleika's not around to see it but Cecile is so he'd better not fuck up. He stands straighter, pulls up his chin and runs onto the stage with Matty and Theo, landing the first *jeté* with the timpani.

Trouble is, as soon as he lands and faces the auditorium he sees the creature again, the same one that distracted him before. It's sitting in the stalls, the third or fourth row and it's luminous, like it's covered in glow-in-the-dark paint.

One of the only nuggets of wisdom anyone passed on to him was the thing about not looking at the auditorium. Stuart, with a hand on his shoulder before his first show. *It's kind of freaky out there, mate. Don't look too hard.*

But of course he had. Hadn't been able to resist. The wonders out there, who alive could say they'd seen what he has in the space of only one month? They look nothing like the fairies in the books he used to read when he was a kid, sitting on the floor in the children's section of the library. Those were all plump cheeks and cute wings and neat little wands they'd use to do good, useful kinds of magic. The things that sit on the plush red seats in the Grit are savage and gorgeous. Their skin shimmers in shades of blue and green and their hair is gold or silver like coins. You can see the sharpened points of their teeth glint in the glow of the footlights. Those who have wings sit with them cramped and folded above their heads like enormous feathered parasols, and those who have horns paint and polish them until they shine. They wear dresses made of fish scales and acorns embroidered with shells and beads of sea glass, and Luke hasn't yet worked out if they're like human audiences and dress up to come to the theatre or if this is the way they dress all the time. He's sure Derek's got something to say about that. *I should ask him*, he thinks as he steps into *arabesque – arms go through first,* he reminds himself – and the thought makes a bubble of laughter rise in his belly.

But the creature that shines at him from the stalls has long silver hair studded with tiny droplets of something, dew, diamonds, the tears of a wolf perhaps. She – and he thinks it is a she because of something soft around the jaw – is draped in a cloak made of what looks like moss and as he follows Matty in the *jeté* sequence in a circle he realises that the creature reminds him of his grandmother. The stillness, the flint of her gaze and the icy cast of her skin. He sneaks another glance at the glowing thing in the auditorium as he prepares for the *pirouette*. Yes, there really is something uncanny in it.

Now she's dead, he thinks of his grandmother as a kind of monumental ruin, a lightning-struck oak in the middle of a fallow field that takes four grudging centuries to rot into the earth. In his memory, she's sitting on a kind of throne she'd carved for herself into the foam of her armchair with the remote on the armrest, the numbers on the buttons worn away from the years of pressure of her thumbs.

This Fae creature has a sour look on her face. Perhaps she's not enjoying the show. It's the sort of look his grandmother used to wear at parents' evening, sitting opposite the polite teachers who needed their notes to remember his name, holding her handbag like a grenade. On the bus on the way home: *Why do I struggle and sacrifice if you're going to throw it back in my face like this?*

I'm sorry, Granny. I'll try harder, I promise. But it had never been in his power to promise anything to her and he had drifted like an abandoned crisp packet through school, and now life. His grandmother had come to see the end-of-year ballet shows and sat in her best coat, thunderous. *Didn't I tell you they're hiring at Boots in the high street?*

He'd felt like he was standing in front of his grandmother again this afternoon as Cecile was shouting at him. *I'm sorry, Cecile. I'll try harder, I promise.*

He lands from a *tour* cleanly and with some relief – *We are changing it to a single until our new recruits are able to accurately perform the choreography,* Cecile had said, bitchily, although he knows his *tours* aren't that bad – and sees that the glowing creature is staring at him. A second of eye contact – *Fuck, that's not good* – and then he turns for the final sequence of *pirouettes* of the dance. It had only been a moment, just a second of connection but still he could swear he saw his grandmother in the creature's eyes.

Six months dead and the old woman haunts him, following him here and thrusting her soul inside some supernatural being. He'd thought there was nothing left she could cling to, the contents of her house gone to the charity shop, the lease back to the council. Derek's voice drifts through his mind as he stands in fourth position for the very last *pirouette*; *Happy All Souls.* Fucking thrilled indeed, Derek.

He follows Theo as the three of them run off stage with the last blast of the trumpet and before he can get away Derek's right there in his face, wagging a finger.

'Tut tut, you naughty boy,' he says, and there is a leer in his eyes that makes Luke's palms itch, wanting to shove at him and send him flying into a lighting boom with a crunch of bone.

'What are you talking about?' Luke whispers, trying to sidestep him, wishing he hadn't said anything at all, just ignored him. He thinks of his grandmother, quietly shutting the door to his bedroom. *When you learn how to speak to people properly you can come out.* He understands that he wants to hurt Derek because he can't punch Josh or Zuleika or Stuart or – heaven forbid, Cecile – and he understands everyone on *The Apple and the Pearl* uses Derek this way, as a kind of violence extractor fan. Which hardly makes it right.

But still. *Do you want to be right, or do you want to be happy?* his grandmother used to say, usually after a smack following some minor mischief. And he'd think sullenly, *Can't I be both?*

But the existence of Derek seems to prove you can't, at least not on *The Apple and the Pearl*. Really, the man deserves it, even seemed to relish it. The unwashed stench of him, that manic, high-pitched giggle, the way he has of sneaking up by your side and saying something so foul or so bonkers or so totally irrelevant that it takes you a few long moments to work out what he's just said, precious moments you could be using to get away from him. Nothing is off limits to Derek, no subject too delicate, no thought too banal. The rest of the crew joke that he's more like a species of gnome than a human – and when he saw him in certain lights, Luke wonders if that might not be so far from the truth.

'I saw you, having a good old gander at the audience, that's not recommended, didn't they tell you that?'

Luke tries to go the other way past him.

'Seriously now, I'll stop mucking about. That's fucking stupid, mate. You don't look too long or hard, or something will notice you and come for you. Eight years on this show and I've seen things to make your hair stand on end.'

'Thanks, Derek,' he murmurs, the music for the White *pas de deux* starting. 'I'll bear that in mind.' He tries to push past again but Derek puts a hand on his shoulder.

'You're a human fucking sacrifice, mate, you know that? That's what this whole thing is. They dangle a little meat in front of them to keep them out of the real world.'

He could punch him, he really could. He really should,

if only to put a stop to this nightly barrage of nonsense. But punching Derek is not likely to win any respect. In fact – and this would be just his luck – it might create sympathy for him and then, horror of horrors, recast Luke himself in the place Derek currently occupies in the hierarchy of *The Apple and the Pearl*. He can imagine Josh's sneer in the dressing room – *Clearly the man's got a problem, why would you treat him like that?*

'Right,' Luke says, finally getting past him. 'Thanks for the heads up, but I've got to get changed for the wedding dance or them out there'll be the least of my problems.'

The door into the corridor is heavy and cool on his sweaty hands and he can feel Derek's eyes on him, that vile smirk, that goblin-like pleasure in causing discomfort.

A human sacrifice, he thinks as he walks up the stairs, unbuttoning his jacket. *Of course we are, and you and me more than most, mate. We're the first they'd offer up if the audience were ever to rush at the stage*, Belinda would be there saying, *No! Take Luke and Derek, we shan't miss them!* and he'd find himself trapped for all eternity with that blasted man and wouldn't that be the best way to end this entirely unpromising start in life.

And who exactly is 'they'? Luke thinks as he walks into the dressing room. Derek is always going on about 'them', muttering as he flips a spanner between his fingers or scratches his arse. Sometimes *them* is Belinda and Mackie, an axis of authority Derek feels only exists to give him grief, but often *them* is the government, or the CIA, or the pharmaceutical companies, or the banks, who are either persecuting or ignoring him because of his phenomenal or dangerous gifts, depending on the day.

Luke peels the dark brown tights from the hunting dance off his legs and down over his shins and pulls the silver tights for the wedding dance from the hanger.

'You seen the notice? Mackie's pledge day drinks in the Grub tonight. Should be a good one.'

He looks up, surprised, thinking someone's actually talking to him but the voice belongs to Solomon, talking to Theo, over his head. Luke is piggy in the middle.

'You coming?' Solomon asks, and Luke hears the sly, shy note of hope in his voice and understands that that's it for Theo, he's been absorbed into the social organism and by this time next week he and Solomon will be a couple, stepping out, fucking. *Courting.* Whatever you want to call it.

Luke takes the white jacket festooned with silver sequins from the hanger and shoves each arm inside. It itches like a devil but at his costume fitting on his second day Alina had been unmoved by his discomfort. *And what do you want me to do about that, sunshine? Line it with silk?*

It's not surprising Theo has been – is being, before Luke's very eyes – snapped up. He watches Solomon bossily beckon Theo to stand in front of him so he can do up the buttons on his wedding jacket. Theo is talented. There is a what-do-you-call-it, *je ne sais quoi* about his dancing, a clarity to his lines and an easy facility in his body. He's not quite as magnetic to watch as Matty, but that's probably to his advantage because he can slide in anywhere in the show and look good.

Luke does up his own buttons, craning his neck. He should go to the pledge day drinks tonight. He wants to – well, he wants to want to – no – he wants someone to want him to go. He wants to be invited beyond the generic notice on the board, he wants someone to notice as he's going back to his cabin and say, *Oh, aren't you staying?* He hears his grandmother in his head, her voice drifting from the mouth of that creature in the auditorium, *Well if you won't join in, what do you expect?*

He thinks about the way at ballet school they'd all be sitting around in someone's bedroom at the hostel, too young to go out to a club but old enough for the off-licence round the corner to pretend to check their ID as they bought some cans and cheap wine. They'd all be sitting in the common room that stank of stale weed and chips, with all the others passing through, the dancers, the musicians, the backpackers and the kids kicked out of home and someone used to get out their phone and play music, tinny in the crap little speakers they make so they'll break after six months. People would get up and dance, cans of cider dangling from their fingertips and soon the floor would clear so that everyone could watch the dancers, half admiring, half horny, watching as they took pleasure in moving their bodies just for themselves, not caring for the aesthetic value for once – although they looked good, of course they did, how could they not? They were just loose limbs and easy rhythm and the certainty that the world belonged to them and no one else.

But Luke was always on the outside of it. Like he was rubbing at the condensation on a windowpane, peeking in, trying to look like he was having fun. Pretending that he would get up and dance if he felt like it, that he was appreciating the vibe. But the older he gets – and he knows this is a stupid thought to have at twenty years and three months old – the more he sees that it was stupid to think he'd look stupid. Vain. Delusional, even. Because now he's realised that no one sees him at all, not on those luminous Saturday nights at ballet school and not here. *Which is worse,* he wonders, *to be perceived only to be ridiculed or not to be perceived at all?*

The music for the White Princess's solo starts and Luke joins the trot of dancers heading out of the dressing rooms and down the two flights of stairs to the stage. Sequins and silver and gold everywhere, spangled headdresses for the girls and itchy, sparkling jackets for the boys. Pointe shoes tap on the concrete and the wooden stage floor as everyone crowds into the stage right wing, ready for the finale of the show.

He is relieved to see Derek's boots disappearing up the ladder above Charlie at the prompt desk as he arrives in the wings. *Thank fuck for that.* Luke is gloomy now. He stifles a cough, swallows, feels his throat a little constricted by the beginning of swelling in his tonsils. Bollocks, he's definitely getting ill. Maybe that's what he'll say in the unlikely event of anyone asking after him tonight. He'll give a wry smile and shake his head. *Think I'm coming down with something. Don't want to pass it around.*

There is an air of relief in the wings. The bright smiles are beginning to sag and the mascara starting to smudge. *One more push and we're through until tomorrow,* say the wriggles inside the too-tight costumes. *Looking forward to my dinner,* say the rolled necks and massaged shoulders. There they gather, all the dancers of *The Apple and the Pearl*, everyone watching Stephanie as she steps into *arabesque* and the last few notes echo around the Grit.

The finale is no one's favourite part of the show, except in the sense that it's all almost over, with showers, hot food, cold beers and soft beds awaiting them all in the Grub. The music is brassy, a little bit vaudeville or Hollywood musical for most people's tastes, but there's an undeniable sense of joy that comes from the pit as the tune goes *pom-pa, pom-pa, pom-pa-POM* and they all surge onto stage together, sequins spangling, catching the light, letting all that trombone blast through them as they surge onto the stage to surround Stephanie, kneeling centre stage with her eyes on the floor.

Romero's advice: *Travel the* assemblés *and then you'll be right in front of the King* mingles with Cecile's voice in his ear: *Keep the spacing, hold the* coupé *for a count of two and watch Ritchie if you're too stupid to count for yourself. Watch the line of the chin, you're not a woodpecker.* He follows the circle as it swirls, then spins out to the stage left corner – *Feet tight in the* chainé, *Luke! I could get a bus through there!* – and throws his arms out in what he hopes is a nobly celebratory manner towards where Greg and Mara stand at the back of the stage.

He watches the wave of bows and curtseys as Greg sweeps Mara past everyone, trying not to dip his own head too early or too late – *This is the climax of the show, I am begging you not to fuck it up.* Snot drips out of his nostril and into the groove under his nose and resignedly he stands, arms aloft, waiting for it to curl over his top lip and into his mouth. So undignified but that's ballet for you. A shiny parcel bedecked with ribbons and gilt with nothing but humiliation and pain inside.

He is facing upstage and glad of it, because the temptation to stare into the stalls for another glimpse of that creature is strong, but his fear of Cecile shouting at him if he faces the wrong way is stronger. This must be what Belinda warns you about. *Stronger and stranger than you can imagine. Do not think you will be able to dally, you will not.*

The Princesses are dancing in unison with their Suitors and this is it, they are wed and they will live happily ever after, and there are only a couple more steps to be danced tonight and he performs them, *chassé pas de bouree, glissade – Sharp second foot please, I don't care if it's late in the evening, I don't want to see sloppy footwork* – and then he melts towards the wings with all the rest of the dancers, but before he goes he contrives to turn to face downstage towards the audience for one last glimpse – and he will defend himself if he must, but he has to see that creature again – but it's too late, he is already in the wings and the creature is out of his sight, on the other side of the proscenium. His disappointment is a warning to him. That creature is not his grandmother, it's a fairy creature from another world. And it's not like he particularly wants to see his grandmother again, but the hollow feeling in his stomach is another warning. He must be lonely if he's missing her.

The timpani starts for the Crow's solo and Luke stands in the wings, shoulder to shoulder with the full cast of *The Apple and the Pearl* and all their accompanying sweat. Benji is sitting on the floor behind Charlie, looking slightly green, Romero grinning and rubbing his shoulders. Harriet stands in a gaggle of silent well-wishers in sparkly silver dresses, and from here they look like they're in a kind of cult doing some type of spiritual healing, laying their hands on her to absorb some of the adrenaline coursing through her. That's an unkind thought. They're just congratulating her for a good show, just telling her she did well. So easy to be a dick, or at least have dickish thoughts, when you're on the outside of things.

Luke would like to say something to Harriet or Benji, or even both of them, *Well done* or *Hope you had a good show* or *I thought you did great*, but he has no idea if it would be welcome. Is it too familiar, an assumption of some kind of connection they definitely don't have? Or is it rude not to say anything at all? Does everyone know these kind of things, or do they just bet and win more often than not? Is everyone just pretending? He imagines a stage full of wooden marionettes, their puppet masters and mistresses sending out their stiff simulacra into the world to keep their own meat safe. Only idiots like him and Derek didn't get the memo, wandering about the world all soft and squirmy and squishable. *It's legerdemain, mate*, he imagines Derek drawling, wiggling his fingers and waggling his eyebrows like a drunken pier-end conjurer. *It's all an illusion*.

The discordant cello and clarinet fall off and now it's just the timpani, beating out the last notes as Josh walks slowly upstage, the cloak dangling from his cruel, broad shoulders. Luke licks away a drip of mucus from his nose that's half the impending cold and half the impending tears. *Not yet,* he tells himself. *Get back to the Grub first.*

Charlie says 'tabs' and from the corner of his eye, Luke can see the curtain start to fall, the drum slowing as it descends along the line of the proscenium. When it hits the stage it makes a clinking sound, bounces a little, and a moment later Luke surges with the rest of the dancers onto the stage and stands on the end of the back row, back straight, eyes determinedly on the swirl of Anita's hair directly in front of him. The voice of his grandmother in his ear, *I know you'll peek, Lukey, you're a naughty little boy at heart and you never do as you're told.*

Charlie's voice from the wings, 'Tabs up', the creaking of the fly ropes and the scarlet tide of the curtain begins to lift.

There is no applause, there never is, but still, some of the company miss it. *Don't you think a theatre needs that sound?* Evelyn used to say to Michael as they lay in his bed together. *Don't you think the very bricks are soothed by it?*

The dancers are arranged on stage with the King, Queen and Crow in the front line in the centre. On either side stand the three Princesses and their Suitors, slick hand in slick hand. Behind them are two rows of corps de ballet, a neatly poised back foot for the women, a dignified bent knee for the men.

In the flies, Kavi holds on to the ropes that haul the curtain. It won't fall, the tension is perfectly weighted, but he likes to keep his fingers touching the rough weave of the hemp so he can feel every quiver. Mackie stands in the stage left wing with an iron rod warming in his palm – an old tip from Juliet, just in case. In the stage right wing, Cecile, fingering her necklace of polished pink rock salt, plans her *adage* exercise for tomorrow's ballet class as she watches Greg take his bow. Belinda stands next to her, rubbing the salt in her pocket between her forefinger and thumb, leaning to one side to peer into the auditorium. In the pit, AJ stands still on his podium with his baton resting on the music stand and his hands clasped together. His orchestra are on their feet before him, heads bowed towards the scores on their music stands so they don't have to look out into the auditorium and see what's coming next. All except Henry, who looks out into the auditorium as he does every curtain call, desperately trying to catch the eye of something, anything that will take him away.

And then bells ring out into that silence that never fills with applause like in an ordinary theatre, an unholy clanging that comes from nowhere but echoes inside each mortal soul's heart like a bassline, somewhere above Kavi and below Jasper's timpani at the back of the pit. This is what sends the fair folk reeling into a frenzy, that rolling roaring sound, the arpeggios of bells played as if they are harp strings. They start to sing and shout and stamp their feet and the sound is like all your nightmares jumbled and minced for a pie. This is their applause. Maybe. Perhaps the sounds of their displeasure would be the same. Perhaps they are singing in their own ancient language. Perhaps the show is a kind of call and response and this is the bit where they sing back at the mortals, how they tell the story of the curse and the quest and the Crow in her nest, the story of the show they've just danced, a story the creatures of the auditorium probably consider they've told wrong, in the way you always think other people tell the old tales you love wrong. Perhaps there is a kind of harmony underneath it all, based on a scale unknown to mortal ears, made of notes no mortal throat could make.

Up in the lighting box, Derek starts to unplug the follow spot, warm to the touch and humming a little, satisfied with its night's work. Beside him, Zach watches Lara's mouth fall open in a perfect *O*, something Zach thought only happened in books.

A haze starts to drift upwards from the seats, filling the auditorium with tiny speckles of glittering light. They swirl a little, as if shunted about by brisk winds and the haze starts to separate into individual forms. A curly haired child clutching a battered ukulele; an elderly man carrying a severed arm over his shoulder; a woman winding a long braid of hair around her head.

Lara is struggling to contain her tears. All her life alone with all the secrets people hide in their graves and now she's found herself here, a place where every single night everyone else can see the dead too. For she has no doubt everyone else knows what's happening. The dancers on stage and the musicians in the pit have shut their eyes, flinching at the sight of what the dead are dragging behind them as they rise further towards the gilded stucco of the auditorium ceiling. But Lara is used to the sight of the bloodied gashes of stab wounds and failed surgeries, the haemorrhages of childbirth and the organ rot of cancers, and so she keeps watching to see the details of their faces; every one a person with a soul and a story, she tries to catch a glimpse of each of them to be one last witness to their life.

She cannot tell where all these souls were during the show – and she suspects the answer to that is not a simple one – but it's clear they're being called here by both the bells and the fair folk's howling and squalling and maybe also by – there, Lara sees it at last, swooping among the bodies and their parts, the Crow soaring with wings outstretched, herding the dead like sheep into a swarming vortex.

She swallows. Derek's leer in the wings earlier: *A clever girl like you probably knows all about the Crow, don't you?* She has a dreadful sense that something horrible is going to happen, but not to her, not to Zach, not to anyone on stage or in the pit. The dead are getting agitated now because the Crow is pushing the mass of them towards the stage and they do not seem to be able to resist, and now Lara knows she is the only one who knows that this is terrifying for the phantoms – those who had thought that the only good thing about being dead is that they are beyond pain and fear at last – but there is one last portal to enter and they cannot escape it. There, at the back of the stage, sitting in that star-shaped pip-space in the middle of the pink flesh of the Apple, is the Pearl, gleaming placidly. Waiting.

And then the bells stop and the fair folk fall abruptly still and the air is vibrating with the sudden silence, leaving behind a jangling in Lara's ears. The Crow's wingspan widens as it dives towards the stage, driving the dead before it. Lara bites her lip to keep herself from calling out, because the silence is the worst bit of all as the whirl of souls pour across the pit and over the dancer's heads, right into the Pearl. The Crow sweeps upwards at the last moment and turns back into the auditorium, disappearing into the gilt as the last of the dead are gulped up on stage.

On her headset, Lara hears Charlie call 'tabs' for the last time tonight, and the crimson curtains start to descend between the audience and the dancers. The orchestra are starting to leave the pit, with AJ at the very back, as always. As soon as the hem of the curtain touches the vinyl of the floor, Zach turns the dial to bring the house lights up and starts fiddling with the cables by his feet.

Lara has the distinct feeling that Zach is trying to give her space to think about what has happened, while also trying to convey that this parade of the dead is normal, happens every night, and is nothing to get in a stew about.

Derek gives a loud and theatrical sigh and cracks his knuckles. He shifts out of the follow spot seat, kneels among the mass of snaked cables and looks up at Lara with a knowing glint in his eye.

'You see, girl, and I know Zachary won't have told you this because that's not the way his mind works, but the world goes in circles and cycles, and there isn't anything here that hasn't happened before and won't happen again. Every night me and Zachary sit here and we watch the dead go into the Pearl, and every night we pack away this gear and every night we climb up through the tunnel to get back to Charlie and the others, dismantling the show we set up not thirteen hours ago. And I don't ask where the days are going or how they fall away from us because some things aren't given to us to know, you hear me?' Derek pauses to pick up a cable to wind it around his elbow and Lara glances at Zach, who is concentrating on his switches and dials and pretending not to listen. 'Around and around and around. That's the problem with humans. You forget the earth is a circle.'

And because all the little creatures crowded into the lighting box around Derek are staring at her with wide, dumb eyes, Lara takes the cable Zach hands her and starts to wind it up, squeezing the heavy thickness of the plastic in her palms.

Half past nine and Belinda stands just inside the stage door with her clipboard pressed to her chest, leaning against the wall, listening. Members of the orchestra wait behind her in a quiet, patient queue, instruments packed up in their cushioned cases, evening dresses and tuxedos safely stowed away in the dressing rooms. As always, Wilf the cellist and Steve the bassoon are at the front. They like to get to the dining car first to crack open new bottles of whisky before Gino serves dinner.

The dancers start to join the queue at the other end of the corridor, sweaty hair covered with hats, tide marks of make-up at their chins and foreheads. Soon, there will be queues in the Grub for the showers and the drains will run with the watery residue of sweat and hairspray and blister fluid. Gino never lays out all the food until the first dancers arrive, soap-scented and starving. He has a soft spot for their hollow legs and little patience for the cavernous appetites of Wilf and Steve and that gang of carousers.

The bell rings with a single, solemn peal, its deep bass humming through the mist, and Belinda twists the iron key in the lock and stands back as Wilf and Steve shuffle past her.

'It's completely black out here, Belinda!' Wilf booms as he stops at the top step of the Grit and rests his cello on his large paunch. 'Could you sling us a torch or two? This isn't health and safety.'

Belinda rolls her eyes but before she can answer the corridor is awash with bright yellow light and it spills out onto the steps to illuminate the avenue between the mausoleums.

'It's called modern technology, Wilf,' says Max the second violin, trotting down the steps with his phone held up in front of him, screen shining out across the graves like a beacon. 'You should try it some time.'

The bell is supposed to be an all-clear, to tell them that the last of the Fae have slunk back to wherever they came from and everyone can walk freely again. But it doesn't always work that way. That's why it's safest to leave the Grit in a herd; stragglers get picked off. That's one of the first things Belinda tells them, on the day of their first pledge. *It's a little grey area, that part of the day, and if you're sensible you'll not try and make it black or white. Stick with the others, at least three is best, and if any of the fair folk catch you at the stage door and ask you to take a drink with them after the show, then you smile and you shake your head politely, and you'll find it a good idea to bow or curtsey a little so you're not looking at them in their violet eyes, and you say you'd love to but you really mustn't, such a long day and another show tomorrow, and you back away slowly but surely and you don't stop until you're inside the iron carapace of the Grub and you count anything you call lucky that they didn't take you by force.*

Cecile and AJ are last, as always. They check the green rooms and the dressing room, and when they are empty they meet at the noticeboard, then proceed to Belinda at the stage door. She watches them coming, raven and blackbird,

AJ's tall and lanky frame next to scrawny Cecile, and she wonders if they feel the weight of this show as she does, if they wake in the night with something black and fearful squatting on their chest.

'*Ça va*?' Cecile asks Belinda as they pass.

'All fine, thank you.' Belinda says. She never knows whether to try to answer in French or not. She fancies she might have a few sentences in her, just from listening to Cecile over the years, but she wouldn't want to embarrass herself. 'Just to say, I'll be posting the notice of next day off later and it looks like it'll be a station just outside Oxford if you want to make your arrangements.'

'*Très bien*,' says Cecile and she pulls her phone out of her black leather handbag.

AJ gallantly offers Cecile his arm. 'Goodnight, Belinda.' he says, and they walk down the steps of the Grit and out into the night.

Belinda watches the procession of lights up the avenue towards the Grub. She sees one light peel off from the others and zigzag through the maze of graves. The changeling, taking his chances again. She sighs. The Crow says to wait, Gino says *please can we have milk we can drink*, Derek says *he's more human than me but that's not saying much*, the bells ring kings and queens and suitors in a dream. Likely he'll find himself back in the Grub by midnight, ready to try again tomorrow but wouldn't the simplest thing for him to get his wish and go to Faerie so they can all move on and forget about him?

She looks back to the train. The first musicians are there now: she can see their phone torches reflecting on its sleek surface, rectangles of light blinking on as they reach their cabins, sink onto their beds, release the tensions of another day. Good. Inside the Grub they're safe. If they stay there.

She turns the iron key to lock the stage door and goes back into the heart of the Grit to start the next job she has to complete before midnight. A quick stop by her office to pick up her sack and her litter picker, and then out into the stage right wing where Shirley is flicking the clasps on a flight case, through the pass door and into the auditorium.

She starts with the stalls as always. The house lights are up so all the little trinkets glitter as she methodically works her way along each row picking them all up and dropping them in her sack. It looks a little bizarre, this bag, with the canvas rotted and threadbare with unexplainable stains near the drawstring, but the Crow keeps it looking like an artefact from a tomb to deter light fingers.

Tonight she finds little sprays of diamonds like raindrops; turquoise earrings; silver coins that would cover her palm; an emerald as big as an egg. Some of it will be trick gold, of course, but there'll be enough here to pay the salaries of the cast and crew and settle all the bills Gino racks up.

Percy Montgomery used to wear thick leather gloves for this task, crawling along the rows like a penitent monk, but she has no desire for the stage crew to witness her on her knees each night and her sciatica wouldn't have it anyway.

The litter picker was £5.99 from Asda and the Fae-cursed trinkets are handily confused by the plastic.

She pincers a rope of dull gold coins and the thing explodes in successive puffs of green smoke. The sounds of hammering and drilling on stage stop abruptly.

'It's all right,' she calls down to Mackie. 'I'm fine. As you were.'

Josh hangs upside down, stretching his hamstrings with his towel draped over his neck and his washbag at his feet. He pedals through his arches, releasing one tense calf muscle at a time, listening for the sound of the shower in the bathroom cabin switching off. Really – and it isn't just him who thinks so, loads of the guys moan about this – there should be a strict policy about who can shower first and it should go: principals, soloists, corps de ballet, finishing with the newest pledges who did nothing more challenging in the show than standing around holding hands. That's how it used to be, seven years ago when he first pledged. He remembers getting into his bed salty from sweat, leaving black smudges of eye make-up all over his pillow, getting up early to shower the previous night's show off him before he went up to the Grit to class.

But now it's a new, egalitarian era. *We're getting rid of that toxic shit,* Mara says, jabbing her finger whenever the subject comes up, *the only fair way is first come first served.* Fine. It's socialist showers, whatever. But it doesn't actually make things easier. There's a stampede for the Grub as they leave the show, especially on a night like this where the water ran cold in the dressing rooms in the Grit and no one could even have a strip wash to get the most offensive funk off them at the sink, and now the corridors of the Grub are filled with dancers in varying states of undress, stretching aching muscles in the steam that seeps from the bathrooms.

The sound of shower spray stops and he stands up. Whoever's in there better be out in a few seconds or he's going to start banging on the door: maybe he'll even pull rank, sod Mara, she can't hear him. Behind him one of the corps de ballet girls is on her phone, the key sounds left on so it beeps with every touch. The noise is beginning to get on his nerves. He's always sensitive to sounds after dancing the Crow. It's all that intense concentration on the irregular rhythms, all that furious counting. The others say after a few months of shows even the Crow's music comes naturally to you and you stop having to count your way through the entire show, but that's not happened to him yet. Tonight was his fifteenth show of the Crow and still he was in his head the whole way through, relying on the memory of Cecile's voice shouting *un-deux-trois-NON!* at him during the weeks and weeks of rehearsals.

The bathroom door opens and Ritchie comes out, towel wrapped around his waist and clothes slung over his arm. He sees Josh and his face falls blank as he presses his naked back to the fogged-up window to let Josh past. Josh murmurs, 'Thanks,' and shuffles past him into the bathroom with his gaze squarely on his feet so there's no chance he might catch Ritchie's eye again. Josh shuts and locks the bathroom door behind him and the phone beeping in the corridor fades to nothing.

The water is still running hot and he gets under the stream, turns it up hotter, and lets the water sweep everything away. All the tension from his back, all the thick, black make-up on his face and shoulders, the sudden rush of desire at the sight of Ritchie's bare, dripping torso. He squeezes his eyes shut and leans on the tiled wall behind the shower, letting the almost scalding water pummel his back.

A rhyme his grandfather used to mumble comes into his mind, something about pigeons and crows and seeds growing. It puts him in mind of the Saturday afternoons when Mum was working at the Woolworths in town and Dad was at the scrapyard. Josh was judged too young either to tag along with them or do his own thing, so he'd have to go down to the allotment with his grandfather. In the summer it was golden, squeezing raspberries between his thumb and forefinger until he could feel the give of the sweet, pink juice in each cell of the fruit, carting watering cans from the tap to the tomatoes with cold, dank water slopping onto his trainers. In autumn he was put to work, digging up carrots and building net cages and hoeing up potatoes. In winter it was boring, sitting in the cold shed with icy fingers and toes while Grandad sipped on whisky and told the same three stories about the war. But the best days on the allotment were in spring, those weekends where the light was eager and new, with the daffodil trumpets proud on the verges and the hawthorn hedges shyly unfolding their emerald buds. That's when his grandfather would haul himself off his stool, open the twists of brown paper with his fumbling, arthritic fingers and pour a tiny pile of last year's saved seed into Josh's waiting, careful palms. *One for the pigeon, one for the crow, one to rot and one to grow,* his grandfather would murmur like a prayer to the earth, as he'd point to where Josh should press the seeds into the cold ground. Years later, after Josh had swapped Saturdays at the allotment for ballet classes, he stood by his cousins and his dad as the undertakers lowered his grandfather's coffin into the waiting grave. *One to rot and one to grow,* he'd whispered, feeling like the ponce his family accused him of being, but knowing Grandad, wherever and whatever he now was, knew exactly what he meant.

He turns off the shower and grabs his towel. He's hungry now, the adrenaline of the show seeping out of his blood and leaving behind it something clawing in his belly. He presses his face into his towel, trying to wipe Ritchie's face from his mind. That disapproval, that sting of hurt, that sense that he's carrying that night like a bomb he could drop at any moment.

He leaves the bathroom without looking at the girl still waiting and goes directly to his cabin where he dresses hurriedly. Now something for the pigeon, the greedy, gobbling thing that lives inside him and makes him do stupid things from sheer appetite. He pulls the door to his cabin shut and shrugs a jumper over his head. It smells musty, like all his clothes, but the personal washing machine in the Grit is fully booked for tomorrow. He'll just have to wait and smell in the meantime.

Like every night, the dining car is full of musicians starting on their second bottles of wine and dancers sitting cross-legged on chairs pushing food around their plates. Lance the trumpet is nuzzling Yolanda's neck but as he takes a sip from his beer Josh notices him glance at Mara, deep in conversation with Stuart. Michael sits on his own, writing in a notebook with his empty plate pushed aside and in the next booth sits Henry the new violinist, who is staring at Michael with that usual hungry gaze. What exactly is it about Michael that has driven this extremely good-looking man to distraction? What is it about the earplugs, the greasy hair and the weird shit like the mushrooms earlier that gets Henry's blood going when he could have almost anyone on the Grub? Perhaps it's the helplessness that's a turn-on, the tragedy of it, the sheer magnitude of the love Michael must have borne for the old harpist that makes Henry a fool. If only Michael was like Anita, locking up his old love behind a wall of silence and taboo. That's the proper thing to do with feelings. Tie them up in a bin bag and give them to Belinda for her to take to an incinerator on the next day off.

The queue moves slowly and Josh glances around the dining car. The feeble attempts at decorating the carriage for Halloween are still up: the four plastic skeletons looming over them in each corner; the orange and black streamers strung with Sellotape from wall to wall; and a pumpkin squatting on an empty table without its candle. Two nights ago a few of the corps de ballet girls were wearing nylon witches' hats and he was genuinely amazed by the sight of them. Is there not enough spooky shit going on here? Tonight the fancy dress has disappeared and everyone is miserable again. Good.

But Josh remembers seeing something on the notice-board about a pledge party and he curdles. Sod that. He'd rather go to bed and browse bullshit on his phone while Greg reads his boring books about anatomy – he's studying to be a massage therapist after he retires, following the obvious route off the stage for a lost and limping ex-dancer, and God forbid he should actually do anything out of the ordinary – and they both pretend to be sitting in companionable silence.

The hunger in his belly is beginning to sour into a bad mood. Shouldn't he be able to go straight to the front? To walk past all these others and get a tray of something hot and filling and eat it wherever he likes? He's the Crow, tonight at least. He's been here for seven years, obeying the rules, paying his dues. This place is constant lines and sharing and trying not to get in anyone else's space. It's like nursery school without the naps and gold stars. He watches Luke meander through the booths with his full tray, looking for somewhere to sit. *Just sit the fuck down,* Josh thinks viciously. Why does that kid wind him up so much? *I seem to remember you also found the orchard dance hard in your first couple of months,* Greg had said mildly last week at breakfast and Josh had ignored him so as not to throw his cereal at the wall.

He shuffles forwards in the queue as Gino doles out steaming plates of food and all around him the noise of the dining car drifts like smoke from its little islands around the tables and booths. Just in front of him is the table where the three musicians sit each evening, holding court on any and every topic under the sun, especially those they know little about. Wilf the cellist and Steve the bassoon and Jasper the timpani, who he feels as if he knows well now, after the traditional rehearsal with just him, Jasper and Cecile, counting and stamping out the irregular rhythms of the Crow's solos. They remind him of his granddad and great-uncles, sitting in the kitchen or on the patio or on the fold-up chairs at the edge of the common, the whisky draining from the bottle, the years-old conversations, the jokes, the soft silences, the hard gazes.

'…So that's why he'd say that there'll never be harmony aboard this train, because we're all trapped in a hierarchy that privileges the already powerful.' Wilf sits back with a smirk and takes a sip of his beer. Josh tries not to listen, tries to keep his mind on the queue and the menu options but their voices boom, dominating everything. They are the lords of the Grub. The dining car is their feasting hall and they know everyone knows it.

'But we *are* a collective,' Jasper is saying as he adjusts his eyepatch, the pointed tip of his grey goatee quivering.

'We don't have a dictatorial leader. We have customs and traditions we all follow because we want to and we see the value in them.'

'No dictatorial leader! Have you heard the way Cecile talks to the dancers!'

'But she's not in charge of me, I do what I want.' Steve sits back and folds his hands over the belly he's cultivated over years of beer and bassoon.

'As long as you play the right music for the show,' says Wilf.

'But that's what I mean! I'm held here by the conventions of classical music, yes, but also everything that's special about this place.' Jasper clicks his fingers. 'The pledge and the bell and all that, not by some authoritarian crackpot holding me hostage.'

'I think you're forgetting Belinda.'

'She's not in charge. She's an administrator.'

'And you'd say that to her face, would you?'

'Come on, Belinda's at best a lieutenant.'

'So who's in charge?'

'No one,' says Jasper.

'*The Apple and the Pearl*,' says Steve.

'The Crow,' says Wilf.

And just then, Josh reaches the front of the queue and Gino beckons him forward to the serving hatch. He passes the table where the three men sit each evening and as he shuffles past they look up from their table, catch his eye, and as one tip their pint glasses to him.

'To the Crow,' says Wilf with one of his booming chuckles.

'To the Crow,' say Steve and Jasper, and they all drain their beers and slam them on the table with a crack that echoes like a shot.

Gino waits with a ladle in one hand, a plate in the other and an expectant smile on his face. 'What's it for you this evening?'

'The sweet potato, please Gino.'

'Good choice,' he says, spooning dumplings and curry onto the plate. 'A new recipe and it needs a little adjustment but not too bad.' He slides the plate across the serving hatch. 'Here's yours and I've got the other in the hot drawer when you're ready.'

'Thanks, Gino, I'll be back for it.'

One for the Crow, he thinks, as he weaves his way among the tables to where Greg, Mara and Stuart sit, eating quietly. Greg shifts his chair and slides his thumb over Josh's hand as he sits down. 'Good show?' he asks gently. Greg does everything gently. He's the kind of guy who'd hold your hair back as you're puking from too much tequila and never try to worm his way into your bed as payment, let you store the stupid things you bought online in his cabin while you sort the returns and wait for a day off to lug them to the post office, turn up to meet your parents with flowers for your mum and a firm handshake for your dad. Josh doesn't deserve him. He never has.

'Yeah, fine,' he says, shovelling sweet potatoes with his fork. 'You know.'

'Your second act solo was good.' Mara says. 'You landed

all those *tours* perfectly. Cecile won't have a thing to say about it.'

Josh waves his fork morosely. 'I'm sure she'll find something.'

He eats without pausing, plunging forkful after forkful into his mouth, only half listening to the conversation. Stuart is talking about an article he read this afternoon about spiders that roam the sky, and Greg is chiming in with stories of his brother's pet tarantula. Josh has heard these stories, first from Greg and then from his parents during that awkward lunch two years ago, when the Grub stopped in Chelmsford for a day off and Greg's dad picked them up at the station. He's heard all the stories Greg has to tell by now. They live the same lives, know the same people, live the same day over and over again. All that changes is Gino's menu and their roles in the show. Although Greg's knees are too shot to perform anything but the King or the corps de ballet these days, so his life is even more boring. He should retire. Josh can see he's in pain, has to lie there every night while Greg faffs about with pillows between his legs, has to help him to the ice bath, has to watch him grimace his way through the first part of ballet class while he waits for his threadbare, creaky cartilage to warm up.

It's obviously Cecile's job to say something, except she won't because the last time she sacked someone it was Charlotte, who was snatched a few days later. It's a chink in Cecile's armour, that day when Charlotte got taken. Never spoken of anymore, never mentioned, but a small nugget of power the dancers have clawed back from her. Sometimes Josh catches her watching Greg do an exercise with something like grief twisting her mouth, and when he's had a couple of beers he fantasises about Cecile telling Greg he has to leave, and then Greg being snatched. No, the fantasy is not about Greg being snatched, it is about how Josh will behave afterwards. How he'll empty out their cabin of Greg's things and give them to Belinda without a single tear. How he'll sit in dignified silence in the dressing room as he gets ready for the show. How he'll bow his head in curtain calls, how he'll go discreetly to bed with anyone he wants: Ritchie, Theo, Solomon, Jack the double bass, Henry the violinist. Unbidden, the memory of Ritchie's bare torso flashes through his mind. He was drunk, they were all drunk, it was a pledge renewal and Greg had – unusually for him – peaked early and gone to bed. The night before a day off and the Grub was a carnival of bacchanalia. Even Belinda was there, sipping on a G and T, masterminding the gentle *hissssss* of pressure from the assorted cast and crew, letting just enough desperation escape for them all to be able to get through the next month of shows without mutiny. It was enough to send him to bed with Ritchie. The smell, the taste, the difference of him, the way he moved so surprisingly Josh was knocked him off his metaphorical feet again and again.

Greg is saying something. Josh doesn't bother to listen because it barely matters and he'll have either heard it before or will hear it again, and Mara and Stuart laugh.

'All right, that's me.' Mara stacks a couple of the dirty

plates on her tray and stands up. 'Going to get an early night.' She'll dance the Crow tomorrow and she's conscientious these days about her sleep and her warm-ups. 'The privileges of age, gentlemen.'

Josh glances at the clock on the wall. Ten thirty-two. There was a time when he'd have thought that was early, a party only just started. Now he's bone-weary at this time every night, especially after a big show. Ballet is ageing: it disintegrates your cells until you're nothing but ash covered in sequins. He's twenty-seven and already feeling his ankles freeze and his shoulders seize. No wonder Greg can hardly move on cold mornings. The privileges of age.

'Night, Mara,' he mumbles through his dinner.

Stuart, who only has to do the orchard and wedding dances tomorrow, slaps Josh on the back and follows Mara, stopping briefly to chat to Benji, Zuleika and Romero, who are sharing a plate of the tiny chocolate truffles Gino makes for you whenever you debut a role. Josh and Greg sit alone at their table while the noise of the dining car swells with alcohol and the sweet, blessed release of another show done on this eternal tour.

There's a little tap on the table and Josh looks up, fork half to his mouth. It's the oboe, Jean, smiling at Greg. She looks distracted, clutching her phone in one hand, the grey wisps of her hair breaking free from the old lady barrette she wears.

'Is tomorrow still okay for our appointment?' she asks. Greg's giving out free massages to anyone who wants them, trying to get his hours in for his qualification. Josh used to volunteer but now he makes excuses because it is too terrible to lie there with Greg's hands on him and feel nothing but irritation.

'Of course! I don't have any rehearsals, so I'll see you at three.' Jean's phone trills and she glances at it, flushes and hastily excuses herself.

'There's a bloke,' Josh mumbles as he chews a parsnip.

'What?'

'Jean. Giddy as a bride. I bet you anything she's seeing someone.' So much easier to gossip about others rather than deal with the sterile wreck of his own life.

'Someone in the outside world?' Greg sips his beer. 'I've always thought she and Mackie would suit each other.'

Josh shrugs. 'Could be Mackie. He might be texting her from the Grit, sending her cheeky photos.'

Greg laughs. 'No! Mackie's a gentleman. That's the sort of thing Derek would do.'

'Maybe Jean's secret lover is Derek.'

Greg grimaces. 'Now you're going too far. Jean is a lovely lady and I absolutely refuse to think of her involved with that gremlin.'

Josh grins, but he wishes Mara and Stuart were still here. They would get a lot of comic mileage out of the idea of Derek's romantic relations.

Silence again, filled only with Josh's sticky mouthfuls and Greg slurping at a beer. He is jealous of Jean, he realises, jealous of that secret blush on her neck, jealous of a passion that he is now not sure he has ever had with Greg. *Just break up with me already,* Josh thinks, *let this thing rot.* Because of course it is rotten. They planted something years ago and it had all the potential of a seed tucked up tight in the warm, damp soil, but nothing ever germinated, no shoot or roots ever troubled it. Yet still they're here. Sharing a cabin, sharing a stage, sharing a life.

Greg takes a breath ready to say something and although he loathes himself for it, the long force of habit makes Josh look up from his plate.

'Yeah?'

'What?'

'You looked like you were going to say something.'

Greg smiles, that faraway expression still on his face. 'No. I don't think so. No. Just that I think I'm going to get in the shower.' He puts his empty bottle on his tray, screws up a paper napkin between his palms and Josh has the terrifying, elating thought that his partner has a secret from him. Perhaps he really does know who Jean's screwing. Maybe he wants to tell him that Michael finally gave in to Henry the hot violinist's relentless pursuit and that business with the mushrooms in class was actually a sex thing. Maybe he's had sex with Henry himself!

But he says none of that. Habit wins. 'You'll have a clear run,' Josh mumbles. 'Everyone's in here by now.' The mundanity of it, the sheer idiocy of their conversations.

He slides out from the booth to let Greg past and gets a pecking, chaste kiss.

'I'll be reading, okay, so don't worry about disturbing me when you come.' Josh nods, munching on his rice, deliberately not turning to see Greg leave the dining car.

It's difficult to imagine now, but when he first joined he was desperate to get Greg into bed. He can't remember what it was that did it for him. If he's honest with himself – which he might as well be now – it was that Greg was the only one of the cast or crew who reminded him of the world he came from. Ballet is filled with posh people and bohemians, or quirky individuals who were some mixture of the two, and by the time he joined *The Apple and the Pearl* he'd sat silently through enough conversations about skipping family skiing trips for fear of breaking a limb, flute lessons, holidays in Tuscany and birthday treats at the opera. Greg's dad was a postman, his mum a dinner lady at the local primary school and his accent – as well as the fact he didn't even seem to be trying to hide it – made something inside Josh unclench. Even before they got together, Greg's mere presence quietened that insidious inferiority in him. He could be all of himself with Greg, the gay man, the dancer, the scholarship lad from Preston. He still can. He mops up some curry with a hunk of bread and chews on it. If nothing else, he should remember that.

He seduced Greg with facts about crows and ravens and jackdaws. Greg's Crow rehearsals started a couple of months after Josh's first pledge and Cecile was vocal in her disappointment. *You are a boy in a stupid costume!* she'd shout at him during run-throughs. *Be a bird, dammit!* It did not help that Cecile was, as usual, right.

Did you know crows can recognise human faces? he'd said one day after class, when he looked up from the noticeboard and found Greg beside him. He'd blurted it out before he could change his mind and regretted it instantly. What sort of fucked up come-on was that? But Greg had looked interested. *Really? That's cool.* Emboldened, Josh continued. *And they hold funerals for their dead.* Greg had given him a wry smile before climbing the stairs to the dressing room. *Don't give Cecile any ideas.*

Four months ago, when Cecile beckoned Josh over at the end of class and told him to start learning the Crow, Greg had reminded him of those first awkward conversations. He'd gone rifling through an old box and pulled out the card Josh had written him for the first time he performed the Crow. He'd read it aloud, the earnest, hopeful message and the silly rhyme written out in its entirety in his best handwriting. They'd laughed and curled up in bed together from something more than just habit. That was the last time he'd felt anything more than quiet contempt for Greg. He can't remember the time before that.

Josh swallows the last of his dinner with a heartburn-inducing gulp and picks up his tray as he's chewing. He's got a job to do, the last obligation of the day.

He slides his tray across the kitchen hatch, where Romero takes it with a nod – he should be getting paid for this extra kitchen skivvying, or maybe he does it for love, the thought of it is unimaginable – then he hangs around the serving hatch, trying to catch Gino's eye.

Just over a month ago, the night of his first show as the Crow, Stuart had put a hand on his shoulder as he returned his plate to the kitchen hatch. *Before you get stuck into your truffles,* he'd said, *there's something I need to show you.*

He'd taken a tray from the serving hatch bearing one of those old-fashioned embossed silver cloche things over a plate. Next to it were two shot glasses filled with a clear, oily liquid that barely swayed as Stuart pulled it off the counter.

Follow me, Stuart said, and Josh followed him out of the dining car and along the corridor, leaving the noise behind. They walked through eleven carriages of cabins and bathrooms, Stuart confident, with the tray secure in his hands and Josh confused, stumbling behind him, a dread mounting behind his breastbone that Stuart knew something about Ritchie and he felt panic rising. Stuart and Greg were pledge-mates. Maybe there was some honour thing involved, some vow to punish your pledge-mates' cheating partners.

They reached the caboose and Stuart wedged the tray between the wall and his hip while he wrestled with the doorknob.

Mate, Josh had said, trying to keep a lightness in his voice though he was starting to panic. *What the fuck are we doing?*

Did Greg not tell you? Stuart bent to put the tray on the floor of the caboose and moved it across the flaked-paint floorboards with one trainer-clad toe.

Josh shook his head, swallowing. *The sly bastard,* Josh thought. *Can there really be anything, anything at all that teddy bear's kept from me?*

Good man. It's supposed to be a secret, but you know what things are like.

Who is this for?

Stuart grinned. *The Crow.*

There was a silence. Josh stared at the tray on the ground. He wasn't sure what to say.

Is that a metaphor?

Stuart burst into laughter. *You don't need to take it so seriously! Gino gives you the tray, you bring it here, you go to bed with your boy safe in the knowledge you've kept the spooky creatures at bay for another day.*

Do I have to pick up the tray too? he'd asked, stupidly, wondering what the penalty might be if he overslept, if he forgot, if it was simply a freezing morning and he couldn't face wandering the cabins in his pyjamas.

Nah. Belinda sorts that out. Josh thought of the times when he'd woken up early and left his cabin to go to the loo to see Belinda walking briskly through snow or slanted golden light with an empty tray crooked in her elbow.

Is it— dangerous out here? Like, has anyone ever actually met the Crow? Josh was more than familiar with the Crow's keening after a snatching, but the idea of ascending to a new level of weird and having a tête-a-tête with the creature now that he was dancing this role was making him feel sick.

Stuart had shrugged. *I haven't but Mara's good mates with it, apparently. Shouldn't say you're in danger. Crow probably thinks you're a grumpy old git.*

Stuart reached down, picked up one of the shot glasses

and bent over the railing. He poured the shot onto the dark ground and Josh stood back as if he were waiting for something to catch alight. *I'd not worry about it if I were you. You know what it's like. Weird shit comes looking for you, you don't need to worry about finding it.*

But weird shit has never really come looking for Josh. He's not like Romero, with that curl to his upper lip that suggests he can smell the supernatural on you like a dog or a deer, or Michael the violinist with that trick with the mushrooms he pulled this morning. Seven years he's been here, seven years of standing on stage while whatever beings have turned up in the audience cavort, seven years of rehearsals and classes and petty rules and pettier rebellions and never a whiff of anything interesting, never the slightest hint that the Crow sees him as anything but another boring body to do the show and spit out when the mortal knees start to creak and groan.

He opens the door to the caboose and places the tray on the rough floorboards. He shivers. The night is foggy, illuminated only by the floodlights set up so the crew can pack the front carriages of the Grub with the set and the lights and costumes, all the tools of this oldest of trades. Muffled voices swear as the doors to the cargo carriages of the Grub whine and clank. He takes one of the shot glasses and leans over the railing to pour the viscous liquid onto the wet leaves, leaving the other by the plate like Stuart told him. He almost thinks he can hear a slurp.

Despite the damp chill that seeps through the wool

of his jumper, Josh props his elbows over the railings and leans out into the night. He waits, listening to Danny, Zach and Mackie calling to each other through the fog, trying to sense something in the night, something other than his own leaden dread of going back to his cabin to lie next to Greg's lumpen body and wake up to the faint yellow stain on his pillowcase. He can see the shape of dark trees against the shadows cast by the floodlights and he thinks about how long it's taken those things to get so big and gnarled and deep. Who cast their seeds into this enchanted mud and when?

One to grow, Josh thinks, and he remembers his grandfather scattering breadcrumbs all around the gate to his plot. *They remember those who do them a kind turn, and they tell their friends. You don't want a crow for an enemy, boy.* What would his grandfather say if he could watch the show? He would not be very interested, probably, or would not show it. For a moment Josh fantasises about going back to his cabin and getting out his phone to order seeds online, to have boxes of courgettes and leeks and carrots and parsnips delivered to his parents' house to sleep in the darkness of their shed until he's done with this ballet stuff. Done with this show that pickles you inside a timeless, placeless world even while your joints fall apart. Done with Greg and all his gentle, suffocating love. And done with showers slick with other people's soap. Then he'll go, and he'll grow again.

Beside him, the Crow settles on the floor of the caboose, right by the tray. Josh feels hot and cold needles prickling on his skin. It ignores him, pecks at the sweet potato on the tray and dips its beak into the shot glass.

He would like to say something, but his tongue is heavy and his mouth dry. He has the feeling it's waiting for him to do something – leave, perhaps – but this is the first, and perhaps last, time he has ever seen this creature so he needs to grab this chance. He puts both hands in the pockets of his jeans, finds a couple of hair grips and an elastic band. Josh puts one of the hair grips onto the tray and the Crow gives it a couple of cursory pecks. It cocks its head and looks up at him, black eyes gleaming in the lantern light. Now it's listening.

'If I told him, do you think he'd forgive me?'

The Crow is silent.

'I just don't think I can do this anymore.' Josh rubs his fingertips over the worn denim on the inside of his pockets. 'I mean, I made a pledge to you, not to him.'

The Crow goes back to its dinner. Josh knows he is dismissed. He pushes himself off the railings and something twinges in the back of his ankle. He circles it a little to release the gunk. White Suitor tomorrow, and as he opens the door to the caboose the first steps of the solo come to his unwilling feet and he starts to mark them as he steps into the corridor and pulls the door shut, leaving the Crow to its feast.

He wanders past the cabins, moving through each carriage in turn, until he gets to his own cabin door. Inside, the bed is creaking as Greg moves around, piling up pillows around his knees to get comfortable. Josh puts his fingers on the door handle but he cannot make himself go in. He shuts his eyes, thinking of all the other things he could do instead. Go back to the dining car and get another beer. Pretend he's got something to tell Romero or Benji. Knock on Stuart's door and ask to borrow something. Go to Ritchie's cabin and lurk outside, hoping he's not planning to join in Mackie's party. Lock himself in the bathroom, stare at the smudges of black make-up he couldn't get off his face. Go for a walk among the graves. Try and make it to whatever place Belinda warns you that you don't want to go to.

He leans his forehead on the door and listens to Greg humming to himself inside their cabin. *Did you know crows mate for life?* he told Greg once, lying together in a small cabin two carriages over, their limbs entwined and rocking with the gentle motion of the Grub. Greg had laughed. *Enough about crows now. You got me, I'm here.*

But he is not a crow. Just the bone and sinew and lumpen blood of a man no longer in love. He puts his hand on the door handle to his cabin. He will go inside. There is nowhere else to go. He just needs a little minute to resign himself.

Cold as a witch's tit, her breath pluming into the darkness. The Crow sits on the damp wooden floorboards of the caboose, wraps the black serge skirts around her legs and pulls the tray onto her lap. An owl hoots into the night and the Crow caws softly in answer.

Hark, she thinks, *the owl on silent wing in the darkness, the softly dripping mist from the yews, the crew hauling the Pearl and the rest of the set down from the Grit to stow it in the belly of the Grub. Familiar voices of the Crew, muffled by mist. The wandering man who serves the Grit so well, tending it like a lover; the troll man who Crow brought here to fuck with everyone; the seamstress who carries the chick in her belly and the poet whose words Crow is eating. Of all humans aboard the Grub, the crew are most beloved to the Crow. Because isn't that who Crow was, once upon a time? Long ago now, perhaps a thousand years. Crow was a fixer, a dealer, a messenger, a half-this half-that, a betwixer. Crow was behind-the-scenes, pulling strings. Now Crow gets humans or sort-of-humans to fix for her. Belinda to hold back Faerie with the force of her father's blood, before that Percy Montgomery with his charming smile and quick understanding of how it was, how it had to be. Yes, the crew are most beloved.*

She belches, and drains the shot glass in one gulp.

Belinda woman will come for the Pearl soon, nestle it into the engine, listen for the little hum of satisfaction from the Grub. A gift from a Fairy Queen long since gone into the West. What were her words? Crow would like to forget but they are engraved on her heart, her feathers, the Pearl itself if you know where to look. We will exile you, shape-shifter, but catch the souls of the dead and you will not starve.

Starve? Fuck you, witch queen, Crow does not starve. Crow feasts. Crow has two nests and moves her treasure from between them each night and day; Crow perches on each gate to Faerie and shits all over the railings; Crow brings the humans here to dance the old story of The Apple and the Pearl *to tease the Fae bastards with what Crow has built to spite them because you don't want a Crow for an enemy, and surely Faerie has found that out by now—*

The snap of a twig, a rustle in the loam. A scuffle of black serge and Crow is in wing again, peering out into the darkness. Hoof-beats, a dim and distant thudding. She caws furiously and takes off from the caboose.

Mara knocks on Belinda's office door. There's no answer, she must be still in the Grit, and Mara almost goes back down the corridor and away to the cabins. Then the carriage door opens and there's Belinda, her clipboard poking out of her handbag, her shoulder laden with that medieval-looking sack she carts to and from the Grit each day. She raises her eyebrows and Mara stands back to let Belinda pass and gestures to the office door.

'Can I talk to you for a moment?'

Belinda unlocks the door to her office and shoves it open with her foot. 'By all means.'

She sits on the chair, lets the bag sink onto that chest in the corner where it makes a merry clinking noise. Mara hovers in the doorway, unsure. Really, she could come back another day, she tells herself. Tomorrow even, there's no rush.

But Belinda draws the chair up to her desk and steeples her fingers. Mara knows that she is out of time, it's now, Belinda knows exactly why she's here and what she'll say and backing away is no longer an option. *It's over*, a voice whispers in her ear. *Time to go.*

'What can I do for you?'

'I just wanted to tell you first,' Mara's voice is croaky, her mouth dusty dry. 'I won't be renewing my pledge.'

As soon as she says it, a warm spread of relief rises from her toes. She wonders if Belinda can feel it too, like a soft, fragrant wind in the room. No more aching calves. No more spooky curtain calls. No more waiting in the caboose for one-sided conversations with a bird.

'Have you told Cecile?'

'Not yet.'

'Well, don't leave it too long. She'll want to know so she can mope.' Belinda takes off her glasses and rubs at the indent on the bridge of her nose.

'Remind me again of your pledge date?

'Twenty-second of December.'

'Your family will be pleased.' Belinda smiles and turns her chair a little away, letting Mara know the audience is up. 'Home for Christmas for once.'

She pauses, and for a moment Mara thinks she'll say more. But Belinda shrugs, puts her glasses back on and reaches to her desk for a pen. She's dismissed.

And that's it. Mara feels that burning itch at the bridge of her nose that means she's about to cry as she shuts Belinda's office door behind her. She'll leave the Grub the morning after her last show and later that day she'll be sitting in her mother's living room with the gaudy Christmas tree blinking in the corner, the rest of her life stretching in front of her. Something splinters in her heart. Sitting on her mother's sofa in front of *The Sound of Music* with a bellyful of over-boiled Brussels sprouts is not where she belongs. It's too late to take it back. She leans her forehead on the window. The Crow won't have her anyway. It'll throw her things onto the tracks, change the locks, reject her like an unwanted transplant.

Footsteps. She takes her forehead from the cool glass and brushes tears from her cheeks. Zach the lighting guy is blundering down the corridor, waving his hands at the blonde girl following him, listening intently and frowning. He ducks under a light, sees Mara and waves.

'Hey Mara, this is my new assistant, Lara – hey, you two should get on, your names rhyme!'

Mara smiles weakly at the girl. She hates her. About to take her first pledge, the Crow listening like a lover to the particular rhythm of her heartbeat to fold her secrets into its magics.

'Welcome,' Mara says as she passes under Zach's arm in the direction of the cabins. 'Lovely to have you here.'

She walks away and lets the carriage door slam behind her.

Zach stops in front of Belinda's office door. He shoves his hands in his pockets, suddenly nervous. Until this moment he's taken it for granted that she'll pledge, that she's as fascinated by the show as he is and will want to stay, but now he's not so sure. She looks exhausted, with smudges under her eyes and wisps of blonde hair escaping from her plait. She looks at the door thoughtfully, and Zach realises with a physical pain in his chest that he would be strangely hurt if she chooses not to pledge.

'You know how this morning you said I could ask you anything?' she says quietly.

Zach nods. There's a static between them now, of the kind he knows he is liable to misinterpret. He's done it before. He tells himself to back off. It's her moment. 'I also said I might not know the answer.'

She pauses for a moment, looks up at him then back at Belinda's closed door. 'Is it another taboo, to talk about what happens in the curtain call, like it is to talk about someone who was taken?'

Zach swallows. That isn't what he was expecting her to ask. 'I don't know how to give you a yes or a no. It's not forbidden, but people don't usually like to talk about it. It's kind of terrifying, I guess, to think that one day that will be you.'

He falls silent. Lara is wrestling with something, her eyes unseeing, her thumb worrying at the cuff of her jumper. He would like to make it easier on her, he would like to strip the Grit and the Grub of all their secrets, to make her feel like she can give her pledge to the Crow and not regret it.

'I'm not sure where the dead come from and I'm fucked if I know where they're going but the show attracts them.'

Zach says. 'Maybe because they want to go wherever the Pearl takes them. Sometimes you can see bits of bodies and that, which is horrible, but you learn to shut it out. Some say you can recognise the people you've loved. The old LX lady, Juliet, she used to swear she saw her father go into the Pearl one night.' Zach pauses. 'It sounds a little fucked up but she said it was a nice thing. She got to say one last goodbye.'

Lara nods. She's turned away from him and the office door now, staring out of the window past his shoulder, past her reflection and out at the huddled mass of dark, silent graves.

'Maybe it's the other way round.'

'What?'

'Maybe we do the show to release the dead from wherever they are towards wherever they're going to, and those – creatures – are the ones tagging along.'

He stares at her. 'I don't know if anyone's ever thought of it like that before.'

She shrugs, and knocks on the office door.

Zach's belly twists with longing. This is inconvenient, at best. The last time he fell in love it was with Juliet, who took him to bed a few times and then bought him a drink in the Grub one night, patted his hand and told him it was nothing personal. *I just like variety, young buck. No hard feelings, eh?* He can hear Juliet's cackle as if she could see the way he's looking at Lara now.

'Come in,' says Belinda and she gives a tired smile when she sees them. She hands Zach a piece of folded paper.

'Zachary, please take this to Gino and ask him to display it in the usual place.'

Belinda's gaze slides past Zach as footsteps echo in the corridor. 'Ah, Mackenzie, good evening.'

Zach gives Mackie a mock salute as they pass each other and ducks under the light.

He tucks the piece of paper in his back pocket and heads down the corridor, towards the dining car. Already he can smell something curried and warm and sticky, but it's not dinner time for him, not yet. The rest of the crew are still hauling gear from the Grit down that avenue of dead bodies walled up in stone, and that's what he needs to be doing right now. Not making a tit of himself mooning over a girl who won't ever look at him twice.

Back in the office, Belinda is watching Lara over the half-moons of her glasses. She's accompanied again by the woman sitting beside her, stitching up a hole in her goose-feather cape.

'So, have you decided to join us?'

Lara thinks of everything she's seen today: the spots on the mirror in the guest cabin; the Grit rising above the mausoleums through the mist; the dancers sprawled on the stage before class; the weight of the spanner in her hand; the melody of the Pearl waltz; the star at the centre of the pink-fleshed apple on the act three backdrop; the Crow veering away from the Pearl at the last moment; the warm, animal smell of Zach's hair as they were pressed together in the confines of the lighting box; the sound of the yews dripping through the ghosts that watched them push the flight cases between the graves. The woman in the goose-feather cape smiles sadly at her.

'Yes.' She swallows, makes her voice clearer. 'I have.'

'Excellent.' Belinda slides a piece of paper across the desk. 'The pledge I need you to read and repeat back to me, but the contract you can take away with you. You have seven days to sign and return it to me with your details. Any questions?'

'Does anyone ever break their pledge?'

'Yes.'

'Is it usually grim?'

Belinda shrugs. 'You had a better vantage point to watch the show than most. You saw our audience. Not the most powerful, not the most dangerous tonight, but creatures who do not belong to the world you joined us from this morning. The pledge – like so much else here – keeps us safe.'

Lara nods. 'Thank you. I'd like to pledge please.'

'Good.' Belinda turns to Mackie and raises her eyebrows.

'I trust, Mackenzie, that you do not need me to provide you with the words to read?'

Mackie shakes his head, plants his feet wide apart and clasps his hands behind his back.

'I, Mackenzie Boswell, so named by my father Harrison Boswell, do pledge my heart and body to *The Apple and the Pearl* as technical director, to hold the hearts of the crew in my hands, to watch over every part of the Grit behind and including the curtain, to care for the scene and the set including the Pearl when nesting in the Grit, for a year and a day.'

Belinda sits with her head a little cocked, staring at the blank wall above the cartoon-like treasure chest next to her desk, apparently listening for something. Then she starts and nods curtly.

'All fine, thank you.' She looks at Lara. 'Your turn.'

'I, Lara Pearson, so named by my mother Edith Pearson, do pledge my heart and body to *The Apple and the Pearl* as—'

She pauses, looks at the paper in her hands.

'Lighting assistant, to care for the equipment given to the Grit, to light the above show as I am instructed, to aid in the care for the set and scenery, for a year and a day.'

This time, Belinda doesn't stare off into the distance. She nods, takes the bunch of keys from her desk and swivels around on her chair to one of the thick, iron-bound chests that sit behind her. There is a clinking noise, and when Belinda faces them again she holds two tiny crystal vials in one hand and two long needles in the other.

She nods to Mackie as she wipes one of the needles with an antibacterial wipe, and he holds out his index finger. She pricks it, squeezes a bead of crimson blood out of it and holds the vial labelled *Technical Director* underneath to collect it. She plugs the vial with a cork, leaves it on the desk and gestures to Lara as she wipes down the next needle.

Of course, Lara thinks as she holds out her finger for the prick. *What part of you thought you weren't going to have to sign in blood?*

Belinda stands up, brushes her trousers down and gestures to the door.

'Thank you, all complete.'

Mackie beckons to Lara, holding the door open for her. 'You're one of us now,' he says, and although he means it as a joke, his voice has a severe edge to it. 'The cargo carriages aren't packed yet and the rest of them're no doubt ballsing it right up without me. We'll sort that out, then it's dinner time. No fun until the work is done.'

When they're gone and she's finally alone, Belinda sits down heavily in her chair. There is still the pile of offerings to be catalogued and stored, then she has to get the Pearl from Mackie and take it to the engine, and then get back here to her office to hear and count the tolls of the bell. Only then will she be able to go to Gino and get the plate he'll have saved for her. *You eat last*, says the phantom voice of Percy Montgomery, the old company manager, in her ear. *Don't even think of relaxing until after the midnight bells and the Grub is on the move again. We're the first and last link, the Crow's right-hand man. We are responsible for them all and you must never forget it.*

She remembers the week she spent with Percy, shadowing him as they moved from forest to moor and back again, walking all over the Grit and the Grub, him talking at her without pausing for breath. *I know everyone else gets a day to find their feet*, he told her, *but your job is more complicated.*

He showed her the ledger and the chest and the bank records and the engine carriage and the bell. They sat in the caboose and leaned over the railings and waited for the Crow, came back the next day and the next until the creature showed up, all black wings and sparking eyes and a voice like a scream in the distance and teeth stained with dark, old blood. Putting on a show just to mess with her. The next time she saw it, the creature was just a large black bird with a twinkle of mischief in its yellow eye. They watched the beings in the audience every night and Percy Montgomery put his curiosity about Belinda's lack of curiosity in a pocket to look at later. And all the while, he talked. Snippets of gossip, nuggets of wisdom, old tales she's never forgotten.

Recruitment will be far and away the hardest bit. Always has been. It won't be the best dancers and musicians who see your job adverts, only the ones with something missing. A cast and crew of misfits and mavericks, that's what this place is.

And afterwards? Do they just go back into the world after all they've seen here? In those days Belinda found that hard to believe.

Oh yes. I have a PO box in Birmingham that gets filled with Christmas cards from ex-musicians and dancers of The Apple and the Pearl *every December.*

And those that end up in Fae?

He sighed. *They represent our failures. Sheep lost to the wolves. The Crow relies on you to make sure that doesn't happen.*

And so, at the end of that week, as Percy Montgomery stood on the platform at Liverpool Lime Street station at dawn and waved at the cast and crew who were sorry to see him go, she stood here in this office and decided to make changes.

Barrels of salt. A blacksmith to repair the rusted hinges on the Grub's carriage doors. A new curtain.

She learned it all from her mother, and her preparations each year for Belinda's annual summer holiday with her father. Each July she packed Belinda a suitcase with changes of clothes (*please always be presentable and do me proud*) books with reading and maths activities (*we don't want you forgetting everything you've learned this year at school, do we*) a packet of salt (*you never know*) plenty of soap (*it will annoy them if you're smelly, please wash at least twice a day*) and an iron padlock with a screwdriver *(please install this on your door as soon as you arrive and do not forget to lock it each and every night)*.

Her mother would drive her to the country park after dinner, park the car and lead her along a bridle path to a thicket of gnarled hawthorn. They'd wait, her carefully packed suitcase at her feet, watching for sunset. At last she'd hear hoof-beats, first distant and then nearer and nearer and her mother's face would set hard but implacably reasonable.

The first sight of her father was always a shock.

The glow of him, the way his horse danced and snorted in the twilight, that shifty twinkle in his violet eyes. He would hand her mother a clinking bag which she would reach into, take a coin from and bite before accepting it with a tight smile. She would kiss Belinda on the forehead, hoist her up onto her father's horse and say, '*The first of September, Linden, not a day later*'. Her mother never, ever used her father's title or honorifics and these days Belinda understands that is part of how she corralled him. A named thing is a tamed thing. Belinda never asked how she knew that.

But her mother died when she was twenty, and she never thought to ask the other questions that now itch at her each night. Like how she kept her father – Earl Starmist, Prince of Vryders Heath, Duke of the Moorlands – half tethered to mortal time. Like how she ensured that not a single Fae in the court, from the Queen to the lowliest scullery maid, treated her with anything less that polite respect. Years ago, she began to suspect her mother only managed it because she was not entirely human herself, but she doesn't dwell on the thought, for fear of what that makes her. Percy Montgomery, in one of his retirement letters to her after he had worked it out: *Advisable to keep your family situation under wraps, I think. I know you're the best for the job, and so does the Crow, but one little doubt is all it takes to foment a mutiny.*

No matter. She hasn't seen her father since her mother's death and hasn't been to Fae for at least two decades. She would not be able to find her father's queendom without an invitation. And if someone finds out, or the changeling violinist unmasks her, or Derek shows his hand, so what? They're like children here, helpless little sheep. Are they going to pay themselves? Make a rota to take care of orders and deliveries? Collect the take at the end of shows, transport the Pearl to and from the Grub, form a committee to deal with the Crow?

Perhaps they might surprise her. People often do, she's found. They might be accepting, ask her questions, try to understand. She imagines them all assembled on stage, fifty faces turned warily to her, one hand up at a time. *What's it like there, Belinda? Cold and glittery, with everything slipping away as you try to hold it. What do the humans do there? Play music and dance, much like you do here. What do you eat there? Pear and mallow fruit and honeycakes. Can you go in and fetch Alex or the French horn or Charlotte or Bob the technical manager or Mungo St John Fitzwilliam back again? I have never tried, and yes, that weighs like a sin on my conscience.*

A slam of the connecting door to the carriage brings Belinda to herself. She pulls open the drawstring of the canvas bag, settles the ledger on her lap and moves her chair over to the chest. It will take her until past the midnight bells to account for everything left in the Grit as payment. She must record everything in the ledger, even what she discards as nothing more than beans coated in pollen and glamour, and make sure all of it goes neatly into the chest. In ten days' time, when they stop at Didcot Parkway for the day off, she'll stuff the contents of this chest into a duffel bag and haul it into a taxi to take it to Oxford, slipping the driver an extra tenner to wait for her while she empties the bag all over the counter of some pawnbroker who will stare for a long moment at the heaped gold and jewels before him and then go to the door to turn the sign to *Closed*.

She'll take the cash, deposit it at the post office and, free at last from her responsibilities and swinging the empty bag from her wrist, she'll find a restaurant and sit with a glass of Rioja and stare out of the window at the world going by, letting the wine dull her senses until she can lean back with her eyes half closed and feel the thrum of the land through the soles of her feet.

The flood-lights make triangular glows across the graves, tendrils of mist swirling between each lichen-ridden stone, and Kavi thinks, *you got to hand it to the Crow, it knows how to do atmosphere*. He's wondering how he would describe this scene without cliché – he imagines a reader turning a page and tutting, thinking *we get it mate, it's really foggy* – when Danny, bundled up in a grey parka jacket with the hood pulled over his head, steps into the light.

'Kavi, mate, could you yank that door? This bastard won't budge.'

He puts his shoulder to the edge of the door and heaves. The iron of the Grub cuts into his coat and onto the sharp places of his bones and the creak and whine of the carriage door as it moves makes him shiver. There is something in the Grub that protests against this nightly ritual, some grumpy distaste Kavi feels in its metal skin every night as they pack away parts of the Grit inside it. He imagines the theatre and the train as an ancient couple, married so long they know each seam on each other's skin, bickering every evening as they get into bed and breathe on each other all night until the sun comes up.

Danny fixes the ramp in place and thumps it twice with his fist to tell Charlie it's good to go. Charlie and Shirley start to push flight cases of scenery and lights up the ramp and into the carriage where the new girl and Zach stand ready to strap them to the walls.

Every night they do this, a dance as tightly choreographed as anything the dancers do on stage. Wheeling flight cases along mud and sand and stone paths, heaving them up to the Grub, tightening the straps, slamming the doors shut behind them, leaving the show to do whatever it does in the dark when no one can see it. There is a comfort to it. A few months ago he didn't see how anyone managed to stay here for all the long years of Mackie or Belinda or AJ – the man first set foot on the Grub over fifty years ago, although fair enough, he's come and gone since – how anyone could bear to do the same thing over and over again with nothing to distinguish the days except the passing of the seasons and then the years, but now he begins to see it. The familiar grooves of habit, and the enduring perfectionism of theatre folk.

The first cargo carriage is full, so Charlie shouts to Danny to move the ramp. Kavi slides the door until he hears the click of the lock and they move down the train to the next carriage where Mackie's waiting with the next set of flight cases.

He sees now that it's – at least partly – all the unanswered questions that keep you coming back and the one that pushes itself to the front of his mind now, as he struggles with the stiff handle on the next carriage is: what exactly is *The Apple and the Pearl*? What is the show made of? Is it the melodies of the score? But what is the score if it's not being played? Just a heap of black marks on a heap of paper? Same thing with the choreography – if it's not being danced right at that moment, is it really there? It's just some information encoded into twenty dancers' synapses. So is the show the material things, the pieces of painted MDF and fireproof backdrops that lie disassembled in the flight cases they're shoving around? The sequins and the Lycra of the costumes?

He asked Danny this, once, after a few pints in the dining car. Haltingly, his words skipping and sliding about in his mouth, some sense of recklessness propelling him on, almost not caring if there was something to the magic here that punished you if you spoke of it.

But Danny had frowned and shrugged. *Dunno mate. Just what you do, isn't it? Set up, pack away. I try to not think about what the show is or what Grit gets up to after curfew or those things in the auditorium to be honest. Makes me come over all funny.*

And that's Danny all over, a straight-up, honest bloke who seems to genuinely be able to turn his mind away from anything that might unsettle it and still go about his daily business. Kavi envies it, but he can't leave it there. He worries away at his questions like a gap in the gum and this is the one that troubles him most because it's one that applies to all the shows in all the world, not just the eeriness of whatever happens in the Grit each night.

He catches the flight case Charlie shoves up the ramp and wheels it over to Zach. He wants to stop and grab a pen to write some of these questions down, but he knows better than that now. Seven months he's been here and the Crow hasn't let him write anything more than a text message to his mum since he took his pledge.

He hadn't meant to tell Bella that this afternoon. He hadn't even meant to talk to her at all, let alone go on like a proper dick about poetry and dance and whatever he was gobbing on about. He feels his face redden in the dark thinking about it. He'd been taking a shortcut past the stage on his way back to the Grub for lunch and he'd seen her orange-encased legs poking out from under the props table and he hadn't been able to stop himself. What had he said? Some bollocks about ballet being different from music and poetry. His memory of the conversation is hazy, missing detail and sense, like he was ill or drunk or high as it happened. Poetry! Bloody poetry! What was he thinking? What the fuck does he know about poetry?

He knows about not writing poems. He knows about all the times he sat down to write something when he was a kid – about his mum, his dad, the streets of Wembley where he grew up – and nothing came. Or, what came was trite and flat, nothing that anyone would want to read. He knows about not-writing from when he was working sixteen-hour days on panto with two toilet breaks.

Since starting at *The Apple and the Pearl*, he has become even more expert at not-writing. The notebooks that he's filled with observations and anecdotes after the show that end up shredded into tiny flakes of paper scattered all over his cabin in the morning. The notes he's taken on his phone that make the software glitch, the error messages he gets until he does a factory restore that mysteriously retains everything but the hastily typed messages. The emails he's tried to write himself from other people's phones and laptops that refuse to send. He really doesn't know why he told Bella all that this morning. It just came out. Something about the way her body was turned to him made him want to dredge his secrets and pour them at her feet.

'Heads up!' comes the shout, and Kavi only just turns in time to catch the flight case trundling towards him, about to crash into his legs. He stops it with a foot and almost tumbles into the stack behind him.

'Sorry mate,' Derek calls from down by the track. 'Got away from me.'

The case is labelled *STAGE RIGHT PROPS* in Shirley's neat handwriting. Kavi holds up a hand to show no hard feelings, but it's difficult not to suspect Derek of shit-stirring whenever something goes even a tiny bit wrong. He's just got that air about him of wanting to mess with you, almost in revenge for something you're yet to do to him.

Kavi wheels the case into place and fastens the straps around it. He wonders where Bella is right now, if she's planning on staying in the dining car long enough to join in the pledge day drinks, but the thought skitters in his mind. All the ways the night might go, branching away from him as he thinks about her orange-clad legs under the props table: she doesn't stay for the drinks; she stays for the drinks and he smiles from across the room, saying and doing nothing; she stays for the drinks and he finds some courage from somewhere, the bottom of a can of Stella, perhaps, and he talks to her. More branching fates from there: another can of Stella; an offered hand; a slow walk along the corridors to one of their cabins. *Hold on*, he thinks as he fastens a strap around a flight case labelled *STAGE LEFT PROPS*. *Hold on. You aren't there yet, and you might never be.*

Because there's something he needs to do before he goes to the pledge day party and if Bella's gone by the time he gets there it can't be helped. He needs to dump these words that have been rising in him all day, like a burn of indigestion making its way up from his stomach to his throat. One more of his never-ending questions: why does the Crow make my words hurt me if it won't let me get them out?

He's nowhere near answering this one, but he has found a way to trick the Crow and it seems to be working. After the cargo carriages are packed he leaves the Grub – and of course he knows it's a risk, but he cannot bear the rising tide of words – and he finds a place to write something. He uses his fingers in sand or mud, or he arranges leaves, or he carefully places pebbles. He doesn't take a photo. That makes his phone glitch too.

Then on days off, when he's far from the Grub, he buys a cheap notebook, finds a cafe, gets a cup of coffee and a sandwich and sits there for hours until all the words jumbling in his head that the Crow won't let out, and all the poems he left in earth and water and stone, are safe and on the paper. He sends it to his mum, with a letter inside for her, and a few days later he gets a text thanking him for the letter and renewing her promise that she hasn't looked inside and is keeping the notebooks safe in a box under his bed.

One day, he'll go home and lock the door to his childhood bedroom and sit with those scraps of paper and make something of them. He won't come out until he has enough for a book, like a writer in a film. He's going to call it *The Apple and the Pearl*. And although nobody will read it, although he has little idea how to go about getting anyone to read it at all, he will know it exists and – perhaps – that will be enough.

They're starting to load the last cargo carriage now. The costumes are done and Milly and Alina are gone, safe into the warmth of the Grub and the comfort of the smells wafting from the dining car. Charlie and Mackie wrestle the ramp into position, swearing when it gets stuck. Danny and Shirley wait with the last of the flight cases, those last, unwieldy pieces of set packed away neatly inside, and Zach stands behind them with the new girl, muttering and pointing down the train. Kavi, waiting in the carriage and adjusting the straps that hang from the iron to be ready for when the ramp is in place, hears Belinda's voice call through the mist.

'Mackenzie! It's gone eleven and I still don't have the Pearl.'

Mackie says a quiet *fuck* under his breath and finally clicks the ramp secure.

'It's coming, Belinda, we're almost done here.'

He always has the urge to stand a little straighter when Belinda's around. Or hide, whichever is easier. She comes to stand beside Shirley, the lapels of her smart black coat turned up against the mist, and Kavi shrinks into the shadows of the carriage. He has the feeling that if she were to catch sight of him, she'd see right through his – let's be honest – somewhat dubious intentions towards Bella and chase him with a broom.

Mackie and Charlie jump up into the carriage and Danny shoves the remaining flight cases up the ramp towards them. There are two hard clicks and two triangles of light disappear back into darkness. Shirley comes with the floodlights packed away and hands them up to Kavi for stowing.

There is one flight case left by the tracks, labelled *PEARL* in Mackie's scrawl. Mackie jumps down from the carriage and flicks open its latches. As if reaching into a cradle, he picks up the teardrop-shaped thing that sits atop a podium in the last act, a spotlight trained on it. On his first day Danny told him that Belinda fines you three days' salary if you touch the Pearl and as he'd lifted the lid of the flight case to show him the thing, glowing in its nest of black sponge, Kavi had instinctively reared away from it. No fear, he'd never touch that thing. The eerie smoothness of its skin, the way no shadow ever fell over it, the faint smell of smoke.

Where does Belinda take it? Kavi whispered to Zach a few weeks after his first pledge as they packed away the third floodlight and slammed the last carriage door shut.

To the engine, Zach had replied. *How else d'you think we'd get anywhere?*

And although Kavi had felt a hot and cold tingling all along his spine, he'd only shrugged and turned away, though really he'd wanted to slump onto the grass beside the tracks and think about what Zach had just implied. That the Grub powered its movement not on anything so ordinary as diesel, or as retro as coal, or as futuristic as solar panels, but whatever was contained inside the Pearl. Which was not discussed – at least in the circles he moved in – but seemed likely to be the essences of whatever soared above the auditorium during the curtain call, which it didn't take Kavi long to realise is dead people.

Amazing, how that's bothering him less and less. That's how it happens, that's how you stay here for years and years. You get friendly with the dead, with the idea of them, with the sight of all those streaming wisps of souls above or below you during the curtain call. Nice, in a way, of the Crow to offer answers to other questions even as it gives you more to think about. *What happens when you die?* said the little boy to his mother as they walked home, hand in hand after his father's funeral. Well, now he knows.

With Belinda gone and the last floodlight packed away, Kavi jumps down from the carriage into darkness and shivers.

'Good work everyone,' Mackie says, laying one hand on the side of the Grub tenderly, as it were a horse. 'Go and get your dinners, and remember it's pledge day drinks tonight, if any of you are up for it.'

He follows Zach and the new girl back along the carriages, stumbling in the darkness.

'Done your pledge already?' he asks the new girl as they follow the light on Zach's phone along the Grub. Lara, her name is. He should use her name, he's going to be working day in day out with her for the next year. 'Belinda capture a piece of your soul?'

She laughs. 'Yeah, it was a bit like that.'

Kavi would like to say something else, practice a little of that small talk he's going to try out later tonight on Bella, but now they're at the dining car and Zach is saying, 'Fuuuuuuck I'm hungry,' and pulling Lara and Kavi up the steps and into the warm hubbub of the dining car.

Kavi peers in as Zach and Lara go straight to the serving counter and looks at the dancers and musicians and crew assembled, the noise already raucous. Vagabonds and wanderers all, the kinds of people who would have been burnt at the stake, branded and outcast in centuries gone by.

Jasper, with his one eye turned towards the ceiling as if he can see patterns in the stars. Wilf holding the two sides of his woollen cardigan over his protruding belly with one hand, mouth agape as he holds his beer to his lips with the other. Lance and Steve huddled over a phone, leering over whatever they see there. AJ and Cecile sitting quietly in a corner, Cecile's eyes uncharacteristically unfocused as she glares at Stuart, who is plugging in a speaker. Romero behind the counter with Gino, wearing an apron and a fixed mask of politeness as Derek leans towards him and waves a fork around. Mackie concentrating on his dinner with a pint in front of him. Danny pulling out the chair next to him. Alina, sipping on a glass of white wine, sitting with Sandra the clarinet who is knitting something in a violent shade of orange. Belinda weaving between the tables with her clipboard tucked under one arm and her handbag swinging on the other.

And there, at the other end of the dining car sitting with two other dancers, Bella. A mug of tea in her hands, legs tucked underneath her, hair wet and dripping down her back. He stands at the doorway, aware he only has seconds to decide what he's going to do. In a moment or two someone, hopefully not Derek, will see him and shout across the dining car to pull him into the drinking, shouting, table-thumping testosterone vortex that will be tonight's pledge party and he will lose his chance.

But what exactly is the plan? To walk over there, sit down next to her with the other girls smirking at him, their barely suppressed titters shrivelling his balls to dust? To wave from afar while some fucker like Lance the trumpet sidles up to her and whispers something irresistible? To grab her hand, lead her out of the dining car and into the night to lunge at her in the darkness? He imagines her cringing away from him, murmuring in that worried, trying-not-to-offend way girls have: *Sorry, I think you've misunderstood, I like you just as a friend.*

Everyone will know that he's an idiot by the half tomorrow. Danny will shake his head, wincing, *You fucked it up mate, you really did.* Derek will be vibrating with glee. Mackie will beckon him over to the prompt desk in the second interval, *Belinda says I've to have a chat with you about sexual harassment in the workplace,* and all the dancers – in disgusted, disapproving solidarity with Bella – will simply look past him like he doesn't exist.

No. He'll leave. Now, while no one's clocked him.

He turns quickly, lets the door click softly behind him. He's hungry but there's a curdle of nausea in his belly he has to deal with first. If Bella is still in the dining car when he comes back then great, but he won't be able to concentrate on anything – let alone a girl – while there's all this pressure building up inside him.

He jumps down from the Grub and stumbles away through the mud. He swipes the torch open on his phone. Eleven thirteen. Plenty of time. He holds the light out in front of him, illuminating the droplets of mist and his other, groping hand, seeking the cool, rough dampness of a grave.

His fingertips brush against soft, spongy moss and he stops, runs his hands over the pocked stone. The grave bears the name of Desmond C Jones and as he digs inside his jacket pocket for a screwdriver and starts to work away at the stone, he silently thanks whatever remains of Mr Jones for his understanding. Bits of stone crumble in his hands and fall away onto the crunch of needles underfoot. His mother would flinch to see him. *Desecrating a grave, beta? Surely you're not in so much pain as that.*

But it doesn't feel like a desecration, honestly it doesn't, although he would say that, wouldn't he, to justify what he's doing so he can keep on doing it. It feels like giving this hunk of stone an afterlife, something else to commemorate other than the poor soul long returned to ashes beneath it.

He tucks the screwdriver into his pocket and feels with his finger for the hole he's been working in the pitted stone and kneels in the mulch of leaves at the ancient grave's base. Dampness starts to spread through his jeans, up his thighs and down his shins into his socks and as the wet rises so do the words, up from whatever's left of the body decaying in the soil beneath him, through his skin and into his belly, up his gorge until he thinks he's going to vomit and he opens his mouth and whispers into the hole he's made in the limestone.

And all the things that have happened this short day and long night of the dead come flooding out of him: the spooky gothic vibes of the Grit this morning, looming through the mist; the message from his mum thanking him for the money; the feeling of his fingers tingling as they thawed when he got inside the Grit; the bubble of guilt that floated in his belly as he ducked into the wings rather than stop to exchange small talk with Derek; the violent longing rising from the root of him at the sight of Bella's orange-clad legs under the props table; the way he'd had to clutch at his jeans to stop himself from running his palms up her thighs; the garbled idiocy of the things he ranted to her about; the ache of pleasure as he noticed their bodies leaning towards each other; the little stalks of mushrooms Mackie made him pick out from the edges of the dance floor this afternoon; the softening of Zach's mouth as he handed the new girl his spanner; the way the second act violin solo made him think of the smell that pervaded his house in the weeks after his father's death, that sex-and-death stench of lilies, decaying in their vase; Michael's flood of grief washing up the memory of his mother chanting when he broke his arm; her prayers in Hindi, English, Sanskrit, a trifecta of languages woven and threaded through him from babyhood, words knotted in his every cell so tightly that no one would be able to unravel him, no matter where he went in his life, *No racist, no thug, no belittler, no boss will ever silence you in this world, beta;* the rawness of his palms after a show; Mackie handling the Pearl with devotion, like it was a holy relic; the way his own mind can't quite hold thoughts of the Pearl, sliding and skating all over the attempts to work out what exactly it is or is not; the openness of the secrets here, the way you can think you know everything about the show but there's always some part of it you can't see, some further mystery you're blind to; his hunger; his lust; his wonderings about which is stronger right now; the thought that he needs to reply to a text from his cousin; the chill on the back of his neck as tendrils of fog reach through the gaps in his clothes; his hunger; his lust; the vague idea that he would like to elevate both of those feelings and make something new of them, something that does not shame him like these stuttering attempts at something like intimacy.

Emptied, as though he has truly vomited everything inside him up to and including the bile, Kavi pulls some mud from the ground and presses it into the hole on the gravestone. He wipes his hands on his jeans and tucks the screwdriver up his sleeve. Steel wouldn't do much more than irritate anything lurking in the shadows, but it might buy him time to run.

He turns the torch on his phone back on and holds it up to where he thinks the Grub should be. There it is, fuzzy squares of light dotted along its length, muffled sounds floating between the deadening droplets of water in the air. Voices, the hiss of a shower, the dripping of the drains and quiet, tinny music from a speaker.

He loves this feeling, this ache of the stranger, the yearning you get when you're on the outside in the dark, looking in at life going on in the cosy yellow light and you know all you have to do is step over the threshold, that there is a place for you somewhere inside one of these squares but still you linger in the cold. How many pledges does it take before that feeling leaves you, before you can no longer look at the Grub as it rests in the darkness and feel all the weight of its strangeness, of its occasional and inexplicable hostility, of its essential not-you-ness?

He slips the screwdriver out from his sleeve, nestling it into his pocket, and his fingers curl around a piece of paper there. He pulls it out, holds it under the light of his phone and brushes off the smears of mud. He sees his own scrawl, reads something about starlings in a hay meadow, chittering in a belligerent gang.

He remembers scribbling this, from his second or third week here when he was still trying to figure out what was happening, starting to choke on the welling up words.

And I think Derek thinks he's some kind of oracle, he reads, *but really he's more of a jester, a holy fool on a good day, but I've heard him come out with some blinders and it's as if something's speaking through him, moving his mouth with words that make you stop dead still and think. This morning, during get-in: Mackie telling Danny that when he retires he'll be free to stay in bed all morning, but until then he needs to get his arse out of bed and get to work; Danny muttering something foul from under the shadow of his hangover; Derek, hanging the act two backdrop with me, like he's soliloquising at the RSC. 'The problem with humans – well, there's a lot of problems with humans but this is one of the biggest – is that you don't know you're free. You parcel up the land and say you own it and you draw lines on maps and you say you can't come here or there and you shut yourselves up inside boxes of bricks and you say we envy the birds their wings when all the while you could be flying.' Of course I didn't know what to say. And even though I've been thinking about it all day, I still don't.*

A slam of a door to the Grub, footsteps, and his heart lurches. He stuffs the paper into his pocket and crouches behind Desmond C Jones' gravestone, swiping the torchlight off. *Fuck fuck fuck, Belinda will kill me,* he thinks, but how stupid to think of her first. Belinda in full, raging wrath will be nothing next to the horrors that await those – like him, it seems – stupid enough to get caught out near curfew.

There is a rustle of someone sitting down and rooting in a bag. A humming, and it's the tune to the Pearl waltz if he's not mistaken, and the sound is so human that Kavi relaxes. A triangle of light beams up through the mist and there's a sound of teeth crunching on biscuit. Kavi peeks over the stone to see Michael sitting on the steps to the Grub, eating from a napkin in his lap. Fuck.

Kavi checks his phone. Eleven thirty-two. He can still make it. He'll have to just brazen it out, wander up to Michael, nod a casual hello and brush past him onto the steps to go and get his dinner.

And if Michael asks him what he's doing out so close to curfew Kavi will ask him the same question and he'll give him a conspiratorial grin and say *well I won't tell Belinda if you don't*, and then they'll be locked in the complicity of this against-the-rules secret and tomorrow night he'll have to do something else, go somewhere else and make sure he's nowhere fucking near Michael and his death wish.

All right. Michael isn't moving. He's still sitting on the steps, munching his way through what seems like a whole sodding pack of biscuits, still humming. The White Suitor's solo now. Eleven thirty-six. He really should go.

But then the door behind Michael opens and there's a man silhouetted there against the warm yellow light inside the Grub and Kavi swallows his groan.

'Oh. Hi.' says the man. Squinting into the light from Michael's phone, Kavi can see it's another musician, one of the second violins. That creepily handsome guy who follows Michael around.

'Late, isn't it? Mind if I join you?'

Michael murmurs something and shuffles over on the steps, offering a biscuit.

Fuck. Two of them to get past now. It's not a disaster, not yet, he can try and get in at some other door. He'll just have to stay close enough to the line of the Grub not to lose it in the mist. He takes the screwdriver out of his pocket and wraps his fingers around the cold steel.

There's a tinkle of bells in the distance, not like the loud, deep clang of the curfew bell but the jangle of a tambourine. Hoof-beats. Starting faintly then drumming louder, vibrating through the mud and up through the stone of Desmond C Jones's grave. The soles of his feet start to tingle. He knows that if he doesn't go now he will be caught, and it will not be what they call a close shave, he will not even get back to the Grub to tell this tale.

Voices. At first he can only hear the faint murmur of

someone talking but they come closer and he can make out each word, though the speech is odd, sing-song.

'And there you go, we are not too late. We will not be disappointed, not tonight.'

'One of them stinks of melancholy. Quite exquisitely.'

'Do you want it?'

Kavi hears the soft pad of feet on the needles. It makes him think of a tiger. Can't Michael hear this? Of course not, he goes about with those bloody ear plugs. Well, ignorance is bliss until it isn't. Fuck. What about the other guy? How can he warn them, how can he get their attention?

A long, animal sniff. 'No. Not that one. It's lost its heart.'

'Careless.'

'Given it up to the Crow, I believe.'

A prim little tut. 'Barbaric.'

Another long, animal sniff. 'We'll leave it well alone. It's pathetic. No kind of tribute.'

'The other? It's beautiful enough.'

'You'd have us take a repudiated changeling back to the queendom? You are tired of the queen's favour and wish to spend the next hundred years in the sculleries?'

An annoyed sigh. 'There is sport to be had with such a one, but all right. We'll leave it.'

The mist begins to glow and they're there, in front of Kavi, impossibly tall but he is on his knees, looking up into the night at these two, beautiful looming faces with violet eyes gleaming with hunger. It occurs to him now he is exactly where he should be, and he has a fleeting sense that the whole day has been leading up to this perfect moment, from the moment he rolled over this morning in his cabin to ducking away from Derek – bless him – to seeing Bella's legs sticking out from under the props table, to watching Mackie cradle the Pearl, to kneeling here at this grave. A great, awed peace comes upon him. Is this what Belinda's so afraid of? That we'll like it? And the thought of Belinda almost makes him smile. Why think of such a person at a time like this? What does she matter now?

But maybe these creatures know Belinda too, he thinks stupidly, because they begin to laugh, and he hopes Michael and the other violinist can hear this at least. It is so loud, the pulse of it thudding and aching in his ears, he hopes they've dropped their sodding biscuits and got inside the Grub at last. Great peals of giggles echo on the stone, and Kavi thinks about peals of laughter and peals of bells, the metallic clang of them and what the bell is made of, perhaps bronze. Yes, probably bronze, a fairy metal if there is such a thing, a bronze bell tolling midnight, his midnight, signalling curfew to all without the Grub that it is time to seek shelter, the time has come to go.

Kavi finds himself on his feet, face to face with the creatures, and he has never seen anything so beautiful in all his life. He thinks they're male but it's hard to care. All he can think of is their violet eyes and the way they make tunnels, long passages of darkness he'd like to leap into.

There is some kind of shouting behind him, someone making a racket in the Grub and dimly Kavi wonders if someone is coming to rescue him even though Belinda always insists she doesn't do heroics. One of the creatures leans towards him and takes a long sniff of his neck and his throat, making a long, juddering sound of contentment.

'But this one, on the other hand. This one might do.'

'Yes, this one. It calls itself a poet. Thwarted by the Crow.'

'Poor thing.'

'We can help it.'

The shouting is right beside him now and someone is trying to push in front of him and knock him down but he is held fast by those twin dark pools edged with violet.

'Yes.' And one of the creatures holds out its hand like he's a child and beckons kindly. 'Will you come with us, poor little poet? Will you come sing with us awhile?'

And he would like to say no thank you, and he realises that if he says no thank you they will not be able to take him, and for a moment he has the strength to say it, to force out the words *but my mother will be all alone* or *but there is a girl in there I was trying to get into bed* or *all right but I want to come back soon*. But the moment of strength passes, draining from his muscles into the mulch and his hand is in the creature's and it's cold and smooth, like porcelain, and he murmurs yes, or something like it. Then he is atop a horse and the wind is in his face and he can smell peaches and words are flooding into his mind again, filling him up and up and up and up.

Just before midnight and the cast and crew of *The Apple and the Pearl* are aboard their train, not a one among them still dawdling among the dark graves or lingering in the muffled shelter of a yew. The shriek of a whistle – the very last warning call to stragglers – and the train starts to heave itself along the track, a groaning moaning sound of carriages awakening, spitting and spluttering as they gather speed. The *chug chug hiss* of the curved steel on the track. The sigh of cool air on the nose of the locomotive as it hurries through the darkness, its lurching the loudest thing in the night. Outside, a hunting owl's wings brush the air. Tiny icicles dangle from the fir trees, growing a hair's width every hour as the snow water *drip drip drips*. A fox cub sniffle-snuffles as he digs at a hedgehog nest.

Now the bell rings, tolling in the new day and bidding farewell to the old. It rings loud outside the train, echoing solemnly from the stones.

A clang for the King, a clang for the Queen,
three clangs for the sisters never to be seen.

In the first carriage behind the set and costumes and paraphernalia a touring ballet takes on the road, a woman called Belinda sits with a heavy hidebound ledger open on her lap. She scrawls quickly down the columns, dropping necklaces and bracelets and tiny gleaming gems into the iron-bound chest at her feet. As the fifth bell tolls she puts the ledger in the chest, locks it and puts the key on a chain around her neck.

A clang for the orchard, a clang for the sea,
three clangs for the suitors who lie in a dream.

In the dining carriage in the middle of the train the musicians are drinking, the usual crowd of cellist, timpani and bassoon sipping on their shot glasses and slamming on the tables to make syncopated rhythms. They hum Strauss and Handel as they get drunker and drunker, and when the tenth bell comes they weave it into their wobbly melodies and toast the coming of the new day.

A clang for the curse, a clang for the quest,

The sleeping cabins in the back half of the train are starting to fill up with those who hear the curfew of the midnight bells with relief rather than challenge. Yawning, the assorted dancers and stage managers and woodwind and strings spit out toothpaste, pull pyjamas out from under duvets and slip on eye masks, rolling out their shoulders and necks from another day of leaping and turning and humping and hauling and blowing and plucking to sink into the soft lull of the train gently rocking their tired bones.

And one last for the crow who sings in its nest.

At the very back of the train in the caboose, a woman sits with her legs dangling off the deck, a broom across her lap. She wears a voluminous dress of black serge and hums a little tune as she points her toes and swings her legs. Beside her is a tray bearing a chewed-up and spat-out sweet potato dumpling, a smear of pear crumble and two empty shot glasses. She watches the lichen-speckled graves and haughty mausoleums of the day before dissolve as the train staggers into a new landscape, and with the toll of the thirteenth bell she opens her beak and caws out into the night.

ACKNOWLEDGEMENTS

My profound and heartfelt thanks to everyone who had a hand in supporting me as I worked on this book:

George Sandison, who has been a fairy godfather to my work since the beginning.

Margaret Halton, for her intuitive understanding of my writing.

Julia Lloyd for a wonderful cover that perfectly represents this book to the world.

Charlotte Kelly and Katharine Carroll for helping this book to find its readers.

Kevin Eddy for his sensitive copy editing of the manuscript.

Dancing teachers and mentors from throughout my childhood training and professional career, who lovingly passed this most beautiful, exacting and maddening art form on to me and hundreds of others who continue to grace stages around the world.

Anne, who made me a reader.

Dave, who holds us all.

Djamel Eddine, for his support.

Lorna, early reader, champion and cheerleader.

Otis, for his steadfast friendship.

Marianne, for the long, encouraging conversations.

Roisín, for her excellent taste.

Clare and Charlie, for their dedicated care.

Ed, who does not waver.

And finally to my daughters. Without the two of you around this book would have been finished much more quickly but it would not have been so rich with life.